EVEREST ▓▓▓ LIBRARY

3 5056 01496 9458

MYSTERY

ANOTHER ONE BITES THE *Crust*

Ellie Alexander

Author of *A Crime of Passion Fruit*

Killing can be as easy as pie.

D0054407

ST. MARTIN'S
PAPERBACKS

U.S. **$8.99**
CAN. $12.50

Dig into the whole series!

MEET YOUR BAKER

A BATTER OF LIFE AND DEATH

ON THIN ICING

CAUGHT BREAD-HANDED

FUDGE AND JURY

A CRIME OF PASSION FRUIT

Ellie Alexander's Bakeshop Mysteries

From St. Martin's Paperbacks

ISBN 978-1-250-15935-9

9 781250 159359

5 0 8 9 9

Praise for Ellie Alexander's Bakeshop mystery series

"Delectable." —*Portland Book Review*

"Delicious." —*RT Book Reviews*

"Quirky . . . intriguing . . . [with] recipes to make your stomach growl." —*Reader to Reader*

"This debut culinary mystery is a light soufflé of a book (with recipes) that makes a perfect mix for fans of Jenn McKinlay, Leslie Budewitz, or Jessica Beck." —*Library Journal* on *Meet Your Baker*

"Marvelous." —*Fresh Fiction*

"Scrumptious . . . will delight fans of cozy mysteries with culinary delights." —*Night Owl Reviews*

"Clever plots, likable characters, and good food . . . Still hungry? Not to worry, because desserts abound in . . . this delectable series." —*Mystery Scene* on *A Batter of Life and Death*

"[With] *Meet Your Baker,* Alexander weaves a tasty tale of deceit, family ties, delicious pastries, and murder." —Edith Maxwell, author of *A Tine to Live, A Tine to Die*

"Sure to satisfy both dedicated foodies and ardent mystery lovers alike." —Jessie Crockett, author of *Drizzled with Death*

St. Martin's Paperbacks titles by Ellie Alexander

Meet Your Baker

A Batter of Life and Death

On Thin Icing

Caught Bread Handed

Fudge and Jury

A Crime of Passion Fruit

Another One Bites the Crust

Till Death Do Us Tart

Death on Tap

Live and Let Pie

The Pint of No Return

A Cup of Holiday Fear

Nothing Bundt Trouble

Beyond a Reasonable Stout

Mocha She Wrote

Another One Bites the Crust

Ellie Alexander

St. Martin's Paperbacks

NOTE: If you purchased this book without a cover you should be aware that this book is stolen property. It was reported as "unsold and destroyed" to the publisher, and neither the author nor the publisher has received any payment for this "stripped book."

This is a work of fiction. All of the characters, organizations, and events portrayed in this novel are either products of the author's imagination or are used fictitiously.

ANOTHER ONE BITES THE CRUST

Copyright © 2018 by Kate Dyer-Seeley.
Excerpt from *Till Death Do Us Tart* copyright © 2018 by Kate Dyer-Seeley.

All rights reserved.

For information address St. Martin's Press, 120 Broadway, New York, NY 10271.

ISBN: 978-1-250-15935-9

Our books may be purchased in bulk for promotional, educational, or business use. Please contact your local bookseller or the Macmillan Corporate and Premium Sales Department at 1-800-221-7945, ext. 5442, or by e-mail at MacmillanSpecialMarkets@macmillan.com.

Printed in the United States of America

St. Martin's Paperbacks edition / January 2018

St. Martin's Paperbacks are published by St. Martin's Press, 120 Broadway, New York, NY 10271.

10   9   8   7

dedicated to Judy Faulkner

Chapter One

They say that absence makes the heart grow fonder. After a week away from my beloved town of Ashland, Oregon, I knew this to be true. The sidewalks along the plaza seemed merrier, the budding spring trees looked cheerier, and the southern Oregon sky glowed in warm pink tones as I made my way to Torte. It was as if Ashland had rolled out the welcome mat to greet me. I smiled as I passed sleepy storefronts and drank in the cool, early morning air. Our family bakeshop sat at the corner of the Elizabethan-inspired village. Huge Shakespearean banners announcing the new season at the Oregon Shakespeare Festival danced in the slight breeze. Torte's front windows had been decorated with matching maroon and gold banners, ribbons, and twinkle lights. Platters of cupcakes adorned with edible, hand-painted theater masks, busks, and scrolls made for a colorful and tempting display.

"I'm home," I said to no one as I took a deep breath and unlocked the front door. Inside, the bakeshop was blanketed in darkness. I flipped on the lights and surveyed the dining room. Torte was divided into three unique spaces. The front served as a dining room with red and teal walls, corrugated metal siding, an assortment of small tables, and cozy booths lining the windows. An espresso bar and pastry counter divided the dining room and kitchen. A large chalkboard menu took up most of the far wall. One of Torte's youngest customers had colored a stick figure family with a dog, cat, and what I could only guess might be some kind of a bird in the bottom corner of the chalkboard. We keep an assortment of colorful chalk on hand to entertain youngsters while their parents nosh on pastries or linger over coffee. It's been a tradition since my parents opened the bakeshop to reserve a special section of the chalkboard for budding masterpieces.

The same was true for the rotating Shakespearean quote on the top of the chalkboard. My father had always been a fan of the Bard's work and enjoyed sharing his passion for poetry with customers. When he died, Mom continued the weekly quotes as an homage to him. This week's quote was from *Antony and Cleopatra*. It read: "Give me some music; music, moody food. Of us that trade in love." Not only was it a lovely quote, but it was also a teaser for the new season at OSF which kicked off in a week with the premiere of *Antony and Cleopatra*. Everyone in Ashland had been buzzing with excitement. The commencement of another season meant that soon our calm streets would be packed with tourists in town to take in a show and shop and dine in our little hamlet. I liked Ashland's seasonal rhythm. When the theater went dark for the winter, so did we. GONE FISHING signs hung from storefront windows, locals packed up and followed the sun south, and business owners spruced up their shops and planned for the coming year. Having a cold and snowy reprieve where things quieted down and assumed a more leisurely pace for a few months was always nice, but by February the entire town was ready and eager to welcome tourists from around the globe.

I'd been away on a temporary assignment as head pastry chef for the luxury cruise ship *The Amour of the Seas,* where I had spent many happy years with my now estranged husband, Carlos. Our time together had been blissful, although perhaps not grounded in reality. Traveling across oceans had allowed me to explore the world and taste exotic pastries, like Taiwanese buns with dried jujubes and traditional star plum pastries from Finland. My palate expanded with every bite at each new port of call. I credit my years on *The Amour of the Seas* for making me the chef I am today. Yet, when I left it behind I never looked back. From the moment my feet hit the pavement in Ashland I knew I was home.

That changed a few weeks ago when Carlos called out of the blue and begged me to fill in. The ship's pastry chef had stormed off in a huff, leaving the kitchen in a lurch. At first I had resisted the idea, but the timing had been perfect. Plus, Carlos had offered an all-expenses-paid vacation for Mom and the Professor. A week at sea under the tropical sun had been just what the doctor ordered for all of us. I got some much-needed clarity on my relationship and future with Carlos, and the Professor finally popped the question, getting down on one knee under a glowing sunset to ask for Mom's hand in marriage. Every time I replayed his romantic proposal in my head my eyes began to mist.

Being back on the *Amour* had been a reminder of the life that I'd left behind. I didn't harbor any ill will toward my memories or my years spent sailing on calm, azure waters. Nor did I regret marrying Carlos. What I had come to understand, though, was that it was possible to love more than one person or thing. I knew that my heart belonged in Ashland, even if Carlos would always hold a piece of it. It was time to let go of the past, even if that meant saying good-bye to Carlos. The ache of leaving him this time felt different. I knew that things were shifting, and I was ready to dive headfirst into my life here.

For starters that meant focusing on the task at hand—preparing vats of homemade soups, breads, and sweets for the incoming crowds. I tugged off my coat, grabbed an apron from the rack next to the espresso bar, and headed for the kitchen. In addition to gearing up for the busy season, we were in the middle of a major expansion. The basement property beneath the bakeshop had recently come on the market and Mom and I had decided there was no time like the present to take the plunge. While we were on the cruise, the first phase of construction had begun. The space had been waterproofed by adding special drainage and shoring up the foundation. With that project complete we could now turn our attention to the fun part—designing a state-of-the-art kitchen.

Our current plan was to roll the remodel out in stages. The next step involved gutting the current floor plan to make room for an industrial kitchen and small seating area. Once that was complete, baking operations would move downstairs. Then we would knock through the current kitchen, add stairs, and expand the coffee bar and dining room. I was most excited about the open-kitchen concept that the architect had drafted. We had discovered a massive brick oven that would serve a dual purpose—baking wood-fired pastries and pizzas and offering a cozy spot for guests to watch our team of bakers at work and nibble on buttery croissants. For the past week, I'd woken up in the middle of the night dreaming about pulling beautiful charred crusts and bubbling ramekins of macaroni and cheese topped with applewood bacon from the new oven.

It all penciled out on paper, but I was nervous about how everything would come together and keeping the contractors on track. But with one glance at our current kitchen I knew whatever stress this project brought would be worth it. We had reached maximum capacity in the current space. If we wanted to expand our offerings, and continue taking so many special orders for weddings and catering, we had to have more square footage.

One task at a time, Jules, I told myself as I fired up our shiny new ovens, which would eventually be repositioned downstairs, and studied my to-do list on the whiteboard. There were wholesale bread orders, four custom cakes, two corporate pastry orders, and the daily Torte menu to complete. I quickly sketched out a plan of attack. Stephanie, our pastry protégée, and Bethany, our newest recruit, could tackle the bread and corporate orders. I would work on the custom cakes. Sterling, our chef-in-training, would be responsible for soup and sandwiches, and Andy would man the espresso counter. Fortunately, Mom had decided to scale back a bit to focus on wedding plans. I would miss having her steady energy around, but honestly, I wasn't sure how we could squeeze one more body into the tight space. Our expansion couldn't happen fast enough.

As I turned on the sink and began washing my hands, the front door jingled and Stephanie and Andy arrived together.

"Morning, boss!" Andy grinned and waved.

Stephanie made some sort of grunting sound, hung her head, and shuffled inside after him.

"Someone needs a java—stat." Andy mimicked Stephanie's posture.

She shot him a harsh look. "Do you pound espresso before you get here?"

"Nope. But my mom always says that the early bird catches the worm." He winked and tipped his baseball hat at her.

Stephanie scowled. "Will you please just make me a coffee?"

I hid a smile. I was used to their unique personalities. They were both students at Southern Oregon University, but that was where their similarities ended. Nothing ever appeared to fluster Andy. He was perfect in his role as Torte's lead barista with his jovial attitude and easy ability to chat with anyone. Our customers loved him. They also loved his coffee. He had a natural talent for combining unique flavors and was a master at latte art. The things he could do with nothing more than foamed milk and a toothpick would make a professional sculptor's head spin. From a swan floating on puffy white clouds to a pirate ship, complete with a skull and crossbones, Andy could create almost anything on the top of a cup. As of late he had been perfecting Shake-speare's bust in foam, and starting to take requests. Watching him flourish had been one of the highlights of my career thus far.

Stephanie might not have Andy's laid-back attitude, but I had learned that sometimes there's a soft and sweet center under a crunchy exterior. Her goth style, shockingly purple hair, and tendency to dress in all black paired with her sometimes-surly smile made her appear uninterested and aloof. But nothing could be further from the truth. She was loyal, dependable, and a quick study. Mom and I had been teaching her the tricks of the pastry trade, and I was impressed by how much her skills had grown in the last few months. She often surprised me. Like the fact that she binged on hours and hours of Pastry Channel baking shows for entertainment and her own education. Or that she had forged a strong bond with Bethany and seemed genuinely excited about taking on independent projects like Torte's Web site and social media accounts.

Andy removed his baseball cap and gave Stephanie a half bow. "My pleasure. I'm here to keep you caffeinated."

"You better make that a double," I hollered from the kitchen.

Stephanie tied on an apron and joined me while Andy began to steam milk and grind beans.

"Late night?" I asked, handing her the wholesale order sheet.

"Don't even get me started. A new girl moved in next door. She's a music major and likes to belt out show tunes all night long. All freaking night long. It's been going on for a week and I think I might snap."

I couldn't help but chuckle. "Show tunes, really? Somehow I don't think of your generation being big into show tunes."

Stephanie scowled. "We're not."

Andy turned to face us. "I second that! Man, I feel for you, Steph."

"Thanks." She rubbed her temples. "If I hear the soundtrack of *Oklahoma!* one more time I'm going to lose my mind."

"Only in Ashland." I shook my head and laughed. "You know who would love this? Lance."

"No. Don't give him any ideas," Stephanie pleaded. "Gawd, can you even imagine? He'd probably want to have her come in and audition or something."

"Good point." I gathered mixing bowls and nine-inch round pans. "I promise this will be a show-tune-free zone today. Are you okay with working on the bread orders? Once Bethany gets in I thought the two of you could focus on the corporate deliveries, too. They want an assortment of pastries, so we can double up our daily offerings."

"Sure." Stephanie's eyelids, which were coated in purple shadow, drooped as she read through the bread orders. Upon closer inspection, her deep-set eyes were puffy with heavy bags beneath them. Her skin looked pale, but not from makeup. She absently twisted off the lid to a flour canister and nearly dropped it on the floor.

I felt sorry for her. Having a noisy neighbor was the worst. I was fortunate to have complete privacy in my apartment in Ashland. It was located above Elevation, an outdoor store that closed at seven every evening. However, I remembered my early days working for the cruise line when I had to bunk with three other women. The crew quarters were often an all-night party, which did not lend itself to bakers' hours. I had invested in an expensive pair of earplugs to get to sleep. I wondered if I still had them. I would have to check later and bring them in for Stephanie.

We worked in silence for the first thirty minutes of the morning. I creamed butter, sugar, eggs, and vanilla in the mixer and then sifted in dry ingredients for the first cake. The order was for a vanilla sponge with vanilla buttercream. A simple but classic request. The customer hadn't specified any design preferences so I planned to use an old method called spooning. After frosting the layered cake with generous amounts of buttercream I would pipe vertical dots all over the cake. Once the cake was covered with dots of buttercream I would use the back of a spoon and start at the base, making small swirls up to the top edge. Then I would repeat the process around the entire cake. The final product would look like fluffy clouds or flower petals. It's a gorgeous vintage look that never goes out of style.

Andy cut the silence by bringing us two brimming mugs of black coffee. "Coffee anyone?"

I poured the creamy vanilla batter into the cake pans, slid them into the oven, and turned toward Andy.

He handed a ceramic mug to me. "I went with a straight-up light roast. It's delicate and floral and I think it's best without any cream or sugar."

Stephanie, who was up to her elbows in bread dough, frowned and stared at Andy's offering. "Light roast. I need caffeine—like an IV of caffeine. I can't stop singing 'Oklahoma!' in my head."

Andy bit his lip to keep from laughing and rested the cup next to the mound of springy bread dough Stephanie was kneading. "Trust me. This will do the trick. There's no difference in caffeine when it comes to roasts. People assume that dark roasts have more caffeine because it's a bolder coffee." He paused and shook his head. "Nah, total myth. Roast has nothing to do with caffeine. Nothing. It's kind of a big controversy in the coffee world, though. There's a whole camp of people who think that light roasts actually have more caffeine. You know, because roasting the beans for longer brings out oils, so I guess you could say that more caffeine burns off in the process."

Stephanie stared at him as if he was speaking a foreign language.

Andy looked to me for confirmation. "Right, boss?"

I shrugged. "Don't look at me. To be honest, I've never considered the caffeine content of a roast." I wrinkled my nose. "How do you know all of this?"

"YouTube." Andy's wide smile made his face look even more boyish.

"Really?" I cradled the coffee mug. The scent of floral notes hit my nose.

"Sure. I have to know what I'm talking about. When it comes to caffeine people get kind of crazy."

"Light roast, dark roast, I'll drink whatever you brew." I held up the mug in a toast and took a sip. As promised the coffee was smooth with a sweet complexity and a fruity tanginess. I inhaled its fragrant, almost floral scent and took another sip. "This is fantastic."

"Glad you like it. I'm going to experiment with this blend today. It should be a nice spring drink. I'm thinking of trying to pair it with some infused rose water or maybe orange blossoms. I'll bring some stuff for you guys to try in a while." With that he returned to the espresso bar.

Stephanie took a long drink of her coffee and then punched a mound of bread dough on the island. "Oh my Gawd, I'm such a tool."

"What?" I looked up from the next order sheet.

She dug her black nails into the pillowy dough. "I accidentally put sugar in this instead of salt." Then she pointed to a row of canisters next to her flour-coated workspace. Sure enough, the sugar lid was off and had measuring spoons resting inside it.

"It's okay." I set the order sheet near my coffee and walked to the other side of the island. "We can salvage this, no problem."

Stephanie brushed flour from her hands with such force that I thought she might injure herself. "This is supposed to be French bread."

I ripped off two tiny pieces of the dough, popped one in my mouth, and handed the other to Stephanie. "Taste it."

She rolled her eyes. "Yeah?"

"Improvise," I said, swallowing the sweet, stretchy dough. "Any good chef will tell you that some of their most revered dishes were nothing more than happy accidents."

"Right."

"It's true." I cut off a hunk of the dough and formed it into a round ball. "Here's what we'll do. Why don't you coat the loaf pans with olive oil? Then we'll drizzle each loaf with honey and a dusting of sea salt. Suddenly, you'll have a crisp crunch, a light sweetness, and a touch of salt. Ta-da! Honey French Bread."

"But that isn't on the order list."

"No problem. We'll make another batch of standard French, but I guarantee you this is going to be a hit."

Stephanie shrugged. "If you think so."

"I *know* so." I thought about patting her on the shoulder or giving her a quick hug to reassure her, but decided against it. Even in the best of circumstances Stephanie wasn't effusive. I didn't want to make it worse for her.

Sleep deprivation had rattled my young apprentice. I was going to have to keep an eye on her. I returned to the other side of the workstation, sipped my coffee and studied the next order. It was for a two-layer chocolate marble sheet for a fourth-birthday party. The customer had requested a unicorn and rainbow theme. That should be fun, I thought as the door jingled again and Sterling and Bethany arrived.

"Everyone's coming in pairs this morning," I said to Stephanie and waved hello to Sterling and Bethany.

Andy offered them a cup of his spring blend on their way back to the kitchen. They both gladly accepted drinks and joined the activity.

"Morning," Sterling said to both of us, but I noticed his gaze linger on Stephanie for a moment. His eyes shifted ever so slightly. Was he worried about her, too?

Sterling had become like a brother to me. We shared a common love for food, we had both experienced losses, and we had tender, romantic souls. He had been holding a torch for Stephanie for a while now, and I just hoped that she wouldn't break his heart. Not that he would have any difficulty finding someone new. Ever since we'd hired Sterling a rotation of young girls came into the bakeshop every day to catch a glimpse of the handsome, dark-haired chef. His brilliant blue eyes and poetic nature often sent groups of teenage girls into giggling fits in the dining room. Sterling was oblivious to the attention. He only had eyes for Stephanie.

"Are you up for a busy morning?" I asked Sterling and Bethany.

"At your service, Jules," Sterling said, heading straight for the sink. "Put me to work."

"Same here," Bethany echoed. She savored her coffee. "Have you seen our social media accounts lately?" She wore her curly brown hair in two braids and had on a pale pink T-shirt with a silhouette of a cupcake and the words BAKE THE WORLD A BETTER PLACE.

"No." I shook my head. "Love your shirt, though."

She grinned and gave me a thumbs-up. Bethany had come on board initially to cover while Mom and I were on the cruise, but she'd been so helpful and blended in with our staff so well that we asked her to stay permanently. She had started a brownie-delivery service, the Unbeatable Brownie, so part of our contract had been a partnership where she retained a portion of the profits from those sales. She had also agreed to work with Stephanie to bring us into the twenty-first century and create a stronger online social media presence. They had been snapping pictures of cakes, pastries, customers, and life in the kitchen and posting them online. So far the response had been great. It was fun to have fresh ideas and energy in the kitchen.

Bethany tied on an apron, hiding the sweet saying that could be Torte's new mantra. "Well, Stephanie and I came up with this idea while you were gone and it's been working really well. We've been posting a secret brownie flavor of the day. Anyone who comes in and mentions the flavor gets a free one. They have to take a picture and use the hashtag #SecretSweets. We've doubled our followers in less than a week."

"That's amazing. I love the idea. A little touch of mystery in the bakeshop never hurts. How have you been deciding on flavors?"

Stephanie patted the last round ball of bread dough into a bread pan and brushed flour from her hands. "We started with a crazy flavor just to see if anyone would bite." She placed our experimental French bread in the ovens and unleashed the heavenly scent of my vanilla sponge cakes.

"Ha, bite!" Andy clapped from the espresso bar. "Well played."

"Anyway," Stephanie continued with an eye roll at Andy. "Bethany thought of adding sriracha to the brownie batter and we sold out in like an hour."

"Sriracha brownies? Wow. I'm impressed, you two."

"Thanks." Bethany gave me a sheepish grin. "It sounded weird at first, but they were good. We went easy on the sriracha. And don't they say that chocolate and spice go well together?"

"Absolutely," I replied over the humming sound of the espresso machine.

"Well." Bethany hesitated for a moment and fiddled with her hands. "You know my friend Carter? He's working in Portland now and they are doing all kinds of unique things with macarons. Like Doritos and Fruity Pebbles. I've been wanting to learn how to make them, so I thought if you were up for it you could teach me and Steph, then we could mix it up and do macarons and brownies. I mean, only if you think it's cool. No pressure or anything."

"I think it's a great idea. Let's do it. Macarons are one of my all-time favorite desserts. We should definitely be offering them here."

"Awesome." Bethany reached over to Stephanie and gave her a fist bump.

We reviewed the task list and everyone started on their individual projects. I couldn't keep the smile from my face. Our team at Torte was more than I could hope for. They were hard workers, self-starters, and innovators. How had I been so lucky? The morning was confirmation of my decision. Ashland and Torte were home, and nothing—not even the stress of a major renovation— could get me down.

That was until we opened for business an hour later and Lance, my friend and the artistic director at the Oregon Shakespeare Festival, pushed his way past the small line queuing at the coffee counter. He balanced a pie box with one hand and used the other to snap at me. "Juliet, I need you!" Pausing for dramatic effect, he glanced around the dining room to make sure that he had everyone's attention. "Darling, it's an emergency. If I don't talk you—*now*—I simply might die." He stopped, gave a half bow to his audience, and raised the pie box. "Or rather, I might pie!"

Chapter Two

"It looks like Lance is already on the warpath," I mumbled under my breath to Sterling.

"Ha!" Sterling didn't bother to try to hide his amusement. He rolled up the sleeves of his hoodie, revealing a hummingbird tattoo on his forearm, and rubbed his hands together. "Jules, this is all on you. We endured a week of Lance while you were away. It's your turn."

Stephanie held up a rolling pin. "Yeah. Don't let him back here. I'm in a show-tune nightmare and can't be trusted. I might go postal if Lance says—anything."

I threw my hands up. "All right. All right. Don't panic. I'll handle Lance."

The team breathed a collective sigh of relief as I reached for a lemon raspberry tart and popped it on a plate. On my way to the dining room I stopped and poured a cup of Andy's spring blend. The only way to deal with Lance this early was with pastry.

"Darling, you look positively refreshed." Lance greeted me with a kiss on both cheeks. He tossed his cashmere scarf on the back of the booth and motioned for me to join him.

"Thanks." I set the tart and coffee in front of him and took a seat.

"The tropics were good to you." He narrowed his eyes behind his thick-framed black glasses and stared at me. "That porcelain skin of yours has a slight touch of sun. It works, darling. It really does. But honestly, how many times do I have to tell you to do something more than a boring ponytail with your hair?"

My hand betrayed me as I instinctively touched the back of my head. Lance had been begging me since we first met to let his makeup artist and hair stylist "work their magic" on me. I'm not much of a makeup girl, mainly because it isn't practical. The steam and heat of a commercial kitchen tend to make mascara run. The same was true for my hair. Wearing it up in a ponytail was quick and easy since I was usually awake long before the sun, and it allowed me to concentrate on piping designs and stencil work without getting hair in my eyes. Not to mention that it's also the rule of the state health authority.

"Well, don't sit there staring; don't you want to see what I've brought for you?" He pushed the white pie box stamped with a simple black silhouette of a hummingbird and the words "Grandma J's Hummingbird Café" toward me. Then he loosened his gold and eggplant striped tie and opened the box to reveal a gorgeous toasted coconut cream pie. "Darling, wait to be amazed. I've brought you a little slice of heaven."

"Grandma J's Hummingbird Café, I've never heard of it." I ignored his commentary on my appearance and studied the beautiful pie that had been finished with mounds of whipping cream and golden brown toasted coconut.

"Of course you haven't. It's off the beaten path. *Way off* the beaten path." He glanced around the bakeshop to see if anyone was listening and then whispered. "As in Medford—next to a truck stop of all places."

I couldn't picture Lance trekking to a truck stop in Medford for pie, or anything for that matter. As if reading my mind, he swept his hand across the top of the box. "Don't believe me? Take a bite. I'll have you know that Grandma J and her pie-baking daughter, Donna Marie, make the lightest, fluffiest crusts you've ever tasted, filled with the most decadent custards and freshest of fruits. One bite and you'll be swooning."

"Truck stop pie. You never cease to amaze me, Lance."

"Not truck stop pie. Don't make it sound so uncivilized. Next to a truck stop. And really, Juliet, you of all people should know that the best things come in the most unexpected places." He pointed to the pie. "Now, shall you do the honors, or shall I?"

Lance drummed his long fingers on the table. Had he been chewing his fingernails? Lance had impeccable style. He tended to wear expensive three-piece suits and ascots. No one else in Ashland could get away with his regal look, but it worked on him. As artistic director of OSF he saw it as his personal duty and responsibility to give the people what they wanted. According to him they wanted a leader who embodied the theater vibe and could connect with the upper crust. Typically, every inch of Lance's outfit was put together with thought and care. But today something was off. His nails had been gnawed and his silk tie was slightly askew.

"Should I get some plates?" I asked. "And what were you doing in Medford?"

"Nothing," Lance snapped. A woman waiting for her latte turned her head in our direction. Lance recovered and offered her a noble wave. "It's nothing. You might call it an exploratory trip."

An exploratory trip to Medford? I was about to ask for clarification when Lance thrust the lid on the pie box down and pushed it to the edge of the table. "Never mind about the pie," he said. "We have bigger things to discuss."

"We do?"

Giving me an exasperated sigh, he reached for his fork. "I feel like you've been gone for ages. Where to start?"

"Lance, I was only gone for a week," I said, trying to get a grasp on his erratic behavior. "How is everything coming along for the new season?"

He stabbed the lemon tart with his fork. "Don't get me started. It's a disaster. An absolute disaster. One might even say we're setting ourselves up for a tragedy of Shakespearean proportions. There's more drama in our tiny hamlet than can fit on any OSF stage."

"Why?" I wrinkled my brow. Lance was known to exaggerate and embellish as much as he was known for his tailored style and his award-winning productions. There was something unsettling about the way his hand shook slightly as he put a bite of tart to his lips. When Lance fell into character his mood was usually light and playful.

"This is delicious," he said, after swallowing the bite and dabbing a bead of sweat on his forehead with a napkin.

I leaned across the table and lowered my voice.

"Lance, is everything okay? You don't seem like yourself."

His cheeks sunk in as he wiped even more sweat from his brow. "Juliet, you know I tease, but what would I do without you?"

For a minute, I thought he was going to say more, but instead he placed the napkin over his uneaten tart, rested his elbows on the table, and massaged his temples.

"Lance, what is it?" I repeated.

He pursed his lips and shook his head. "They're conspiring against me. They want me out, Juliet."

"Who?"

"The board," he whispered. Then he sat up and glanced around the dining room. A handful of early risers waited in line for coffee and breakfast to go, but otherwise things were relatively quiet. An hour from now, once most of Ashland was up and moving, the place would be packed. "It started with that young diva I hired. He's out to get me. I know it."

"Wait, slow down." I reached my hand across the table. "Is this the actor you were complaining about while I was on the cruise?"

"One and the same. Antony." Lance shuddered as he said the name. "I gave the kid a shot. As a matter of fact, I gave him the break of a lifetime. I'll admit that he has talent, I won't argue with that, but the ego on this one is out of control."

Lance and I had exchanged e-mails while I was away, and I remembered him mentioning an actor who was driving him crazy. At the time, I had figured it was because Lance didn't like sharing the spotlight. Maybe there was more to it.

"What has he done?"

"The question is what hasn't he done? He refuses to break character. He only answers to Antony—not his real name, FYI."

"Really? He's that method?"

Lance rolled his eyes. "I can't even."

"What's his name?"

"Good God, if I told you I'd risk upsetting the little prima donna." Lance scowled. "It gets worse. He parades around in his toga and expects everyone to jump at his every command." Lance's voice hit a high octave. "He's staging a coup. He's plotting against me. Quite ironic if you think about it. When Shakespeare wrote *Antony and Cleopatra* he was making a statement on world politics. The battle for power. East versus West. A play written four hundred years ago resonates today, doesn't it?"

He didn't pause long enough to let me respond. To be honest my Shakespeare knowledge was limited at best.

"They're both superstars—Antony and Cleopatra. Ancient Rome versus ancient Egypt. That's exactly the battle raging on my stage and in my personal life."

"How?" I asked, waving to one of our regulars who left the bakeshop with a box of pastries for her office.

Lance looked distracted. "What?"

"Well, for starters, Antony. What is he doing to plot against you, and why don't you just fire him?"

"Please." Lance gave me an exasperated stare. "You should see the OSF contracts. They're iron-clad. Not to mention that he has the entire company and board wrapped around his little finger. That's why they hosted that disgusting preseason dinner at Richard Lord's. He and Richard teamed up against me. Richard offered the board a ridiculous price break. For what? Glorified pig slop? I doubt he made a dime on the dinner. He simply wanted to able to boast that the Merry Windsor was the restaurant of choice this year—blah!" Lance stuck out his tongue. "The board has been looking to cut every penny it can from the budget so when Antony suggested a *gastronomic experience* they jumped at the chance to save a buck. Is this what theater has come to in Ashland? I swear. I think it might be time for me to start packing my bags.

"You don't mean that."

"I do." His eyes bulged. "Antony claimed that his previous company in L.A. always hosted a gastronomic dinner at the hottest eateries. What he failed to mention is that he was nothing more than an extra. He never had a lead, let alone a speaking part in L.A. I gave him his break and this is the thanks I get." The disdain in Lance's voice was thick.

Richard Lord owned the Merry Windsor hotel on the opposite side of the plaza from Torte. He had appointed himself lord of Ashland and made it his business to know everyone's business. Richard and I hadn't seen eye to eye since he had attempted a hostile takeover of Torte. The Merry Windsor was rundown, in need of repair, and served prepackaged frozen and processed meals. As part of his attempt to pull customers away from Torte, Richard had added a coffee bar to the front of the hotel. His latest food escapade involved updating his menu to molecular gastronomy, a trend that first hit the food scene over a decade ago. I couldn't even begin to imagine what his new menu might feature. Probably something like deconstructed grilled cheese. Gross.

I shifted in my seat. "What are you going to do?"

Lance clapped his hands together as a slow, evil smile spread across his face. "Ah, that's why I need you, darling."

"Okay." I could hear the trepidation in my voice.

"I'm going to throw my own preseason party. It's going to be a fully immersive experience. Set designs, costumes, and of course show-stopping food."

"But I thought the dinner already happened."

"We will never speak of that again. The meal was an assault to my palate and a hideous blemish on OSF's tasteful history. I intend to put on the most luxurious fete this town has ever seen, and you, dear Juliet, are going to help me."

"I am?"

"Indeed." Lance leaned across the table. "Now let's get down to details. I want an authentic Shakespearean dessert buffet. I'm talking about a cornucopia of Renaissance delights. No expense shall be spared!"

This was more like the Lance I knew and loved. "What sort of budget have they given you?"

"There's no budget. This is on my own dime. Funded completely by yours truly. And I want this to be *the* party that people talk about for years to come."

"How many people are you inviting? And when is the party?" I asked, wondering if we had the time or capacity to take on another project right now.

"Next week. The night before we raise the curtain on the new season, and everyone is invited. The entire company."

"Lance, that isn't a lot of time, and that's a lot of people. I don't know if we can do it. We have so much going on here with the expansion."

He grabbed my hand and squeezed it tight. "Juliet, you have to." I could see the desperation in his eyes as he continued. "This party is my chance to prove my worth and vision to the board and company. It has to be perfect. It might be my last and only opportunity to save my career. No one does dessert like you. I'll absolutely die if you say no."

"You won't die, Lance." I freed myself from his grasp.

"Please," he begged, and batted his lashes. "For your best friend?"

"I don't know." I hesitated.

"Look, I didn't want it to have to come to this, but you do owe me. I saved your life, remember? If it hadn't been for my superb acting you might be floating at the bottom of the ocean or dead in a ditch. The least you can do to repay me is whip up a culinary masterpiece."

"Fine." I knew it was probably easier to just agree. Lance wasn't used to hearing no, and this conversation could go on for hours.

"You'll do it? Excellent." Lance leaped to his feet. "I'll return later with my set designer. I'll want to coordinate the color scheme, and I have some original recipes from the 1500s that you can use."

Before I could caution him that translating a four-hundred-year-old recipe wasn't my expertise, he kissed both my cheeks. "Ta-ta, darling. Don't forget to cut yourself a slice of Grandma J's pie."

He wrapped his scarf around his neck and practically skipped to the door. Mom came in as he was leaving.

"Lance, how lovely to see you," Mom said while he held the door open for her.

"Dearest Helen, how lovely to see you. Ashland was

positively bleak without your presence." He kissed both of her cheeks. "You are absolutely aglow with the blush of love. I've heard the news and I assure you I'm at your service. Anything you need. Anything, you let me know."

"Thanks." Mom gave him a hug in return.

Lance clapped his hands together. "Now, let me see the ring."

Mom raised her left hand to show Lance her antique platinum engagement ring.

"Stunning. Not that I would expect anything less from our resident bard." Lance kissed her hand. "I must be off. I have a party to plan. Juliet will fill you on all the gory details. Ta-ta!"

He had certainly perked up since the start of our conversation, but I was still worried about him.

"I'm trying to remember if I've ever seen Lance here this early," Mom said, walking over to greet me.

I motioned for her to sit. Lance was right. There was a lightness about her that I hadn't seen for years. Her brown eyes were bright and filled with eagerness. When she caught my eye her expression changed.

"What's wrong, honey?" she asked, taking off her pale green jacket and placing it on the back of the booth.

"It's Lance. He's acting unstable." I filled her in on our conversation and about how I had just agreed to cater a dessert buffet for his party. "He breezed in with a pie from Medford, demanding that I taste it." I pointed to the untouched pie box. "Then he completely shifted gears and launched into a rant about his leading man and how the board is trying to usurp his power."

When I finished, she glanced behind her to the plaza.

Ashland was beginning to wake up. Storefront lights had been turned on, sidewalk seating and sandwich boards had been placed outside, and shop owners chatted with one another. "I've been wondering about this," Mom said, returning her attention to me. "Lance has been at the helm of OSF for over a decade, and he's taken that responsibility seriously. He lives and breathes the theater. I wonder if he needs a break? He's good at putting on a happy face, but I suspect that the stress and pressure of managing so many personalities, as well as the board, volunteers, and patrons, has to have taken its toll. Can you imagine constantly having to be 'on'?"

"No." I shook my head. Mom raised a valid point. I knew that Lance loved the theater, but maybe it was too much of a good thing. I thought about how even being away from Ashland for a week had given me new insight and perspective. When Lance came back with his set design and ancient menus I was going to suggest that he take a break. A little rest and relaxation was hopefully just the thing my friend needed.

Chapter Three

"What are you doing here, Mrs. C.?" Andy asked when Mom and I brought the pie box to the kitchen.

"Some welcome." Mom winked at him.

Andy's boyish cheeks flamed. "I didn't mean it like that. I thought you were taking a break and doing wedding stuff."

Mom's wide smile spread to her eyes. "I am doing wedding stuff, but that doesn't mean you're going to be entirely rid of me. I have some time between appointments this morning and thought I would come by and get my hands sticky for a while."

"Cool."

"You want a slice of pie?" I asked.

He shifted his eyes from side to side. "Boss, come on, you had me at pie."

"Don't you want to know what kind it is?"

"If it's pie, I'll eat it." Andy flexed his muscles. "Coach wants me to add some weight for next season."

"You're perfect, just as you are," Mom assured Andy. "Don't let anyone tell you otherwise."

I brought the pie box into the kitchen and grabbed

plates, forks, a knife, and a server. "Anyone else want to try Lance's pie?" I asked the team.

Sterling stopped peeling eggs for the egg salad he was making. His cobalt-blue eyes widened. "Lance bakes?"

"No." I pointed to the logo on top of the box. "It's from a shop in Medford."

Bethany had arranged cupcakes, each frosted with a different color of buttercream, in the shape of a rainbow. "Is that from Grandma J's? I love that place!" She twisted the legs of a miniature tripod that she would use to take photos of her rainbow art. "My dad always gets a pie from Grandma J's for his birthday."

"Weird, I've never heard of it and I've lived in Ashland nearly my whole life." I removed the pie from the box.

"You kind of have to go looking for it. It's on the far end of town, on the way up to the mountains," Bethany replied.

Sterling held his arm next to the box. "Get a shot of this, Bethany. Hummingbirds unite." The tattoo on his forearm mirrored the bird logo.

I sliced through the snowy mounds of whipped cream and cut into a flaky crust. The first piece slid out of the tin in one fluid motion. That was the sign of a well-crafted pie. After cutting generous helpings for my staff, I put Grandma J's pie to the fork test. It passed with flying colors. My fork stood straight as a statue in the custard pie.

"This is amazing," Bethany said through a mouthful. "Can I have that piece for a sec?" She framed Sterling's tattoo, the logo, and my slice; then stepped back to assess the angle. Satisfied with her layout, she lined her phone up even with the island and knelt to take a few shots. Her ability to construct a scene in a photo impressed me.

Stephanie hung on the opposite side of the kitchen. "You want a piece?" I asked. She shook her head and returned to packaging cooled bread in paper bags.

"I doubt that Grandma J's has any social media," Bethany said, handing me back my slice of pie. "If you're cool with it, I'll do a post about them. Maybe something funny like 'the team at Torte dies for pie'!"

Mom chuckled. "You guys are so clever."

"Don't worry, Mrs. C.," Andy called from the bar. "If you ask, I'm sure Bethany will hook you up with wedding hashtags."

Bethany's head bobbed in agreement.

"Maybe," Mom said with a subtle wink to me.

I tasted the coconut cream pie. Each layer offered a different texture. The light-as-air whipped cream blended with the crunchy coconut, and the smooth custard with hints of vanilla bean mingled with the buttery, flaky crust. "This is divine."

"It's really good," Sterling agreed. He finished his piece and returned to his egg salad station.

Grandma J's pie inspired me. When I had a free moment, I wanted to tweak her coconut concoction slightly by adding a layer of strawberry puree and fresh strawberries marinated in a simple syrup. In the meantime, I checked on the dining room and helped prep for the lunch rush. The morning flew by as Andy cranked out aromatic coffees and we churned out cakes and giant cookies.

As promised Lance returned after lunch with an entourage. He hollered at me from the other side of the pastry case. "Oh Juliet!" Lance snapped his fingers together and shifted the attaché case under his arm. "We *need* you." A trim balding man in his early forties and a woman with short red hair and huge orange glasses stood next to him.

Sterling snickered. "They need you, Jules."

"Great." I untied my apron and reached for a stack of cooling cowboy cookies with huge chunks of milk and dark chocolate, pecans, and coconut. "Wish me luck."

"You need it," Stephanie said, not bothering to look up from the meringue she was whipping.

I scooted through the busy dining room and joined Lance and his friends at the only open window booth. He had opened the leather case and was arranging elaborate sketches and recipes written in old scroll on the table.

"Sit, sit," he commanded.

I slid in next to the balding man, who wore thick jeans with a tool belt that stretched over both shoulders and around his waist like a suspension harness. Screwdrivers, hammers, carpenters' pencils, chisels, and a tape measure hung from two reinforced leather pouches. "Thad, set designer." He extended his hand.

"Nice to meet you." I returned his handshake and recoiled slightly at the smell of his garlicy breath.

"Right, right. Jules, Thad. Thad, Jules," Lance said, brushing his hand over the sketches. "These are Thad's designs. He's simply the best."

Thad cleared his throat. "And I've told you that the

best is going to cost you, Lance. A week is an impossible deadline. My crew is focused on last-minute set tweaks for the season. The board is not going to like it if I have to pull them off to work on this. It can't be done. There's not enough time."

Lance slammed his hand on the table. "It has to be done. I don't care what it costs, just do it." Like earlier, he seemed to realize that his outburst was unwelcome. He smoothed one of the recipes and plastered on a serene smile. "What I mean is that as the personal benefactor of this event I assure you that every expense you incur will be generously compensated. If you have to pay your teams double or triple to get the job done, so be it."

Thad shook his head and looked to the woman sitting across from me for support. I'd seen her before, but didn't know her name.

"Boys, let's all calm down." She smiled at me. "I'm Vera MacBohn, by the way."

"You look familiar to me," I replied.

"I've been with OSF forever. You've probably seen me around."

"Enough," Lance interrupted. "We're not here to chitchat. We are here to plan the most jaw-dropping soiree that Ashland has ever seen."

Thad let out an audible sigh. "Lance, this is ridiculous." He adjusted one of the screwdrivers in his tool belt.

Vera gave him a look to tell him to stop from across the table.

In an attempt to break the tension, I offered everyone a cowboy cookie. "Cookie?"

Lance scoffed. "Jules, this is no time for cookies."

Thad snatched three from the plate. "I disagree."

Vera smiled but declined with a curt shake of her head. "If you can believe it, I don't enjoy sweets."

"Really?"

"It's true. With one exception. Carrot cake. I have been known to devour an entire cake, especially Torte's carrot cake. You make the most exceptional cream cheese frosting with fresh candied ginger. I love it because it isn't overly sweet." Her eyes drifted off. "My husband thinks that the reason I like carrot cake is because I'm ginger." She ran her fingers through her short tangerine hair.

Lance threw his hands up in disgust. "Enough. Focus, people. Focus." He picked up photocopied recipes and forced them at me. "Study these. I want everything for the party to be completely authentic. Clotted cream, trifle, pudding, tarts, and royal marchpanes. Understood?"

I started to reply, but he didn't let me finish. "You must coordinate the dessert color scheme with Vera's costumes and the sets." He turned his attention to Vera. "Did you bring the swatches?"

She gave me an apologetic look and then reached into a leopard-print bag. "I did." Then she placed gorgeous swatches of silk, organza, and taffeta in eggplant, navy, gold, silver, and cream next to Thad's sketches.

"You want us to match the desserts to these?" I asked Lance. I had to agree with Thad—Lance's request was over the top.

"Yes, of course, darling." Lance tore off his tie.

"Gold? Silver? I mean we could use edible gold dust and silver pearls, but I'm not sure how we would tie that in with these recipes." I studied the papers he handed me. "I've never even heard of a royal marchpane."

"You'll figure it out I have complete faith in you. Keep the sketches and the swatches. I'll be here at three P.M. sharp tomorrow for a tasting." Lance picked up his case and waited for Vera to exit the booth.

"Mind if I have another?" Thad asked, pointing to the cookies. "These are great." His breath now had a chocolaty garlic scent. I wanted to offer him a breath mint, but instead told him to help himself and moved out of his way.

Lance blew me a kiss and arched his shoulders. "Spare no expense and tell your staff there's a hefty tip waiting for them at the end of this fete." With that he strolled to the door.

Vera patted my wrist. "Don't worry. You know how he gets. Hopefully, he'll come to his senses and rethink this party."

"I wouldn't count on it," Thad interjected, stuffing two cookies into the left pouch in his tool belt. "The man is on a mission and he's not going to stop until one of us kills him." He pushed past us to catch up with Lance.

Vera scratched her short red hair. She only stood five feet and barely came to my shoulder, yet she had a commanding presence. "I have to confess that Thad might be right." She pulled her glasses to the tip of her nose and shot Lance a look of concern. "To tell you the truth, I'm not sure what to think. I've worked with Lance for a long time and I've never seen him like this. It's been a weird start to the season. The entire company is out of sorts."

"Me, too." I was glad that Vera recognized that Lance wasn't himself. "He seems to think that the board is conspiring against him."

Vera's brow shot up. "What?"

"That's what he told me earlier. That the board is trying to force him out."

A strange look flashed across Vera's face. "No. Certainly not. That's ludicrous. The board adores Lance. Are you sure you didn't misunderstand him?"

"Positive."

"Hmm. I'll talk to him." She pressed her glasses back onto the bridge of her nose. "In the meantime, please tell me if you put your carrot cake back on the menu."

"I will. In fact, consider it done. I'll bake some while I try to figure out how to re-create a dessert menu from the sixteenth century."

"Good luck." She looped her bag around her shoulder and left.

"How did it go?" Mom asked while I started picking up Lance's master party plans from the table.

I showed her the sketches, fabric, and recipes. "He wants us to coordinate an authentic Shakespearean dessert buffet that matches these."

"What?" Mom laughed aloud. "He can't be serious." She must have seen the dismal look on my face because she stopped laughing and asked, "Oh, he is serious?"

"Yeah." I nodded and pointed at one of Thad's sketches. It was labeled "Guest entrance" and showed a massive gold spiraling staircase that twisted up to a balcony and then back down the other side where huge marble arches would welcome everyone into the space. The pencil drawings were lush with greenery, candles, garlands of flowers, and handcrafted furniture. "This is just the first of ten designs."

"How can he afford it?" Mom thumbed through the pencil drawings. "Some of these sets are twice the size and scale of shows at OSF."

"I know." I picked up a recipe for fig tarts. "And to color-coordinate food and costumes."

"Why costumes?" Mom ran her hand over a piece of ivory silk. Her skin was still tan from a week in the Caribbean.

"Apparently, he's planning to outfit the waitstaff in period costumes, and the invitations state that costumes are required."

"Hmm." Her lips turned down. "It's almost like he's delusional. Not that I would ever want to say that about a friend. You know how much I care about Lance, but this is worrisome."

"Yeah." I held up a recipe. "Do you know what royal marchpanes are?"

At the same moment, someone approached the booth. "Did someone say marchpanes?"

We turned to see the Professor, Mom's paramour and Ashland's resident detective standing in front of us. He wore his signature tweed jacket and a pair of loafers.

"Doug." Mom's voice was full of delight as she patted the spot next to her. "I wasn't expecting to see you this afternoon. I thought you were in Medford?"

He slid in next to her and gave her a light kiss on the lips. They made a handsome couple. The Professor had a reddish beard that was streaked with gray and matching hair. His thoughtful and intelligent eyes held an inquisitive kindness. Mom's walnut hair was cut in a shoulder-length bob; she tucked it behind her ears and stared up at the Professor. "Indeed, I did make a stop in Medford today, but my business wrapped up early so I thought I would pop by and say hello. What's this about marchpanes?"

"What are they?" I asked.

His lips formed a knowing smile. In addition to being in charge of Ashland's small police department, the Professor was also the town's go-to source for all things Shakespeare. He had studied the classics and dabbled in community theater. The man was a walking encyclopedia of the Bard, as he would say. "Royal marchpanes were a most favored delicacy in the Bard's time. We, however, refer to it as marzipan today."

"Oh." I grinned at Mom. "We can handle that."

"With our eyes closed," Mom bantered back.

"Why, pray tell, do you need to handle marchpanes?" The Professor smoothed his tweed jacket.

"Lance, who else." Mom filled him in on Lance's extravagant party plans.

When she finished, the Professor sighed and stroked his beard with his fingers. "This is out of character, don't you agree?"

We both nodded.

"Perhaps I should stop by the theater and have a talk with him. As fate would have it I need to have a conversation with him about another matter."

"Would you?" Mom looked relieved.

"Of course, but only if I get the first taste of your royal marchpanes." He winked at me.

"We can probably arrange that, don't you think, Juliet?" Mom asked me.

"You bet." I gave the Professor a thumbs-up. "Hey, speaking of Medford, Lance said he was there earlier too."

The Professor's face clouded. "Indeed." He drummed his fingers on his chin and stared outside for a moment. "I might suggest that you follow the old adage of 'letting sleeping dogs lie' when it comes to Lance for the moment."

His reaction surprised me. Then again, given Lance's erratic behavior, maybe it would be better to let the Professor, who exuded a natural calmness, try to talk Lance off the ledge.

I agreed and excused myself. I figured they might want some privacy and I needed to get back to the kitchen. If Lance ended up going through with his party for the ages then I had some long nights ahead of me. I did love a challenge when it came to baking. Re-creating an Elizabethan menu wasn't going to be easy, but after seeing how intense Lance had been with Thad and Vera I was resolved to help him however I could. Even if it meant whipping up a batch of (shudder) black pudding or one of the many other authentic desserts on his approved list.

Chapter Four

"Is anyone up for late-night baking?" I asked the team after Mom and the Professor left and we closed the shop for the afternoon. "There's extra cash in the deal." I explained that I was willing to pay double time and promised tips.

"Count me in," Bethany said. "I'm saving up for a new camera and professional studio lights."

Stephanie shrugged. "I guess I am, too. It's not like I'm going to get any sleep anyway."

"Are you sure?" I didn't want her to overextend herself.

"Yeah, I'm cool."

Andy took off his apron. "Wish I could, but I have a hot date, boss."

Sterling looked injured. "You do?"

"Gotcha!" Andy flipped his baseball cap forward. "I'm taking my grandma to dinner."

"That's sweet," I said, noticing a brief glimmer of relief on Bethany's face. Could it be that we had not one, but two, budding bakeshop romances?

"Catch you guys tomorrow." Andy waved and left.

"Sterling, what about you? You want to join us for some Renaissance baking?" I asked.

He glanced in Stephanie's direction. "Nah, I'll let you guys have a girls' night. I've got some stuff to do."

"I guess it's us, then," I said to Bethany and Steph.

"Do you think you could teach us how to make macarons tonight, too?" Bethany asked as Sterling ducked out.

"Great idea." I waved to Sterling. "I'll order Thai food and we can blast some . . ." I trailed off. Stephanie shot daggers at me. "No, I take that back. No music. Just delicious food and some serious sixteenth-century baking."

We cleared the island and started by reviewing each recipe. I was surprised to find it was much more enjoyable than I had imagined—many of the recipes weren't radically different than today's. Not that I intended to admit that to Lance. Bethany found some videos online of one of Stephanie's favorite British chefs, who specialized in demonstrating traditional methods. We chowed down bowls of spicy yellow curry and pad Thai as we watched the chef meticulously tackle the task of constructing marzipan castles and turrets.

"That looks pretty cool," Stephanie said when the video ended. She twisted a strand of her purple hair. "I kind of want to give it a shot."

"Consider it yours," I said, licking my curry bowl clean with a slice of bread. "What about you, Bethany, do any of these recipes look appealing to you?"

She picked up a recipe for an old English pudding, which was usually made in a mold and more like what we thought of as bread pudding. "You know me. Fine

detail isn't my skill set. I'm much better at baking or taking pics. I could try one of these puddings."

"Sounds good. Let's divide and conquer. I'll work on
a fruit trifle."

We worked in an easy rhythm. I checked their progress and offered suggestions about ratios and potential
proportion sizes. If the entire company did attend Lance's
party, then we were going to have to size each recipe
accordingly. Collaborating with them was seamless.
Bethany documented our progress on her phone throughout the night. Stephanie concentrated on her work, and
drank cup after cup of coffee.

"Are you sure you don't want to call it a night?" I
asked, pointing to the clock on the far wall. "It's after
eight."

She rubbed her eyes. "Nah, it'll be worse at my place.
At least here I'm doing something productive."

"Is it that bad?" Bethany asked, dumping raisins,
dates, and figs into a bowl. The smell of bread soaking
in sherry and cognac gave the kitchen a holiday smell.

Stephanie rolled a sheet of marzipan paper thin. "It's
been over a week of no sleep."

"Cumulative sleep deprivation is the worst." I stared
at her sallow face. "I think we should send you home.
Or, you can come hang out at my apartment. I tend to
fall asleep on my couch most nights anyway. I'll gladly
give you my bed."

Bethany agreed. "Good idea, Jules. You can come
crash with me, too."

"No, I'm good." Stephanie cut the marzipan with a
pizza cutter.

I looked at Bethany, who shrugged. Stephanie was

fiercely independent, which often served her well, but with sleepless nights that trait had become a detriment.

We were about to switch gears and start in on macaron technique when someone pounded on the front door. We jumped in unison. I clutched my heart, which thudded in my chest.

"Jeez, who is that?" Stephanie asked.

It was dark outside, but the streetlights cast soft halos on the sidewalk. I peered out the window to see Lance banging on the door.

"Take a guess," I said.

"Lance?" Bethany asked with a look of trepidation.

"The one and only. Keep at it. I'll go see what he wants."

He didn't let up on his knocking. "Juliet, I've been out here for hours. I was about to break down the door."

"Lance, you've been outside for one minute and you scared us to death."

His top three buttons were undone, his jacket was missing, and he wore a pair of bright red sneakers instead of his leather dress shoes.

"What are you doing here?" I asked, letting him inside.

He paced to the pastry counter and twiddled his fingers on top of the glass. The nervous cloud of energy surrounding him was palpable. "I had to do something. I'm going to kill him. Seriously kill him, Juliet."

"Slow down." I walked closer.

The concrete floor trembled beneath us as Lance bounced his foot up and down. "I've got a plan. A big plan."

"To do what, Lance?" My stomach felt queasy, and I didn't think it was from the curry.

"To ruin him," Lance spat out.

"Look, we've been playing around with your menu tonight. Doing some early recipe testing. Do you want to sit down? I'll bring you a taste of what we've put together so far."

He drummed his fingers on the counter and exhaled. "I don't know if I can sit."

"Try." I placed my hand on his shoulder. "I'll make you a cup of chamomile tea. You go take a seat in the booth and try to relax."

"He looks messed up," Bethany whispered when I walked into the kitchen.

I kept my voice low. "I know. I'm going to make him a cup of tea. Can you guys put a small tasting tray together?"

Stephanie nodded. "I can't believe I'm going to say this, but I almost feel sorry for him."

"Me too." I sighed. I filled a mug with water and zapped it in the microwave. Hopefully a cup of calming tea would bring Lance back to center. I took the steaming mug of tea and a plate of our interpretation of sixteenth-century desserts to the front.

"Here, drink this." I handed Lance the tea and set the plate in front of him.

He cradled the mug in his hands for a minute and then without saying a word tasted every dish I set before him including hand-designed royal marchpanes in the shape of popular fruit from the time like figs, dates, plums, and apples.

"It's perfect. Perfection," he said, finishing a bite of

layered trifle. His demeanor had shifted radically. He leaned against the booth and stared at the ceiling.

"Lance, what's going on?"

He sat up. "What do you mean?"

"I mean your outbursts. Showing up here—now—freaking out."

"I'm not freaking out." He cracked his knuckles and savored his tea.

"You're kidding, right?"

Lance scowled. "Oh, do keep that chin up. Cheekbones, Juliet. Cheekbones."

"Look, Lance, I'm worried about you. Have you thought of taking a little break? Maybe take a vacation? Go get some sun, sip a fruity cocktail on the beach. You're not acting like yourself."

He threw his hand over his heart as if I had stabbed him. "Not acting like myself? Darling, acting is my middle name, and I assure you I'm fine. I need this party to be fabulous and all will be right with the world."

"What happened with Antony tonight?"

He shuddered. "It's nothing. Like I said, I have a plan. And it's not going to matter because your pastries are gifts from the gods." He popped a bite of marzipan in his mouth. "This party is going to solve my problems. Trust me."

"That's putting a lot of faith into one night, Lance." I sighed and looked at Steph and Bethany who had their heads down, focused on baking. "I can't even imagine how much it's going to cost you. Can you afford a party like this?"

Lance threw his head back and laughed. "Please. You do not need to worry about my financial status. I have a strict rule to never speak of politics, religion, or money with friends. It's tacky, darling. But I promise you that money is the least of my worries."

I wondered what he meant by that.

"Do you have anything else awaiting my taste buds in the kitchen?" Lance asked, changing the subject.

"Nope. This is it."

"Excellent. In that case, I'll call it a night. I'm going to write up some notes for my vendors with details and final numbers. Expect an e-mail from me later this evening."

It was futile to attempt to reason with him, so instead I picked up the tasting tray and returned to the kitchen. Getting Lance to open up wasn't going to be an easy task. But I knew that I had to do something. My friend was clearly in bad shape.

Chapter Five

"Jules, is he okay?" Bethany tugged on one of her braids. They had cleaned up our sixteenth-century baking mess and had assembled supplies for macarons.

"I don't know."

"He kind of seems like he's on the edge," Stephanie added. "And if I'm saying that right now, that's terrifying." Her lip, painted with black lipstick, curled into a snarl.

I couldn't argue with them. Instead I let out a sigh and brushed my hands together, as if trying to brush off my worry about Lance. "What do you say, macarons?"

Professional bakers know that there is a huge difference between macaroons, which are basically coconut balls dipped in chocolate, versus macarons, French sandwich cookies filled with everything from lavender and honey buttercream to pineapple jam. Many bakeries use food dyes to color their macarons, but I prefer to use natural flavors to achieve beautiful colors. Like pureed blueberries for purple and fresh raspberries for a soft, subtle red.

I handed Steph and Bethany each a mixing bowl and

French whip (or whisk). "You want to start by whisking almond flour and confectioners' sugar together."

They obliged and I showed them how to beat egg whites, cream of tartar, and a pinch of salt until frothy and then slowly incorporate superfine sugar and beat until it formed shiny peaks. "Be careful not to break the egg whites as you fold this into the flour and sugar," I cautioned.

"Next, go ahead and pick one of the purees to add some color and flavor to your batter." I lined baking sheets with parchment paper. Soon they each had luscious, pastel batter.

"What do you think you should do now?" I asked.

"Pipe the batter?" Bethany sounded unsure in her reply.

"Close." I held up my pinkie. "Taste."

"Right." Bethany chuckled. Steph didn't respond, but she did stick a finger into her batter and look pleased with the final result. I tasted each mixture. No wonder Stephanie had almost cracked a smile. The batter was infused with berry flavor with a hint of almond and scant sweetness.

"Perfection." I gave them my seal of approval and demonstrated how to pipe one-and-a-half-inch round circles onto the tray. "You should get approximately twenty-four cookies per tray. But once you finish piping, you're not quite done yet."

"Why?" Stephanie asked, filling her bag with the delicate mixture.

"These beauties are very particular. It's one of the reasons that most home bakers seldom try to make them.

You have to let the rounds age. It's crucial. Otherwise you'll end up with a wet and sticky cookie."

"Gross." Bethany stuck out her tongue.

"Exactly. Time is your friend. Let them sit and form a nice hard shell, and then you're almost ready to slide them into the oven." French macarons had an exquisite texture with a crunchy exterior and soft, chewy finish. Rushing any of the steps would result in a flat, lifeless cookie.

"Almost?" Stephanie glanced at the clock. "Are we going to be here all night?"

"No. The final step is to gently tap the tray on the counter a couple of times to release any air bubbles, and then they're good to go."

"Finally," Bethany scoffed.

"Yes, but they'll be worth the effort." I stood back and let them finish the process.

Within the hour, we had cheerful stacks of macarons lining the island—minty green cookies filled with white chocolate and a touch of mint, peach-colored cookies filled with a thin layer of buttercream and peach preserves, blueberry cookies filled with lemon curd, and pale pink cookies filled with seedless raspberry jam.

"Nice work," I said, appraising the collection of sandwich cookies.

"Thanks for the tips, Jules." Bethany broke one of the blueberry macarons in half. "I can't wait to get some shots of these."

I glanced at Stephanie, who was leaning against the counter as if it were the only thing holding her up. "Let's call it a night. We've made great progress. I'll store these in airtight containers and you two can head out."

Stephanie grunted something indistinguishable and trudged to the front door. Bethany followed after her. It didn't take long to arrange the macarons in large plastic Tupperware. Refrigerating them overnight would allow the cookies to absorb the filling and make them even softer. They would last for three to four days before becoming crumbly. Although I had a feeling they wouldn't last that long. My best guess was that we'd be sold out by lunch tomorrow.

I left Torte feeling content that we would be able to manage Lance's party and that the top shelf of the pastry case would be filled with exquisite spring macarons. That feeling stayed with me until I returned to the bakeshop the next morning.

It started as a typical day with the scent of rising yeast bread and butter croissants baking in the ovens. Bethany set up a photo shoot of our French macarons. Andy kept pace at the espresso bar and continued to perfect his latte bust of Shakespeare. Sterling watched over a pot of bubbling French onion soup, and Stephanie shuffled around like a zombie.

Aside from my concern about Stephanie's ability to function on no sleep, the morning passed with relative calm. That changed when I checked my e-mail. A message from Lance waited in my inbox, spelling out his instructions, which included the fact that every attendee and vendor would be required to dress in period costumes. Great.

I printed out his detailed spreadsheet and called everyone around the island.

"What's the deal, Jules?" Sterling turned his attention away from the onions he was caramelizing on the stove.

"I have an, er, update from Lance," I said.

"Oh no." Stephanie let out a groan. "I don't like the sound of this."

"What's the bad news, boss?" Andy asked, chomping on the day's special—a roast beef and cheddar cheese sandwich with a thin layer of homemade horseradish sauce and served on a hearty baguette. Mom has always believed that a fed staff is a happy staff. Our team never went hungry. They were the first to sample new recipes and taste whatever was hot out of the oven. We had an open-kitchen policy where they were welcome to help themselves to anything from the pastry case or on the lunch menu. No one had ever abused the privilege. If anything, it boosted sales. We often sold out of daily specials because Sterling and Andy would rave to customers about how the daily soup was the best thing that they'd ever tasted.

"It's not exactly bad news." I tried to choose my words carefully.

"But it's not good news," Sterling interjected. He folded his arms across his chest.

"That depends on your perspective."

"Out with it." Andy waved his baguette at me.

"Lance is requesting that we dress up for the party."

Sterling raised one brow. "Dress up how? Like a suit?"

"Not exactly. He wants all of the service staff in full costume."

"No way. I'm out. You are not going to get me in a

costume," Stephanie said from the opposite side of the island. Her dark, steely glare made it clear that she was serious. I had no intention of forcing any of my staff to do something they didn't want to, but given the look of panic and dread on Stephanie's face, I worried she was going to quit on the spot.

Before I could reassure her, Bethany spoke up. "Actually, I think that sounds kind of fun. I've always wanted to see the inner workings of the costume department, and just imagine the photos we can get for social media. They could go viral."

"See," I said to Stephanie. "There you go, no need to worry." I smiled at Bethany. "Thanks for volunteering."

Andy pointed at Sterling. "Does that mean we don't have to wear tights?"

Sterling crossed fingers on both of his hands. "Please, Jules."

I laughed. "You are all off the hook. Bethany and I will take one for the team."

"I owe you," Stephanie said to Bethany.

Bethany shook her head. "No, I'm excited. I think it will be fun."

The smell of simmering onions, sherry, and thyme made my stomach rumble. "Great." I handed her the printout. "On that note, Lance wants you to go get a fitting at the costume department."

"Really?" Bethany beamed. "This is going to be like being in a show. I can't believe it." She untied her apron. "Do you think I can bring my phone? Or are photos prohibited?"

"I'm sure that Lance would love for you to create a custom hashtag for the event," I said with a chuckle.

"You can ask at the costume department, though. They'll tell you if there's any kind of an issue."

Bethany skipped for the door while Stephanie exhaled. "That girl is crazy."

"She seems genuinely excited," I noted. "That's why we're a team. Everyone brings something different and unique."

Stephanie tucked her violet hair behind her ears. "Jules, you don't even like dressing up."

She had a point. "True. Serving in an Elizabethan costume wouldn't be my preference, but I'm doing it as a favor for Lance, and hopefully some of Bethany's enthusiasm will rub off on me."

"You're a good friend," Sterling commented, returning to the stove to stir the heady onion soup.

Andy shoved the last piece of his sandwich into his mouth. "Truth." He gave me a salute. "Thanks for not making us wear tights. I'd never live that down with the guys on my football team."

"Or the ladies," Sterling interjected.

"Right."

I made a few quick notes about some minor changes for the party. Last night I had served the fruit and custard trifle in a clear glass bowl, but for the party I wanted to find a tall vase or maybe a crystal serving dish to display the layered dessert. I also wanted to embellish the apple tarts with a Shakespearean scroll made of shortbread, frosted with royal icing, and dusted with edible gold powder. Once I finished my notes I set to work estimating proportions and ordering supplies. We could work on the marchpanes first as they would keep for a few days. I sketched out a production plan and assigned

roles to each team member. It was an ambitious project, but we'd successfully accomplished bigger tasks in
the past.

Once I finished our plan of attack for Lance's party
I tucked my notes in the office and headed for the basement. Mom and I had an appointment with the architect to discuss which walls were staying and which were
going and to talk about flooring. Our small office had
been taken over with samples for paint, flooring, coun-
tertops, and more. I hadn't anticipated how many decisions were involved with a major renovation.

When I stepped outside onto the plaza the signs of
spring were everywhere, from the scent of fresh cut
grass to the tulips blooming in the window boxes. Galvanized tins flanked each side of the bakeshop with cascading greenery. Bistro tables with canvas umbrellas
sat on the sidewalk. Bright teal-colored Ashland visitor
maps had been placed on every windowsill along the
plaza, a sure sign that the tourist season was upon us.
The free maps showcased Ashland's shopping district,
hotels and B and Bs, and a plethora of outdoor activities
nearby, like river and lake kayaking and trail running.
Spring fever had hit me. I couldn't wait for alfresco
dining under the stars and afternoon picnics in Lithia
Park.

The sidewalk changed to brick as I rounded the corner to the basement. Moss coated the pathway and stairs.
I held on to the iron handrail as I made my way down
the aging brick steps. We had yet to decide what to do
with the exterior of the building. Mom and the architect were already waiting for me when I made it to the

landing and peered through what used to be a solid metal door.

"Hey," I called, stepping through the opening.

Mom was standing in front of a wall that currently divided the space horizontally. "Juliet, good, I'm glad you're here. We were just discussing whether we should completely remove this wall or leave one section at the end with a pass-through."

"I'm not sure what you mean," I said, waving to Robert, the architect.

He greeted me with a firm handshake. "Follow me." We walked to the far end of the basement. Robert pointed to the vintage brick oven. "One idea is that instead of tearing out the entire wall here, we can leave a section to provide you with some privacy in the kitchen. I would have my subcontractors cut out a six-by-four window if you like. That way you can have the seating area out here and your customers can get a glimpse of what you're working on, but you'll still maintain some privacy."

"That could be good." I looked at Mom. "What do you think?"

"I'm not sure. You said that this wall isn't load-bearing, correct?" she asked Robert.

Robert knocked on the rotting Sheetrock. "Correct. You'd be in a bad way if it was. I could punch through this with my pinkie. If you want to do the pass-through we'll rebuild this section, but either way this entire wall will come down."

It was hard to visualize what the space could become. I turned back to face the direction we had come from. That's where the new stairs connecting the basement would be located. Everything to my left would be the kitchen and the space to my right would be additional seating. Portable shop lights cast a shadow on the floor. Gone was the smell of mildew. An earthy scent remained, but I figured that would dissipate once new Sheetrock went up and flooring was installed.

"When do we have to decide?" Mom asked. I appreciated her practicality and keeping us on task.

"You've got some time. The next round of subcontractors arrives tomorrow. They'll tear everything down to the studs and then we'll start framing everything in."

"Can we take a day or two to think about it?" Mom asked.

"Of course." Robert pointed to the concrete floor, which was brand-new and dry as stale bread. "What do you think of the subfloor? Nice to see it without water, huh?"

Mom and I both laughed in unison. "More like a relief," I said.

"Any decisions on flooring yet?" Robert asked.

"I think we're leaning toward the Pergo that looks like distressed barn wood, right, Mom?"

Mom nodded. "I know you and your team keep reminding us that our water issues are behind us, but I think we both feel safer going with a waterproof floor."

The flooring option that Mom was referring to was a modern laminate. It was completely waterproof, but made to look like rustic barn wood. Not only would it provide another water barrier but also the design should go well with the classic brick fireplace that would become the centerpiece for the basement kitchen.

"Good choice," Robert said with a nod of approval. "Should I go ahead and order it then?"

Mom frowned. "What do you think, Juliet? How many hours have we been staring at floor samples?"

I bit my bottom lip. "Too many."

Robert smiled. "I assure you, it's normal."

"Let's do it," I said to Mom. "If I don't say yes now I'm going to run upstairs and spend the rest of the afternoon second-guessing myself."

"My thoughts exactly." Mom squeezed my hand. "One decision down. Two hundred to go."

"I think you'll be pleased with the performance and aesthetic of the Pergo. It's a great choice," Robert assured us. "Now on to the fireplace." He proceeded to explain a variety of techniques he could use to sandblast and seal the bricks as they were now, as well as options to resurface them with everything from salvaged bricks to a tile façade.

"This one is easy," Mom said when he finished. "We want to keep the bricks as they are. We love the rustic look."

"Sandblasting it is." Robert made a note.

By the time we were done with the walk-through my mind was spinning with decisions—the pass-through, lighting, paint colors, and much more. Mom and I decided to take a short stroll along the Calle Guanajuato. The rushing sound of the creek, swollen from mountain snow melt, murmured to our right. Antique street lamps lined the walk. Local artists had been commissioned to create custom pieces for the pedestrian pathway. During the off-season, a European-style outdoor market, the

Lithia Artists Market, pops up next to the creek, drawing craftspeople selling everything from ceramic pottery to leather shoes, along with hosting live poetry readings and music.

"How are you feeling about all of this, honey?" Mom looped her arm through mine. "Your eyes look a bit glazed."

"It's just so many decisions, you know?"

"I know." She squeezed my arm. We walked in silence, drinking in the sound of birds flitting between trees and the succulent scent of blushing pink hollyhock. The pathway ended adjacent to Lithia Park. We turned the corner to return to the plaza where a group of Southern Oregon students had staged an impromptu protest. They were dressed in toxic-sludge costumes and waved signs reading NO OIL. KEEP ASHLAND GREEN. Ashland was no stranger to rallies. As an artistic, collegiate town it attracted a population that embraced civic engagement. One of the things that made Ashland unique was its openness. Every year, any group was invited to march in the annual Fourth of July parade, from churches to proponents of legalized marijuana. I loved watching our eclectic community finding commonalities while waving American flags and dancing down the street.

We passed Puck's Pub and then A Rose by Any Other Name, the flower shop where bundles of fragrant roses and lilies sat in buckets.

Mom paused in front of the flower shop. "I'm having the same momentary panic about the wedding." She stared at the flowers for a moment. "I keep telling myself to make one decision at a time and stick with it. Maybe years or even months from now I'll be drawn to peonies, but if my heart wants roses today I should go with roses."

Her words were true of so much more than flowers or flooring. They were a mantra for living. Make a decision today and stick with it. I could do that. I had done that. After going back and forth about my future and what I wanted from Carlos, I had finally decided in the moment what I wanted, and I was getting it—the bakeshop, a new expansion, and a joy-filled occasion for celebration, Mom's wedding. I resolved right then and there to stop worrying about making the wrong decision about the basement. There were too many wonderful things to look forward to. I wasn't going to let worry get in the way.

Chapter Six

The rest of the week passed in a blur of happy activity. Mom's wedding plans were coming together, minus the venue. We went to dress fittings, outlined a potential menu and guest list, and started looking at invitations. True to Ashland fashion, everyone had distinct offerings for her, like Save the Date cards written in medieval script that read, "Hear Ye, Hear Ye, Herald the Happy News," and were sealed with bloodred wax. Mom's cheeks glowed and her steps looked lighter. I loved seeing her so excited and full of energy.

Demo began in earnest in the basement. Once Robert's team removed the old Sheetrock and opened up the entire space, my excitement began to build, too. The space was huge. I started daydreaming about constructing six-foot tiered cakes and mass-producing macarons. Even my dress fitting for Lance's party wasn't as painful as I had anticipated. He had picked a silk sheath in pale pink with a shimmering silver bodice. The dress had an empire cut and long, narrow shear sleeves. I had to admit that it accentuated my tall, thin frame in all of the right places. Like Bethany, I also had to admit that I felt a bit like a princess in the ethereal costume.

When the night of the party finally arrived, the entire team helped load and trek carts of our regal desserts and supplies up Pioneer Street. The party was taking place under heated canopies on "the bricks," an outdoor space in front of the Elizabethan and Bowmer theaters where the Green Show takes place every summer. A variety of performers from jugglers to African dancers keep the crowd entertained on the bricks before the main show.

For his soiree, Lance had completely transformed the outdoor space. A white canvas tent covered every square foot of brick. Topiaries and gaslit torches flanked the perimeter. The "show" began with an entrance fit for a king, complete with a spiraling staircase leading to the party down below. I couldn't believe how true the design was to Thad's original sketches. No detail had been spared on the exterior design, from stained-glass window panels to ornate wood-carved balconies shimmering with iridescent lights.

The team and I unloaded via the back entrance, which fortunately did not require navigating the twelve-foot staircase. Inside the tent, heaters shaped to resemble ancient rock fireplaces blazed with warmth. Wrought-iron chandeliers dripping with flowers and ten-inch tapered candles hung from the ceiling. Old-English–style wooden tables and benches were positioned in a U-shape with servants and dogs in the middle. There were keg barrels, silver wine goblets, and platters of fruit on every table. A minstrel band warmed up on the stage. The space was lit entirely by candlelight, giving it a romantic and almost otherworldly feel. Shadows and silhouettes danced on the tent walls.

"Wow," Bethany said with her mouth hanging open. "This is . . . um . . . um . . ."

I couldn't blame her for being speechless. Lance had outdone himself. Waitstaff in Tudor costumes circulated the room with brushed-nickel trays loaded with savory hand pies and carafes of rabbit stew. Two peacocks paraded through the tent, their feathers puffed out in a show of color. Carved wooden crests and ten-foot banners with calligraphy scrolls of Shakespeare's most famous quotes were interspersed among giant candelabras flickering with golden light.

"It's Lance," I offered in reply. Topiaries dripping with jasmine vines infused the tent with the sweet smell of spring.

"Yeah, wow. I mean I don't know if I've ever seen anything like this. I can't even think of a hashtag to use for this." Bethany gawked as a fire dancer on stilts walked past us.

"Over the top?" I shifted a box of royal marchpanes.

"Well, yeah." Bethany pulled a cart of supplies behind her as we made our way to the table reserved for the dessert buffet.

Sterling and Andy lugged in the heavier boxes. "Dude, this is insane," Andy said, gaping at the ten-foot potted trees strung with white paper globes behind our table.

"Seriously." Sterling set a box on the floating wooden floor. "Are those real birds?" he asked, pointing to hanging bronze cages with pairs of mourning doves.

"I think so," I said as one of the birds fluttered his white wings.

"How much do you think something like this costs?" Andy asked, with his jaw still open.

"A lot." Bethany nudged him as a crew member passed by with twelve cases of champagne.

"I almost wish I would have agreed to wear tights just to stay and watch this," Andy said.

Sterling grabbed his arm. "No you don't, man. Let's get out of here before you do something you might regret." He grinned at me and Bethany. "Have fun!" With that they raced out of the tent.

Bethany stared after them. "He would look cute in tights, don't you think?"

"Who, Andy?"

Blotchy red spots rose on her chest. I took that as my answer.

"What should we do first?" she asked, changing the subject.

"Let's unload the trays and then we can start arranging everything." I enjoyed watching a blank canvas, in this case two pedestal tables made of hemlock, come to life. Dessert has always been my medium and for Lance's party we had pored through pages of cookbooks and the Internet to make sure that our pastries and sweets resembled exactly what people would have noshed on in the height of the Elizabethan era. Bethany and I set up gorgeous crystal bowls of trifle layered with silky vanilla and orange cream custard, berries, and pound cake soaked in rum. Small royal marchpanes had been designed in the shape of fruits and vegetables as well as large ones like a chessboard and chess pieces and a replica of the set for *Antony and Cleopatra* per Lance's orders. I had learned in my research that these would have been the main part of the dessert course at a Shakespearean feast. They were often glazed with a combination of rose water, finely ground sugar, and egg whites—what we know as royal icing today. Stephanie had painstakingly crafted each marchpane by hand. The final result was like a fairy tale, from intimidating-knight and statuesque-horsemen chess pieces to a two-foot stage that looked too real to be made from sugar.

We finished out the dessert tables with puddings, tarts, trifle, clotted creams, tea cakes, and cheese and fruit boards. Bethany added touches of greenery and more tapered candles.

"Hashtag stunning," she said, taking a step back to survey our work and snap a few pictures.

"You all really outdid yourselves for this one," I said.

"Stephanie deserves all the credit," Bethany replied, pulling out a chair and standing on it to get a shot from above. "These marchpanes are the dessert version of Madame Tussauds's wax statues."

I was about to agree with her when Lance swept in. "Darlings, this is *très magnifique*." He clapped his hands and blew us both kisses. "These royal marchpanes are absolutely delightful. How will we ever eat them?" Instead of a three-piece suit he wore a Renaissance nobleman's costume with black pants, knee-high leather boots, a black velvet tunic with faux fur trim, a purple satin cape, and a Renaissance-style hat with an ostrich feather attached.

"Lance, look at you!" I'd never seen him in costume before.

He did a little spin. "What do you think?" With cat-like reflexes he reached inside his cape and pulled out a dagger. "You like?"

"I do. It works on you."

Bethany nodded from her perch on top of the chair. "Yeah, totally. This whole place is amazing. Instagram is going to blow up tonight."

"Most excellent." Lance offered her a sly grin. Then he pointed to the bar. "Come, come, we must get you some mead and then get you in costume."

He pulled me to the opposite side of the tent where a cheery mead maker greeted us with two steins of his honey mead. "Drink up, it's good for your health," Lance commanded, clinking his pewter stein to mine.

"I don't think that's true."

"Of course it's true. Don't be daft. In Shakespeare's time water was considered unhealthy so everyone would have imbibed this—men, women, children—*everyone*. Remember, my dear Juliet, that tonight is about authenticity. We are not simply reenacting a period in history. We *are* history."

"Right." I agreed but had no idea what Lance meant by that. "Is mead more like beer or wine?"

The mead maker, who wore a page-boy costume, offered us his expertise. "Mead predates both beer and wine. It's known as the oldest alcoholic beverage and its exquisite taste derives from nothing more than fermented honey." He held up a fluted bottle. "Give it a taste. You should pick up the essence of honey along with hints of melon and tree fruits."

I took a sip and allowed the mead to linger on my tongue. It was semi-dry with floral notes and just a hint of sweetness. It reminded me of a cross between cider and wine. "This is lovely," I said to the mead maker.

He beamed with pride. I wondered how much of his own product he had sampled over the years. The merry craftsman's cheeks were puffy and red. Lance guzzled his drink and thrust his stein to the mead maker for a refill. The maker obliged and filled Lance's stein to the brim. In one fluid motion Lance opened his throat and polished off the second glass before demanding a third refill.

"Lance, don't you think you should pace yourself?" I asked, pulling him away from the bar.

"Nonsense. It's my party and I intend to have a fabulous time." He stared at me for a minute. "Don't wrinkle your forehead like that. Mead is a working man's drink. Farmers drank it all day in the field. Not to worry. I'm not the slightest bit tispy."

"Tispy?"

Lance waved me off. "You know what I mean. I'm not even tip-see. See, I said it. Say it three times fast. Tip-see, Tip-see, tispy."

I wanted to caution Lance to go easy on the mead. Given his erratic behavior of late, getting "tispy" at his party sounded like a disastrous idea.

"Let's go, let's go. You're late. You should already be in costume," Lance said, dragging me toward Bethany. "You and your adorable young helper need to get to hair and makeup—stat! Guests will be arriving on the hour. They cannot see you in jeans and a ponytail. Make haste."

He nudged me and Bethany toward the massive entry staircase, but got distracted by a waiter whose ruffled shirtsleeve cuffs were not up to Lance's standards. We made our getaway as Lance lectured the poor guy about how his sleeves were to be precisely three inches from his wrist.

"Um, he's kind of intense," Bethany said, stopping momentarily to snap a selfie with one of the peacocks.

I frowned and glanced back at Lance. "I know." I had a bad feeling about how the party was going to play out. If Lance didn't lay off the mead we could be in for a long night.

Fortunately, Bethany's excitement distracted me as we ascended the spiral staircase and made our way to the costume department. "This is going to be great, isn't it? My dress is like a real ball gown. I can't wait to share pics."

I smiled and we headed for the Bowmer Theater. I knew my way around the OSF complex. As a kid, I had acted in a few productions, and more recently I had participated in a national baking competition that filmed at the theater. Even though the costume department was located inside the theater, OSF's collection of costumes was so vast that most of it was stored in a warehouse in Talent, a small town just a few miles away. Touring the warehouse was like wandering through Costco. But instead of rows and rows of bulk food there were racks and racks of costumes, organized by era, style, and size. The company rented costumes to other theaters and film studios throughout the country.

To my surprise, when we entered the large room with mannequins, bright-colored spools of thread, swatches of fabric, and racks of costumes, there were actors and members of the company milling around everywhere inside. Apparently, Lance had made OSF's extensive line of period costumes available to anyone who didn't want to purchase or create their own costume. It looked as if everyone had taken him up on the offer. The steady hum of sewing machines whirred.

Bethany and I squeezed past a group of fairies. "We're here on Lance's orders," I said to Vera MacBohn, the costume designer I had met at Torte earlier. She was kneeling on a stool and making a last-minute alteration to a Cleopatra costume. "Suck it in, Tracy," she said to a woman in the elegant white dress.

"I am, Vera," the woman wailed. "I am!" She had to be an actor in the company with her perfectly erect posture and sharp features. I couldn't tell if her jet-black hair was real or a wig. Not a single hair was out of place. Her bangs had been cut in a blunt style to show off her gold headpiece adorned with blue gemstones. The sleeveless dress fell to her ankles. It had a gold braided belt and collar that were trimmed with aqua sequins. A matching aqua cape was attached to gold bracelets on each wrist.

Vera stood up and stuffed a roll of Velcro into her apron. She reached for a pencil tucked behind her ear and made a tiny marking on the back of the Cleopatra dress. "I'm going to have to let this out. Hold on." Then she turned to us. "Sorry to keep you waiting. As you can see it's mayhem back here. When I see Lance, I'm going to murder him. Forget everything I said about being worried about him. He's a dead man walking."

"Why?" I asked.

Cleopatra said something under her breath that I couldn't hear. Vera shot her a warning look, but went silent when a man wearing a white belted tunic, knee-high strappy sandals, gold wrist cuffs, a red cape, and a headpiece interrupted us. He looked like a Greek god. This had to be Cleopatra's Antony, also known as Lance's nemesis.

"Tracy, we need to talk." He didn't bother to make eye contact with the rest of us.

"I can't, Antony. I'm doing a fitting."

"You've been doing a fitting every other week. The dress is good. We need to talk—now." He flipped his cape and seemed to notice us for the first time. Extending a muscular arm, he shook my hand. "Antony, star of *Antony and Cleopatra*. I don't believe we've had the pleasure."

"Jules." His handshake was crushing. I wiggled my fingers after he released his grasp. "Pastry chef."

Cleopatra let out a little scream. "You're the pastry chef! I love your stuff. I've been devouring your macarons. Oh my God! They are the best! Total deliciousness. Who would have thought to do peanut butter and jelly macarons? They are the best."

"Meet my macaron master, Bethany." I pointed to Bethany who blushed with pride.

"They are so good," Cleopatra said to Bethany. "Oh, and the bacon and maple syrup ones, oh yum. Lance brought a box to our last dress rehearsal and I think I ate the entire thing by myself."

"That's why you're having another fitting, Tracy," Antony said with a snarl. "Maybe if you laid off the sugar you could fit in your costume."

Tracy's cheeks puffed out as she glared at him. "Whatever. I could say quite a few things about you, but I'm not going to sink to your level."

He kept at it. "Who wants a fat Cleopatra? I'm surprised Lance hasn't fired you yet."

Vera tapped Tracy with her pencil and nodded toward us. "Why don't you two take this outside, so I can get our pastry girls in to their dresses." Her eyes seemed to speak in code. Tracy held her gaze and nodded.

"Right. Come on, Antony, let me show you my secret stash of sweets. Maybe I can smother you with them. Death by dessert." She winked at Bethany. "I'll be by for more of your macarons. Keep those crazy flavors coming."

She and Antony didn't look exactly chummy as they left the costume department. Although I did notice that she wrapped her arm through his and gave the other actors and company a queen's wave as they made their exit. It was a strange shift. He had just insulted her, but then again, they were actors. Maybe Lance had ordered them to put on a good face.

Vera sighed as they strolled off. "Those two." She caught herself and reached for a pincushion. "Okay, where were we? Costumes. Your dresses are both hanging in the fitting area. They should be ready to go, but if you need a last-minute tuck or trim don't hesitate to ask. Once you're in your dress head on over to makeup."

With that she went to work fixing one of the fairy's wings. "See you in a few," I said to Bethany as we parted ways to change. The costume department had always felt otherworldly when I was a kid. Audiences only see what's happening onstage but the real magic occurs backstage where for every actor there are at least three to four costume designers, stitchers, dressers, and assistants. The constant frenzy of choreography offstage was equally—if not more—impressive than a fine-tuned sword fight or dance number. Tonight was no exception. The costume crafts team was hard at work putting finishing touches on wings, crowns, and light-up hoop skirts. Wig designers checked every strand of hair in magnificent frosted headpieces.

I squeezed past a first hand who was fitting an actor with muslin. My dress was hanging on the back of one of the fitting stalls and labeled "Juliet." It looked like something my namesake would have worn, and despite the craziness with Lance, I fell in love with it the second I pulled it over my head. The pinkish hue balanced my pale skin, giving it a soft, warm glow. Its empire bodice accentuated my narrow waist and the thin silk fabric and silver beading gave it a starry feel.

When I exited the fitting space, Bethany twirled out of hers. Her dress was the opposite of mine with a huge hoop skirt and layers and layers of emerald-green tulle. "Isn't it amazing?" she gushed.

"No wonder you feel like a princess. You *are* a princess."

"And you are gorgeous, Jules. Wow. You look like a model."

"Thanks." I pointed her to the door. "Now it's on to makeup."

She clapped. I wished I shared her enthusiasm, but it turned out the process was less painful than I anticipated. The makeup artists at OSF were true masters. They managed to highlight each of our features flawlessly. For Bethany's young acne-prone skin the makeup team smoothed it with liquid foundation and narrowed her round cheeks by contouring layers of rosy blush. They kept my look simple with sparkling silver eyeshadow, a dusting of pink on my brow and cheeks, and a matching pink shimmering lip gloss. Then they curled my straight, fine locks in loose waves and wove in a rhinestone headband. I studied my reflection in the mirror and couldn't believe it was me. Between the dress and the flowing curls, it was a romantic look. I felt like my namesake—Juliet.

Bethany's hair had been piled high on her head and tied with cascading green and gold ribbons. She touched one of the ribbons and gaped into the mirror. "Is it even us, Jules? Don't you feel like another person?"

"I do." I had to admit that I was swept up in the experience, and part of me wished that Carlos were here to see me now. I quickly pushed the thought from my mind. We were here for a purpose—serving dessert and making sure that each guest had a magnificent evening. I wasn't worried about our buffet. I had a feeling that Lance's guests were going to be as impressed as I was with the work my team had done. Neither was I worried about how Bethany and I might blend in for the party. Our costumes, hair, and makeup had transformed both of us into princesses ready for a grand ball. The only thing I was worried about was Lance. I said a silent prayer, as Bethany and I made our way back to the tents, that Lance would keep his imbibing to a minimum and that he wouldn't cause a scene. However, as we descended the staircase into the party my worst fears were immediately realized. Lance was holding a pewter stein, spitting out insults, and looked like he was about to punch Antony smack in the jaw.

Chapter Seven

A commotion erupted just as my pink ballet slipper touched the wooden floor that covered the grass. Lance flung his cape and tried to flick Antony's headpiece with his free hand. Antony jerked backward. Lance missed the headpiece and swiped the air. "Who invited you, anyway?" His words slurred together. I wondered how many more mugs of mead he'd consumed while Bethany and I were getting into our costumes.

Antony adjusted his headpiece and hardened his dark eyes on Lance. "The last time I checked I'm the star of the show. The only reason this place is going to be packed soon is because of me. Everyone is coming to see *me*."

"Ha!" Lance let out a low chuckle. "Please, honey. You've been part of the company for what—a few months? Trust me, everyone is here for *me*. And your name isn't Antony. Drop the gig. You're hardly Tom Cruise, kid. You can take your method acting and shove it where the sun don't shine."

I wanted to jump in and rescue my friend. He was obviously tipsy. Lance never spoke like that. The doors were set to open in five minutes. Who knew how long this posturing could go on? From my vantage point it looked ridiculous, almost like an overacted production, but I knew that Lance's ego had been badly bruised and it was highly unlikely that he would step down. Why was Antony egging him on? Maybe Lance's paranoia had some validity. I couldn't imagine any other actor speaking to the artistic director like that. While I considered how I might distract Lance, Thad the set designer appeared from out of nowhere. He wasn't in costume, but rather wore a pair of faded work jeans, heavy boots, and his tool belt that looked as if it had every tool he could possibly need at the ready.

"Lance, I need you to take a look at the stage. There's a problem with the fog effect." He ignored Antony and pulled Lance away without another word.

Antony bent over and pretended to fix one of the laces on his strappy sandals. I had a feeling he was trying to save face.

"Um, that was weird, right?" Bethany said, holding up the edges of her ruffled hoop skirt as we walked to the dessert tables.

"Yeah. I think he's about to crack." I sighed and tried to see if I could catch his eye. He was huddled with Thad at the end of the stage watching small puffs of fog erupt from the machine. It didn't look like anything was broken, which made me wonder if Thad had had my idea—to distract Lance from his ongoing feud with Antony. Regardless, it had worked, so I returned my attention to our dazzling display of desserts.

For the next two hours Bethany and I served slices of tea cake with clotted cream and fresh strawberries along with warm pots of chocolate pudding and bubbling tarts. By far the hit of the dessert table was Stephanie's royal marchpanes. I wished that she could have been there to see the reaction when guests oohed and aahed over her delicate creations. Of course, in the same breath I knew that she would have hated having to squeeze into a costume. Although she would have made a great evil queen or dark fairy.

"Instagram is on fire," Bethany said between groups of partygoers. "*Sweetened* magazine just reposted the marzipan pic."

"Excellent." I had met the editor of *Sweetened* at the Chocolate Festival and she ended up doing a cover feature on Torte's wedding cakes. The exposure in the national magazine had been great for business. We'd received calls from as far away as Boston and Florida asking if we could fly our cakes out for a wedding. Alas, we weren't set up for delivery outside of a small radius, but it was flattering to be asked.

The party was flush with color and merriment. From fire dancers to the minstrel band and the entire company mingling and laughing while gorging on an authentic Shakespearean feast, it looked like Lance's bash was a smashing success. I'd been busy managing the flow of desserts and restocking the table but didn't notice any other interactions between Lance and Antony. Thank goodness for small miracles, I thought.

Lance stumbled over to the dessert table as the party began to wind down. "Darlings, darlings, you were perfection." He waved his index finger in the air as if trying to find the right words. "My God, you are perfection. I missed the final reveal. No wonder everyone has been raving about the pastries. You are two pastry goddesses. Those dresses. The hair!"

Bethany blushed. I was familiar with Lance's tendency to flatter, but for once I actually felt like a princess, so I took his compliment in stride.

"How was everything? Did you eat? Did you get more mead?" Lance asked.

"We're good," I assured Lance. "We're going to start packing up the few leftovers and I'll leave them for you before I go. How are you? I'm worried about you."

"Fine. Fine. I'm fine, darling." Lance made a dismissive motion in the air with his hand. Then he came around the table and wrapped me in a tight embrace. I could smell the lingering mead on his breath as he said, "Thank you, Juliet. My deepest thanks." His voice was filled with sincerity and for a minute I thought he might cry.

"You're welcome." I returned the hug. "Lance, are you sure you're okay?"

His shoulders heaved. I thought he was finally going to admit that he was an emotional wreck, but instead he clutched me tighter. When he finally released me, he straightened his cape and shifted into his stage persona. "Darling, you must come join us for a nightcap. We're all heading to Puck's Pub in a few minutes. Leave this for tomorrow and come celebrate."

Bethany had finished packing our supplies and had boxed up a handful of extra marzipans and tarts. "I can't," I said to Lance, nodding at the stacks of plastic tubs. "I need to get these back to the bakeshop and then I'm hitting my bed. Remember, we have baker's hours, which means it's way past my bedtime."

"Nonsense." Lance pointed to the supplies. "You can

send someone up for this stuff in the morning. You have to bring your costumes back anyway, and studies say that a nightcap before bed is just the thing to help you nod off into la-la land."

"What studies say that?" I asked.

"Studies. Professional studies." Lance winked.

I turned to Bethany. "Why don't you take off; I've got it from here."

"Are you sure?" she said with a wide grin. "I mean I'm happy to help and I can stay as long as you need me, but some of my friends are heading to the Black Dog and I thought it might be fun to show up in this." She did another twirl. I wondered if her "friends" included Andy.

Lance clapped. "Oh, dearest angel, you must take that for a spin. You'll be the belle of the ball. Off with you." He shooed Bethany away.

"So how did you feel about the party?" I asked as I wiped down the table with a damp rag. "It seemed like everyone had a fantastic time."

"Do you think so?" He darted his head from side to side. "It was marvelous, wasn't it? I can't wait to hear what the board has to say in the morning."

"What's happening in the morning?"

"I've called a special emergency session to discuss that egomaniac." He nodded toward the bar where Antony and Tracy were talking with a tall thin young actor wearing a toga that looked almost identical to Antony's. The only difference was that Antony was dark with olive skin and black hair. The other actor—or member of the company—was as pale as me with light, almost white hair.

"Do you think that's a good idea, given . . ." I trailed off and reached for a grape marzipan in the container in front of me.

"Of course it's a good idea. Why wouldn't it be? I'm done with his little escapades and his ridiculous need for attention. I want his head on a platter. He's done. Finished. Finito." Lance glared at Antony. "In fact, I've already groomed his replacement." He gave a nod to the young actor in the toga. "My new Antony is dutifully waiting in the wings."

Finishing the creamy almond marzipan, I swallowed and stared at the bar. "Who? That blond guy?"

Lance scoffed. "Brock? No, not him. He's Antony's roommate. He's a stagehand and an extra." He gave me a devilish look and pointed to a tall actor who stood at the edge of the crowd. That is my new Antony. Isn't he dreamy?" He reached for a marzipan shaped like a lemon.

I followed suit and ate another grape. "Sure."

"The best thing is that big-headed, pompous, self-proclaimed actor has no idea it's coming, and he's the one who recommended I audition the understudy who is about to replace him. Karma." Lance's eyes twinkled with mean-spirited delight. "It's going to be quite the shock. Perhaps you should time your costume return so you can watch him go down in flames."

"No, thanks." I shook my head.

Antony noticed us watching him. He knocked back his pint of mead and slammed the sturdy mug on the table. With a dramatic sweep of his cape he turned and stormed toward us.

Uh-oh. I wished I could disappear under the table.

"Nice party." His voice dripped with sarcasm. "The

board and volunteers absolutely loved it." He pointed to a group of older women nearby. One of them caught his eye and he blew her a kiss. She giggled like a school-girl and whispered something to the group.

Lance rolled his eyes. "You've had to sink so low that you're flirting with grandmothers."

Antony shot him a dark look. "I don't see them clam-oring for your attention."

Digging his nails into an apple-shaped marzipan, Lance narrowed his lips. "You need to leave. Now."

"Who's going to make me?" Antony puffed out his chest.

To my horror, Lance squeezed the marzipan in one hand and then stepped forward and took a swing. Antony ducked, but the punch landed on his shoulder. Antony recoiled. Brock, the stagehand, sprinted across the room and leaped between them.

I wanted to pinch myself. Was this really happening? The Lance that I knew was dramatic, but a fighter? No.

Lance rubbed his hands together and bounced from one foot to the other, like a boxer warming up before a match.

Antony fumed. His face turned blotchy with red and white spots. He recovered from the initial blow and tossed off his cape. "You want to go? Let's go," he said to Lance.

Brock, who reminded me of a toothpick, stood be-tween them and held out one arm in either direction. "Bad idea, bro," he said to Antony.

"Bro?" Antony spat. "I am not your bro, man. Do you want to go there? Should we spill our dirty little secrets right here?"

I watched as Brock's feeble arm muscles twitched. For a second I thought he might join ranks with Lance and take a swing at Antony himself, but instead he tugged Lance's arm. "You got a minute?"

Lance twitched. His hand was on his dagger. I figured it was a prop, but then again, I couldn't be sure of anything with Lance right now.

"I need to talk to you about something important," Brock almost begged.

Lance flinched, then appeared to realize what Brock was saying. His shoulders swelled. "Of course. I'm always happy to lend a listening ear."

"Seriously!" Antony threw his hands in the air. "We're not done, old man," he said to Lance with a threatening thrust of his chest before storming over to the group of older women he'd been flirting with.

"Well, shall we?" Lance addressed Brock while absently running a finger under his eye. I knew the "old man" comment had to sting. Lance had never revealed his age. I suspected he was in his mid-forties, but he prided himself on his ageless appearance and wrinkle-free skin.

Antony played up his charm by saying something to the group of women that made them all titter. He gave one of them his arm and escorted her out of the tent with a final look of triumph at Lance. Brock whispered something in Lance's ear that made him tip his head back and laugh. I appreciated the fact that he had distracted Lance, but had a feeling it wasn't entirely selfless. He had seized an opportunity to get face time with OSF's most highly esteemed director.

I took that as my cue to sneak out. What I had said to

Lance was true. I had an early day ahead of me and the last thing I wanted was a nightcap. Instead, I wanted a steaming cup of tea and my warm and cozy bed. The event had been a success and I had done my part for my friend. I hoped that he would call it a night, too. But as I heaved plastic tubs onto the rolling cart I heard him inviting anyone who listened to come have a drink. Good luck, I whispered, and made my exit.

Chapter Eight

I fell asleep before I finished my tea, so when I heard the sound of pounding and someone calling my name I figured I must be dreaming. The pounding intensified as I flipped onto my back and stared up at a dark ceiling.

"Juliet! Open up!" someone hollered.

Was I dreaming?

A series of rapid bangs, like someone was trying to break down my front door, made me shake my head and sit up.

"Juliet! Let me in."

I blinked twice and jumped out of bed. What time was it? I fumbled in the dark, instinctively reaching for my slippers before realizing that I was still wearing my party dress. When I reached for the light switch and flipped it on I was plunged into a temporary blindness. Bright spots clouded my vision as I ran my hand along the wall and headed to the front room. The clock in the living room read two o'clock. Who was at my door?

"Juliet!" the voice called. There was a sense of panic in the man's tone. I recognized the voice, but my head was still groggy from being woken from a deep sleep.

I walked to the front door and peered out the peep-hole. Lance was standing on the other side. "Lance, what are you doing here? It's the middle of the night," I said, opening the door.

He burst inside. His hands were shaking and covered in what looked like blood. That couldn't be blood, could it? I must be dreaming.

He paced from the living room to the kitchen and back again. "Jules, this is bad. It's so bad."

"What? What's going on, Lance?" He never called me Jules. That shook me from my sleepy haze and made me pay attention. His hands were covered in something dark and red and he still wore his costume. There was something bulky behind his cape, and his words came out in such rapid succession that I could barely make sense of what he was saying.

"Antony. Dead. I don't understand. I don't know what I did. Why did I do it, Jules? Why?" His ashen face and trembling hands gave me pause.

"Lance, you have to slow down. What about Antony? He's dead?"

"My God, yes! He's dead, Jules. Dead. Stabbed with a bloody dagger." He held up his red hands that shook violently and stared at them.

His entire body went into shock. He dropped to his knees.

I ran over to help him up. "Come on, let's get you on the couch." I lifted him up and slowly positioned him on the couch. Then I covered his quaking legs with a blanket and sat down next to him. "Lance, you're not making sense. Can you take a deep breath and then tell me what's going on?"

He threw his head back and wailed. "What's going on? A tragedy of epic proportions, Jules. Epic. Antony is dead."

My mind flashed to the worst-case scenario. Had Lance killed Antony? No way. My friend wasn't a killer, but then again had he just confessed? Why were his hands bloody and why was he freaking out? I took a deep breath, partly for Lance and partly for me.

"How do you know that Antony is dead?" I asked.

Lance reached behind his back and pulled out a bloody dagger. "Because of this."

I took another deep breath and thought carefully about my words before I spoke. "Lance, you didn't stab him, did you?"

He threw his hands in the air and shot up from the couch. I saw a glimpse of my friend return as he waved the dagger in the air. "Of course I didn't kill him. Please. He wasn't worth a second of my time."

. "Okay, why don't you tell me what happened, then." I smoothed my party dress, remembering the feeling of floating down the staircase into Lance's soiree.

"I don't know what happened!" Lance's composure quickly faded. "We had that nasty tiff at the party. You saw that. And then I left. We went and had a lovely nightcap at Puck's Pub. Don't give me that look, I only had one drink."

I didn't bother to reply.

Lance paced in front of the couch with the dagger still in his hand. "That's it. Then I went back to the theater to grab a few things and make sure that cleanup had gone according to plan. I walked down the Shakespeare stairs to Lithia Park and stumbled over something."

"Antony?" I interjected.

Lance threw his hand over his mouth and gagged, "Yes. He was sprawled on the ground with this sticking out of his stomach." He held up the dagger. "Jules, what are we going to do?"

"We're going to call the police." I stood up and walked toward the bookcase where I had left my phone.

"No!" Lance screamed and chased after me. He stopped short of grabbing me, staring at my silky pink dress and then at his hands. "You can't call the police. Look at me. They're going to think I did it. Look at my hands. Look at this dagger." His feral eyes darted around the room. "Wait, there's more. I found this, too." He yanked a DVD case out of his pocket.

"What is it?"

He held it like it was a bomb about to explode. "I don't know. It was by the body. An empty DVD case—that must mean something—a clue perhaps? You're good at investigating. Can't we just figure this out ourselves?"

"Lance, stop. You have to calm down. We don't have a choice. I'm calling Thomas."

"Not Thomas," Lance pleaded. "At least call the Professor if you have to call anyone."

"Fine, I'll call the Professor, then." I reached for my phone and punched in his number.

"Are you sure you have to call? Can't we just do something with the body? This looks bad for me, Jules, really bad."

The phone began to ring. "Not as bad as not calling

them, Lance." I pointed to the couch. "Why don't you sit down?" I waited for the Professor to answer. When his voice mail came over the line I left him a message explaining that it was an emergency and to call me back immediately, and then without waiting for Lance's approval or input I dialed Thomas's number.

He picked up on the first ring. "Kind of late for a pastry run, isn't it, Jules?"

"Thomas, can you come over right now?"

"Sure. What's wrong? You sound stressed."

I lowered my voice slightly. "It's Lance. He's found a body."

"What? Did you call 911?"

"No, I called you."

"Hang up and call them. I'm on my way."

The line went dead. I dialed emergency services and explained the situation while Lance rocked back and forth on the couch. The dispatcher assured me that she would send a team to Lithia Park. She instructed me to stay with Lance until Thomas or the Professor arrived. As it turned out, we didn't have to wait long. That was one of the perks of life in a small town. Thomas only lived about five minutes from my apartment. When I greeted him at the door I could tell that I had woken him. Instead of his blue police uniform and shiny badge, he wore a pair of warm-up pants and a zip-up athletic jacket. I wondered if he'd been running again. When we dated in high school Thomas had played football and used to run a minimum of six miles every day to stay in shape. He had maintained his muscular physique postcollege, but it had been years since I'd seen him in his workout gear.

"Hey Jules, I came as quick as I could." He was breathless, as if he had run all the way to my apartment.

I stood to the side to make way for him to enter. "It's been five minutes. I think that's pretty quick."

"You look really nice." His blue eyes stared at my hair and then worked their way down to my dress. "Like a princess."

"Thanks." I willed my cheeks not to blush. Thomas had somewhat recently professed his feelings for me, but I didn't reciprocate them. I cared about him, and loved him as a friend, but my heart still longed for Carlos. Until I set him free I couldn't think about another man.

Thomas's body language stiffened when he spotted Lance. "I should arrest you right now, if that's a weapon you're holding, but the Professor gave me strict orders to wait to do anything other than interrogate you until he arrives."

He gave me a concerned look and then nodded toward the kitchen. I took that as my cue to make myself scarce. However, in my tiny apartment it was impossible not to overhear their conversation. I filled a teakettle and set it on the stove as Thomas began interrogating Lance. It felt weird to stand around in the kitchen pretending that I couldn't hear every word they were saying, so I decided to do the only thing that I knew—bake.

My home kitchen was well supplied with baking essentials, but I wasn't sure how long Thomas would stay and whether any of Ashland's other men and women in blue would show up, so I opted to make shortbread. It was a simple cookie recipe that could be baked in a pan or cut into fancy shapes. Shortbread doesn't require eggs and can be enhanced with a variety of flavors. I'm a purist when it comes to the crispy, buttery treat. I like to bake mine with a hint of vanilla, a touch of salt, and finish it with chunky crystalized sugar.

While Thomas asked Lance to start from the beginning I creamed butter, sugar, and vanilla into a mixing bowl. I heard Lance repeat exactly what I had heard. He left the party and went for a celebratory drink at Puck's Pub. After Brock swooped in, Antony left the party with Judy Faulkner, a longtime OSF volunteer. That must have been the woman that I'd seen him schmoozing with, I thought as I turned the mixer to low.

"That's the last time I saw him alive, I swear," Lance said to Thomas as the kettle let out a shrill whistle. I removed it from the stove and poked my head into the living room. "Would either of you like some tea?"

"Yes, please, that would be divine," Lance said, but Thomas shook his head.

"Sorry. I can't let you touch anything." He nodded to Lance's hands. "We're going to have to swab you. As soon as the Professor gets here I'm sure he's going to want me to take you in."

Lance quivered. "You make me sound like a common criminal."

At that moment another knock sounded on the door.

"That's probably the Professor," Thomas said, getting up and walking toward the door. "Do you mind, Jules?"

"Go ahead."

Sure enough, the Professor stood on my front landing holding a Moleskine notepad and a pencil. "Good evening. Or is it morning?" He acknowledged Thomas and gave me a wave.

"Tea?" I asked.

"Thank you for the offer, but I must decline. Duty calls." The subtle lines on the corners of his lips creased. He sat next to Lance and nodded for Thomas to take notes.

I returned to my shortbread, adding in flour and a healthy shake of salt. Then I greased a nine-by-eleven-inch pan and pressed the mixture into a thin layer. I slid it into the oven and poured myself a cup of honey-almond tea.

The Professor's line of questioning was centered around the dagger. "Help me understand what compelled you to remove the weapon."

Lance flustered a bit. "I don't know. I'm not sure what came over me."

"Did you attempt to resuscitate or administer CPR?"

"No." Lance sounded defensive. "I knew he was dead. It wasn't going to help."

"How did you know?" the Professor pressed.

"He was dead. It was obvious. The dagger was jabbed into his stomach and there was so much blood. So much blood."

I couldn't see them, but I figured Lance was probably staring at his bloody hands.

"I found the DVD case first. I picked it up without thinking about it. I figured I would turn it in to lost and found tomorrow. You wouldn't believe what patrons leave at the theater. But then I realized it had something on it—blood." Lance's voice quivered.

"And yet you opted to come here," the Professor continued. "What made you decide to come to Juliet's apartment rather than calling for help?"

Thomas's cell phone buzzed. "I'll take this outside,"

he said to the Professor. I wondered if the first responders were calling him with an update.

The Professor's voice was calm yet commanding as he dove into a new round of questions. "Tell me why you were at Lithia Park at such a late hour."

Lance's voice was shaky. "I don't know why I came to Juilet's. I suppose instinct." He answered more questions and relayed the evening's events once again. I thought it was a good sign that his story hadn't varied.

"Don't you have a permanent parking space up next to the bricks?" the Professor asked when Lance finished.

"Yes."

"And why didn't you park there tonight? You said that you parked your car near Lithia Creek instead."

I wondered what the significance of Lance parking in a different area was and what it had to do with Antony's murder.

"The party." Lance's reply was shrill. "We needed the space. Delivery trucks were arriving all afternoon. I simply parked down below to make room."

"Hmm."

The scent of the buttery shortbread began to permeate the kitchen. I sipped my tea and breathed it in. Thomas came back inside and went over and whispered something in the Professor's ear.

"I see." The Professor nodded. "I believe that's everything we need for the moment. Thomas, please go ahead and take Lance down to the car for DNA samples. We'd like you to come with us and identify the location of the body."

"Okay." Lance sighed.

I ducked my head out again. "Can I send anyone with a mug of tea?"

"Something smells heavenly as always," the Professor said, drawing in a breath and walking over to me. "Alas, we cannot dally, but someone will be back later to take your statement. I do apologize for the inconvenience. Normally I would never consider interviewing a suspect in your apartment; however, I think you'll agree that these are unusual circumstances. I intend to be as discreet as I possibly can, while still following the letter of the law. When and if word spreads that Lance is involved in . . ." He trailed off in search of the right word. "Whatever this is, I'm sure you can imagine the stir this will cause."

I nodded.

With that the three of them left my apartment. I couldn't believe it, and I couldn't sit still. Lance wasn't a killer, but why in the world would he have taken the dagger and why were his hands covered in blood?

Chapter Nine

My shortbread finished baking not long after they left. Shortbread is only as good as the butter you use. My preference is Irish butter. There's nothing that compares to the smooth, soft milk fat from grass-fed Irish cows. I pulled them from the oven and was pleased with the result. The top and sides were golden brown and slightly crisp. After it cooled, I would cut it in squares. At Torte, we use shortbread for everything from crusts for cream-filled pies to specialty cookies, like at Valentine's Day when we cut shortbread into hearts and dip them into melted dark chocolate.

I considered calling Mom, but it was so late that I didn't want to wake her and cause her any undue worry. Like me, the minute she found out that Lance was in trouble, I knew she would never be able to go back to sleep. The empty walls in my apartment felt claustrophobic as I paced from the living room to the kitchen and back again. Short of my collection of cookbooks, my space was barren. I had hung one print that I purchased at the Lithia Artists Market. It was a pencil drawing of an Italian market on a busy summer day. The vibrant stalls of fresh fruit and hanging salami appealed to the foodie in me and reminded me of my travels with Carlos. With my travels and love life on hiatus it was time to make this place my own, I thought, peering out the window for any sign of the Professor or Thomas.

It felt like hours before Thomas returned, but in reality, it was only about forty minutes later that he knocked softly on the front door.

"Hey, Jules. I've got some news and need to ask you a couple of questions."

"No problem." I let him in. "Do you want some shortbread and tea now?"

"That would be amazing."

Was it just my imagination or did he sound dejected? I piled shortbread squares on a plate and poured Thomas a mug of tea before joining him on the couch.

"So how bad is it?" I asked, handing him the tea and setting the plate on the coffee table.

"Honestly, I'm not sure." He wrapped his hands around the mug. "How do you do this?"

"Do what?"

"Manage to bake something that smells like it's going to be the best thing I've ever tasted in the middle of a crisis?"

"It's what I do." I chuckled nervously. "If I didn't do something I was going to go crazy, so I figured I might as well bake."

"Lucky me." Thomas placed the tea on the table and picked up a cookie. He took a bite and savored it for a minute. "Yep. This is the best thing I've ever tasted."

"It's butter, sugar, and flour. It can't be the best thing you've ever tasted."

"I'll be the judge of that." He took a huge bite. "Yep. It's the best."

"Thanks, but you're the worst judge. You would literally eat anything I put in front of you."

He gave me a sheepish grin. "True, but these are amazing." He finished the cookie. "Okay, on to the bad stuff."

I braced myself. Had they found proof that Lance was the killer?

"Jules, you look like you're going to throw up."

"I feel like I might throw up." My stomach gurgled in response.

Thomas placed his hand on my knee. "I know. I get it."

"It's weird, because as you know, Lance drives me crazy, but he's become a good friend, and I'm worried about him."

"Me, too." Thomas squeezed my knee. It felt calming and reassuring.

"Don't leave me in suspense. What did you find?"

"Nothing."

"What?" My hair had spilled from my headband. I brushed a strand from my eyes.

Thomas removed his hand and sat up. "Nothing. Not a body. Nothing. There's nothing there."

"Are you kidding?"

His bright eyes narrowed. "No. I wish I was. Lance took us right to the spot where he says he found Antony's body, but there's nothing there."

"What?" I couldn't think of anything articulate to ask. "What does that mean?"

"Your guess is as good as mine." Thomas helped himself to another slice of shortbread. "Maybe he made the whole thing up. Lance is prone to wanting attention. Stranger things have happened."

I thought about how out of sorts Lance had been lately. Could he have staged a fake murder? Maybe. But why? Even for Lance that seemed out of character and insanely dramatic.

"The team is sweeping the area now," Thomas said through a mouthful of shortbread. "It's dark, so they're bringing in floodlights. Maybe they'll find something we couldn't see with our flashlights. We'll do a complete search of the park first thing in the morning. If there was a body there will be some kind of a trail—drag marks, bloodstains, that sort of thing."

An involuntary shudder ran up my spine.

"There's also the possibility that someone did stab Antony, but that he wasn't dead. Lithia Park is ninety-three acres of canyonland. There's plenty of space to disappear. Antony could have lost consciousness and be hidden underneath a tree or up in the forest if he tried to get help and got turned around."

I rubbed my temples and pulled off the headband. "None of this makes sense."

"None of it looks good for Lance." Thomas played with the zipper on his warm-up jacket.

"Right. I get it."

Thomas leaned his elbow on the armrest. "Jules, how would you describe Lance lately?"

"What do you mean?" I had a feeling I knew exactly what he meant, but I didn't want to betray my friend.

"Has he been acting like himself?" Thomas kept his face passive, but his sky-blue eyes pierced through me. I recognized the look.

"Not exactly." I twisted the beaded headband.

"Care to elaborate?" Thomas crossed one foot over the other and relaxed into the couch.

I confessed my fears and explained that both Mom and I had been worried about him for a while now. Thomas listened without taking any notes. "Anything else you think I should know?" he asked once I finished.

"Isn't that enough?"

He sat up and brushed cookie crumbs from his jeans. "Yeah, it is. Try not to worry."

"Where is Lance now?" I gathered the few remaining slices of shortbread. It would go to waste in my apartment, so I figured I would wrap them up and send them home with Thomas.

"He was still at the scene when I left. The Professor will look after him." Thomas stood. "Listen, Jules, this might get kind of complicated."

"Why?"

"Well, for the moment Antony is a suspected missing person, but if we find a body the Professor has already said that he's going to recuse himself from the investigation. In fact, he already put in a call to Medford for support."

"Why?" I repeated.

"Lance." Thomas curled his lip down. "The Professor and Lance have known each other for years."

"And he thinks Lance is a suspect," I interrupted.

"Jules, come on. He is." Thomas shrugged. "It's the right move."

"Yeah." I stood and held out the plate of shortbread. "You want to take these home?"

Thomas grinned. "You know I won't turn down that offer."

He followed me into the kitchen with our tea mugs. Without asking he rinsed out the cups and placed them in the dishwasher. "How goes the expansion?"

"It's coming along." I found a roll of waxed paper and layered it between the shortbread. Moisture is a baker's enemy. The waxed paper would serve as a barrier to keep the shortbread from getting chewy. Shortbread is meant to be crisp. For soft cookies like snickerdoodles or chocolate chip, I always place a slice of white bread in my cookie jar to help keep them chewy. The cookies absorb the moisture from the bread and white bread won't transfer any flavor to the cookies. For a crisp cookie like a shortbread or oatmeal Scotties, I store them in airtight containers.

Thomas waited for me to place the stack of shortbread into a plastic bag and seal it. "I'll have to come take a look. Richard Lord isn't giving you any trouble, is he?"

I hesitated. It would have been easy to lie, but fortunately Richard Lord had been strangely silent lately. "Nope. In fact, I haven't seen him once since I've been home."

"He's probably planning his next big move." Thomas rolled his eyes and then took the bag of shortbread. "Thanks. You know you didn't need to go to the trouble of packaging these up. They'll be gone before I get back to Lithia Park."

"Pace yourself, friend." I patted his back as we walked to the door.

"Are you saying I can't polish off an entire pan of

your shortbread and not hate myself in the morning?"
He pinched his waist. "I'll have you know that I'm in
fighting shape. I decided I needed a new challenge, so I
signed up for a half marathon. I've been running every
day."

"I wondered if you were running again."

His eyes brightened. "You did?"

My cheeks warmed. "Just take your shortbread and
go," I ordered with a laugh.

He flexed. "All right, but you're saying good-bye to
these muscles."

"Get out."

With a wink, he left.

I had to admit that I enjoyed our easy banter. Being
around Thomas was comfortable and familiar. But after
I shut and locked the door, my thoughts returned to
Lance. What was going on with my friend? Could he
be having a nervous breakdown? Was tonight an elaborate ruse to get attention, or was Antony really dead?

Chapter Ten

I didn't sleep much, so when my alarm sounded in the darkness I quickly silenced it and yanked off the covers. Who knew what the day would bring. I wondered if the police had found anything—or anyone—at Lithia Park overnight and how Lance was doing. Had it only been a few hours since Thomas had come by? I tugged on a pair of jeans, a V-neck white T-shirt, and a fleece sweatshirt. Ashland mornings and evenings had been cool in the shifting weather. By midday I would be pulling off the sweatshirt and cracking open Torte's kitchen windows. I washed my face with cold water and tied my hair into a high ponytail.

Before I did anything else, I needed coffee—strong coffee. My morning routine rarely varied. I enjoyed a leisurely cup or two of dark roast before heading to Torte. The process of slowly brewing nutty aromatic beans was almost like meditation for me. I could complete each step with my eyes closed, from pouring ice-cold filtered water into the pot to grinding the beans. I appreciated that coffee couldn't be rushed. My mornings started with a cadence and pace that involved breathing in the scent of bright and cheery beans and allowing my body a moment of pause and quiet contemplation before facing the day.

This morning was no exception and I found myself lingering over my second cup for longer than usual. I couldn't stop thinking about Lance. There was no good answer. Either outcome—whether he was having a breakdown or had found a body—came with potentially terrible consequences. If Lance had fabricated Antony's death, what did that mean for the state of his mental health? Was he delusional? Did he need immediate help? Or had Antony met an untimely death? If so, where was his body, and who had killed him?

Questions assaulted my head as I polished off my coffee and placed my mug in the sink. I wasn't going to solve Lance's problems by creating my own, so I put on my tennis shoes. Torte was calling like a welcome reprieve from my spinning mind. "Time to bake," I said aloud, stepping outside. A brisk breeze greeted me as I took the stairs two at a time. Elevation, the outdoor store beneath my apartment, had geared up for spring. Two bright red and yellow river kayaks hung in its front windows along with colorful collections of water sandals, swimsuits, beach towels, and a pyramid of sunscreen. It didn't feel like swimsuit weather quite yet. I rubbed my arms and hurried down the sidewalk. By the look of the other storefronts in the plaza it appeared that everyone in Ashland had a touch of spring fever. Tulips budded in planter boxes, special spring menus had been posted on restaurant doors, and flyers for hiking excursions and drumming circles at Lithia

Park were plastered near the information kiosk in the center of the town square.

When I arrived at the bakeshop the lights were already on in the kitchen. Mom had beat me in. I unlocked the front door.

"What are you doing here so early?" I called, locking the door behind me. If we left it unlocked customers would come in long before we were ready for them. "What are you doing here at all?"

Mom turned off the mixer and rubbed her left ear. "What's that, honey?"

Her hearing had been diminishing over the past few years thanks in part to genetics and a lifetime spent in the kitchen surrounded by whirling mixers and happy, noisy customers.

"I said you're here early," I repeated, and grabbed an apron from the hooks near the office.

Then I glanced at the island, which was filled with trays of cooling cookies, muffins, and pastries. "How long have you been here?" I asked. "I thought you were taking mornings off."

Mom slid loaves of bread into the oven, and then turned to me. "I couldn't sleep. I heard what happened." She brushed flour onto her apron and moved toward me. "Have you seen him?"

"Who? Lance?"

Her eyes held a look of deep concern.

"I saw him last night. He came to my place. He didn't even call the Professor or police."

Mom wrapped her arm around my waist. "How are you doing?" She smelled of honey and vanilla.

I leaned into her. "I don't know."

She held me for a minute, not needing to say a word. Once I found my bearings, I squeezed her arm. She took it as a signal that I could stand on my own and released me. "Doug told me everything. He mentioned the possibility that Lance created Antony's death as a hoax." Her voice held the same questioning disbelief that I felt.

"Yeah, that's what Thomas said last night. I can't believe it, though. What would Lance possibly gain?"

Mom's brow wrinkled. "My thoughts exactly."

"Does the Professor really think that Lance made it up?"

She shrugged. "I don't know. But what I do know is that Doug and Lance have been friends for years. Doug isn't going to jump to any conclusions."

"Is he going to stay on the case?"

She twisted her wedding ring from my dad that she wore on a chain around her neck. "I'm not sure. He's meeting with a detective from Medford this morning."

"I hope he can stay involved. Lance needs him."

Mom closed her eyes momentarily. I wondered if she was saying a silent prayer. "I know. There's not much we can do for the moment. We'll have to see what the day brings."

The kitchen smelled of baking bread and cinnamon. My stomach rumbled.

Mom chuckled. "Sounds like someone skipped breakfast." She walked to the island and handed me a cinnamon pecan muffin. "Eat."

Ever since I had returned home she had been trying to fatten me up. The stress of leaving the ship and Carlos had made me drop a few pounds, but I kept reminding her that I had gained that weight back, plus some. "Mom, I'm fine." I shifted my apron to show her how my jeans fit snugly against my waist.

"Nonsense. You've been rail thin since you were a kid. Your father and I used to joke that it was a good thing we owned a bakeshop. He called you a bottomless pit."

I laughed at the memory. My dad, like me, had been tall and naturally lean. As a kid, I hated being the tallest girl in class and wished I had inherited my mom's petite frame. However, in time I came to appreciate my height. It turned out to be an asset in culinary school. None of the guys messed with me, I think because they were afraid of me.

"Eat," Mom insisted. She returned to the oven to check on the bread. "Are you free to come with me to A Rose by Any Other Name this afternoon? I want your opinion on the wedding bouquets."

"Of course. Count me in." I studied the whiteboard to see what orders Mom had already completed. "Have you and the Professor come up with any other venues yet?"

She sighed. "No. We keep striking out. We talked last night—before everything happened with Lance—about scaling back the guest list, but neither of us feel right about that. Ashland brought us together. Ashland should be there to celebrate with us."

"What about one of the wineries on the ridge?" I asked, biting into the muffin. It was light as air with sweet and spicy pecans.

"They're booked. Summer is peak season for tourists, so between that, private events, and other weddings, everything is full." She lowered the oven temp and reached for a mixing bowl. "We could push the date back. I'm sure we could find something next summer, but neither of us wants to wait."

I savored the muffin. "There has to be something." She was right about space in Ashland being at a premium during the summer season. Lance would have gladly offered up one of the theaters or the bricks for the wedding, but tickets for each production had been on sale for months. Many of the summer shows were already sold out. Weddings were also big business in Ashland from June through September. Brides had discovered that Ashland made a perfect destination wedding. Guests could take in a show at OSF, a whitewater rafting trip on the Umpqua River, or a day trip to the Oregon Coast while in town for the celebration.

"There's always Lithia Park." She cubed butter and added it to the mixing bowl.

The warm muffin had hit the spot. I finished it and then decided I would start on the daily soup special. I had been craving chicken tortilla soup. It reminded me of spring and Carlos. "Why not. The park could be fun. What about a giant, community picnic?"

"Maybe." She measured sugar.

"You're not feeling it?"

"It's not that. You know me, I'm not fancy. I love the idea of a picnic, but I was hoping for something a bit more stylish for our wedding. Not Lance stylish." She grimaced.

I laughed. "Oh no. Please no!"

"Never, but something with a touch of elegance."

"We'll find something. Don't worry." I thought through

some of my favorite places as I went to the walk-in. Last winter I had catered an event at Lake of the Woods. The lakeside resort had a rustic lodge and plenty of cabins for out-of-town guests, but it was a popular vacation spot for families. Many families returned year after year to rent the same cabin. It might already be booked, but it was worth a shot. I would call them later this morning and check. I filled a bowl with organic chicken breasts, cilantro, corn, onions, peppers, and tomatoes and returned to the kitchen.

I started by chopping onions, garlic, and peppers. I tossed them in a pan with a healthy glug of olive oil and sautéed them over medium heat. What other venue could there be for Mom and the Professor's upcoming nuptials? There was Emigrant Park, with a waterslide for the kiddos and plenty of shady space, but Mom didn't sound thrilled with the idea of a park wedding. I glanced outside as the onions, garlic, and peppers began to sweat. The smell opened up my sinuses. What if we shut down the plaza for the wedding? I wondered if the Professor could get authorization for something like that?

Andy and Stephanie arrived as I turned the heat to low and returned to the cutting board. "Morning," I called as I chopped the cilantro stalks, reserved the leafy foliage, and added the chopped stems to the mixture on the stove. Then I added corn and set a pot of water to boil for the tomatoes.

"How are the show tunes?" I asked Stephanie as she trudged into the kitchen.

Mom raised an eyebrow. "Show tunes?"

"Don't ask," Stephanie mumbled.

"Stephanie has a neighbor who is apparently a big fan of show tunes," I said to Mom.

Mom stifled a laugh. Stephanie shot daggers at me. "Don't even say the words 'show tune' around me."

"Sorry. I take it that means the . . . music continued last night."

Stephanie washed her hands in the sink. Her nails were each painted black with white skulls on her index fingers. "All flipping night long."

"That is the worst, honey," Mom said with sincere empathy. I thought Stephanie might bite her head off, but instead she looked like she might cry.

"It's the worst," she repeated, and wiped something from underneath her eye that made her black eyeliner smudge.

"Do you want go home and try to get some sleep now?" Mom walked over and offered Stephanie a hug, which shockingly Stephanie accepted.

She blinked rapidly and forcibly wiped her eyes. "No. I'm here. Plus, it never stops."

"Shoot, I meant to find my old earplugs for you, but got distracted with Lance last night."

"Don't worry, Steph, I'll have coffee for you in two minutes," Andy called from the espresso machine. "And here's my question. Why don't you call the police? Couldn't your neighbor get a noise violation?"

Mom perked up. "Yes, do you want me to talk to Doug?"

Stephanie brushed a hair from her face. "It's not loud, it's just constant."

"Bummer." Andy steamed milk. "How was the bash last night, boss?"

"The party was fantastic, but the rest of the night not so much. Did you see Bethany?"

Andy held a skewer stick in his hand that he used for his latte art. "No. Why?"

"She said something about meeting friends at the pub. I didn't know if that meant you two." I intentionally looked at Steph, too. "Your marzipans were the star of the show. People were literally falling over each other to get a glimpse of them. When Bethany gets in she'll show you the pictures, but *Sweetened* magazine and a bunch of other huge baking outlets shared her posts. You're going to have to start a side business."

Mom clapped. "We'll be able to say that we knew you when."

Stephanie shrugged off the compliment. I went on to tell them about what happened after the party.

Andy whistled as he delivered a cup of coffee to a downtrodden Stephanie. "That's crazy. They can't find the body?"

I appreciated that he obviously assumed that Lance was telling the truth.

Stephanie didn't look as convinced. She gulped the coffee like someone who had been lost in the desert and had stumbled upon fresh water. "It sounds like a freaking publicity stunt to me."

Her words gave me pause. Why hadn't I considered that? What if Lance had staged Antony's murder to get more press for the launch of the season? My stomach lurched at the thought. He wouldn't pull a prank like that on me . . . Would he? It was hardly as if OSF needed more press. Many performances (especially for the outdoor summer shows) sold out the day tickets were released. OSF received write-ups and features in national and international magazines. Why would Lance need publicity, unless it was self-serving?

Mom bit the corner of her lip. "A publicity stunt." She caught my eye. I knew she was thinking the same thing.

"Yeah. That kind of stuff is all the rage. It's like flash mobs. Pranks are huge on the Internet. Stupid frat guys making each other run naked down the streets. That kind of thing."

"Hey, I watch a couple of those shows." Andy pouted. "Pranks are great comedy."

"I rest my case," Stephanie said.

My palms began to sweat. No way. Lance wouldn't use me or the Professor and Thomas in a prank, would he? Filing a false report of a crime could mean that Lance was in big trouble. I wanted to believe him, but my confidence eroded as I thought about his constant need for attention.

Andy distracted me when he came into the kitchen with coffee for me and Mom. "I gave Steph a straight shot, but I want you two to try my new creation." He handed us white ceramic mugs brimming with coffee and steamed milk.

I took a whiff of mine. "Am I smelling flowers?"

"Maybe." Andy's eyes twinkled. "Try it."

The coffee was a lovely beige color that reminded me of a sandy beach. I took a taste. The floral scent invaded my pores, and I could swear I tasted a hint of rose. It blended beautifully with the milk and chocolaty undertones of the coffee.

As if reading my mind, Mom exclaimed, "I'm tasting rose, aren't I?"

"Me, too."

Andy beamed. "You guys are good. Yep. I added a splash of rose water and a touch of vanilla bean."

"It's wonderful," Mom said, taking another sip.

"Agreed. It's like spring in a cup." I glanced at the freshly painted walls. We had spruced up the kitchen with an opaque teal three shades lighter than the dining room. The new paint brightened the small space and matched the springtime sky.

Stephanie frowned. "I want to try it."

"You asked for a coffee IV, a coffee IV you get," Andy said, pointing to the nearly empty mug she was holding. "I call that the show tune stopper. It has six shots. Yeah, you heard me correctly, six shots. If that sucker doesn't get *Oklahoma!* out of your head then nothing will."

Stephanie opened her mouth and took a shot of the coffee. "There. Done." She stuck out her tongue. "Now give me some of the good stuff."

"Hey, all my stuff is good," Andy protested.

"You know what I mean," Stephanie replied.

Andy wisely dropped it and went to make Stephanie a vanilla rose latte. I returned to my soup. The veggies gave the kitchen a wonderful spicy aroma. My pot of water had come to a rolling boil so I cut small slits into the tomatoes and dropped them into the pot. After about a minute I removed them from the water and peeled off the skins with ease. The trick worked like a charm.

Next, I squeezed the skinned tomatoes into a Dutch oven. Juice ran down my hands as I tossed chunks of the bright tomatoes into the pan. There is no substitute for fresh tomatoes. This soup can be made any time of the year with canned tomatoes, but vine-ripe tomatoes would give it a depth that can't be found in a can. I added the chopped cilantro stems and sautéed veggies. Then I poured in homemade chicken stock, diced chicken, corn, and an assortment of spices like chili powder and cumin. I would let those flavors simmer and marry for an hour or two on low heat before adding beans.

By the time Sterling and Bethany showed up for their shifts the kitchen was overflowing with pastries and my soup was bubbling happily on the stove. This was the best hour in the bakeshop, when the kitchen was fully alive with flavor. Our small but mighty staff drizzled chocolate over strawberries and sliced bread for paninis in harmony. Bethany chattered about the party and read aloud comments from people who had seen her social media posts. Her glow faded when I told them what happened after the party.

"Lance is no killer," Sterling said, pushing up the sleeves of his hoodie before sneaking a peek at my soup.

Mom bustled past him with a tray of cinnamon pecan muffins. "Exactly." She tapped his sleeve with her free hand. "I keep telling Juliet not to worry too much. Doug will get to the bottom of this."

While she filled the pastry case, I got Sterling started on making tortillas from scratch. We would fry them and use a pizza cutter to slice them into strips for garnish on my soup. "You worked closely with Lance when we were on the cruise," I said to him in a low voice, and handed him a canister of flour.

"Yeah, why?" He made a pile of flour on the island. Tortilla dough requires just a few ingredients—flour, water, a pinch of salt, and lard. The magic is kneading the dough into a pliable soft ball, dividing it into eight equal portions, and then rolling them into flat round circles. Once customers tasted our soft and chewy homemade tortillas they never purchased mass-produced again.

"I wondered if you noticed anything out of the ordinary. When you e-mailed me updates you mentioned that Lance was driving everyone crazy. I didn't give it much thought at the time because—"

"Because that's Lance," Sterling interjected.

"Exactly, but now with everything that's happened the last couple of days, I'm wondering if it could be more. What if he really was starting to have a breakdown when we left?"

Sterling added water, salt, and lard to the mound of flour in front of him and began kneading it together. He was astute beyond his years and I could tell that he was considering my point as he flexed the sticky mixture into a dough. "You know, you could be right. But I'm not exactly sure what was different about him while you were gone. There was something, though."

I sighed. "Yeah, right?" I trusted Sterling's instincts. His ability to read people was a gift, especially for someone his age.

"Do you really think that Lance would fake a murder? That's pretty out there." Sterling patted the ball of dough between his hands and then broke off eight chunks. "I mean, that's low and cruel."

"And Lance isn't cruel." I reached for olive oil and added a few glugs to a clean sauté pan. In addition to using the tortillas for a topping for my soup we would use them for sandwich wraps. Since I was in a spicy mood, I decided I would have Sterling make up big batches of salsa and guacamole. For our lunch special we would pair my chicken tortilla soup with guacamole wraps filled with shredded lettuce, cilantro, salsa, jack cheese, and beans.

"Except." Sterling held up his index finger, which was covered in flour. "What if Antony was in on it?"

"What?" I nearly spilled oil down the front of my apron.

"Think about it, Jules. Lance is always trying to rope you and anyone else he can convince to get on stage, not to mention creating drama. I can't see him faking something like this unless Antony was in on it. He made it very clear when you were gone that he didn't like Antony."

"Yeah. He made that clear to me, too."

Sterling rolled each of the smaller pieces of dough into balls. "But what's that saying from Shakespeare? The lady doth protest too much?"

"You mean you think that was an act?" He had a valid point. Lance had been over-the-top (even for him) about his low regard for Antony. What if was an act? Was Antony hiding out in Lance's basement right now? If that was the case, I might have to smack him the next time I saw him.

"It's a possibility. Lance is familiar with how to stage a drama, you know."

Vera had mentioned wanting to kill Lance last night. What if she learned about their scheme? Lance had seemed genuinely fed up with Antony, but then again, acting was his business. He could be playing me. I sighed and tried to concentrate on baking.

Sterling tossed one of the dough balls in the air and caught it. "How thin should I roll these?"

It reminded me of when Carlos had visited. He and Sterling hit it off instantly. I figured it was due to the fact that they both had an internal intensity. For Carlos, his intensity came through in his passion for food. With Sterling, it was his intensity for people. If you were Sterling's friend he would do anything for you. Carlos was at his best when teaching young chefs, and Sterling was eager to learn. It had been a good combination and experience for both of them, except for the fact that Carlos had taught his young protégé his repertoire of kitchen pranks. I could hear his sultry voice in my head. "Julieta, the food, it must be fun. Let your team play and the food will thank you."

I pushed the memory away and showed Sterling how to roll the tortillas into quarter-inch-thin circles. Then I fried an example for him and broke it in half for each of us to taste. Carlos's priority in the kitchen was infusing life and energy into whatever he put on the plate. For me, if I taught my staff one thing, it would be the power of taste. It never failed to amaze me how many chefs skipped this imperative step. Without tasting the final product or a work in progress there's no way of knowing whether a recipe is balanced or if it lacks flavor.

"What do you think?" I asked Sterling.

He chewed the warm flat bread. "It's good. Totally different than the tortillas you buy in the store. I don't get it. Where does the flavor come from? This is just water and flour."

"Don't forget about the lard." I winked. "And a nice dose of olive oil doesn't hurt, either."

He folded his bite into a square and popped it in his mouth. "How many of these should I make?"

"At least ten dozen. Wraps are usually a hit and I have a feeling we might see more of the gossip crowd today." I went to the walk-in and returned with avocados, red onions, peppers, cilantro, limes, garlic, and tomatoes. "You want to make the gauc?"

"Put me to work." He tossed a lime.

For the guacamole, I instructed him to finely dice onions, peppers, garlic, cilantro, and tomatoes. Then he could soften the avocados with a fork and add a healthy squeeze of fresh lime juice, salt, and pepper. Mix it all together and serve it on our homemade tortillas with cheese and beans. Delish.

I couldn't stop thinking about Sterling's theory that Antony was in on the gig as I checked on Stephanie's progress and sent Bethany out on the morning bread route. By the time we opened I had convinced myself that Sterling was right. The second I had a break I was going to go hunt Lance down and throttle him. As anticipated Torte was bustling the minute we opened the front doors. Everyone wanted to talk about what was going on at Lithia Park. Rumors swirled throughout the dining room along with the scent of our apple turnovers and bread pudding.

Thankfully, Mom fielded questions in the front. She came into the kitchen with two empty pastry trays not long after we flipped the sign on the front door to OPEN. Mopping her brow with a dish towel, she piled more cookies and muffins onto the empty tray. "I hate to say it, but Lance's phantom body is good for business."

"Mom, that's terrible." I scolded her with a frown.

She shrugged and pointed to the picked-over pastry case. "I'm not suggesting it as a marketing strategy, but you can't deny that anytime something out of the ordinary happens in Ashland people eat their weight in pastry."

I watched as she expertly weaved past the line of customers waiting for one of Andy's vanilla rose lattes and slid the newly stocked trays into the pastry case. A woman stopped her, I assumed to ask whether Mom had any insider information. They chatted while Mom packaged up a box of muffins to go.

I was about to start on the afternoon cake orders when a loud thud sounded on the back kitchen window. We all jumped. Stephanie dropped a tray of cupcakes, sending pastel buttercream sailing in every direction. Sterling grabbed a towel and raced to help her wipe down the countertop and cabinets. I looked up to see Lance standing outside. He wore a black baseball hat and a baggy gray sweatshirt at least three sizes too big for him. It might have been snug on Richard Lord, but on Lance's wiry frame it looked like he was swimming in cotton. His pants—sweatpants—were equally giant. Sweatpants? Was Lance wearing sweatpants? No way.

He rapped on the window and pointed to the front door. "Get out here!" he mouthed.

Chapter Eleven

"You got this?" I asked Sterling, who licked pale yellow buttercream from his finger.

Lance paced outside of the bakeshop. Was he afraid to come in? Lance was never afraid. I pushed the door and held it open.

"You have to come out here." He yanked at a black OSF baseball hat to shield his forehead. "I can't be seen. Not like this."

"Fine. Hang on." I closed the door, walked over to the office and took off my apron. On my way out the door I mouthed that I would be right back to Mom and motioned to Lance. She gave me a thumbs-up and blew me a kiss.

Lance was leaning against a tree with his face focused on the sidewalk when I stepped outside. "It took you long enough," he hissed.

"What? Two minutes? I literally took my apron off and came right outside." My heart rate rose.

"Are you intentionally trying to mortify me?"

"Why would I do that?" I stepped closer. He looked up at me and I almost tripped on a crack in the sidewalk at the sight of his bloodred eyes. He must not have slept at all. "Or is there a reason I would be angry with you?" I gave him a knowing look.

"What's that supposed to mean?" His glassy eyes had a faraway look.

"Look, Lance, I want you to be honest with me." I firmed my lips and swallowed hard. "Was last night a hoax?"

He threw his shoulders back. "A hoax? What are you talking about?"

"I'm serious. If this is an act, then our friendship is over."

He threw his arm up in the air, causing the saggy sweatshirt to flap like a kite. "You think I'm faking this? Look at me. I'm hideous, Juliet. Hideous. I'm wearing sweatpants. My God, sweatpants." Spit flew from his mouth as he spoke. "I found Antony at the bottom of the Shakespeare stairs last night. He is dead. I don't know what happened to the body, but I promise you I had nothing to do with it, and you can't desert me. You're my only friend."

"Take it easy." I kept my tone calm. It might have been a lapse in judgment, but I believed him. "Do you want to go talk somewhere more private?" I glanced around the plaza. The oil protesters from yesterday were starting to gather in front of the Lithia bubblers. Richard Lord, wearing an obnoxious orange and brown plaid golf outfit, complete with a matching hat, stood on the front porch of the Merry Windsor. His beady eyes were lasered on Torte. There was no place private. "Maybe the park."

He reeled backward and conked his head on the tree. "The park! We can't go to the park. It's swarming with police. One sight of me and they'll probably cuff me on the spot."

"Lance, they aren't going to arrest you." I tried to reason with him. "They haven't even found a body."

"I know. You think I don't know that, Juliet? They think I'm crazy. They think that I've made this entire thing up. That I'm a complete narcissist. That's what my entire career has come to? The awards, the accolades, building star after star, putting Ashland on the map, and the thanks I get in return is that I've staged an elaborate hoax because I'm desperate for attention." With each word his voice became higher and higher.

I tried to interject, but he barely paused for a breath.

"This is the end of my career, Juliet. I'm finished. Finished. No one will hire me. I might as well crawl into your kitchen and gorge myself on pastries because I'm done."

"Lance." I grabbed both of his hands and tried to get him to focus on me. "Stop."

He stared back with wild eyes.

"Listen," I said softly. "It's going to be okay, but you have to calm down. We're not going to be able to accomplish anything if you're freaking out."

"We?" Lance dropped my grasp and threw one of his hands over his mouth in relief. "Oh, thank God. You believe me?"

"I think I believe you, but don't make me regret trusting you."

He placed one hand on his heart and the other in the air. "I swear on Shakespeare that I'm telling the absolute truth. Please help me. I'm begging. I'll get down on my knees if I have to. It can't be worse than wearing sweatpants."

"You don't need to beg. I told you I would help you last night, remember?"

"You did? I don't remember most of last night. It's all kind of a blur. It feels like I'm living the pages of one of Shakespeare's great tragedies. *King Lear, Hamlet, Macbeth, Julius Caesar.* Name one. It's me. I'm a walking catastrophe."

I glanced at a group of tourists, wearing matching OSF gear, who piled out of a minivan and immediately began snapping pictures of the plaza. For once Lance didn't have to worry about being recognized. There was no chance of mistaking the sloppy, frantic man standing next to me for OSF's artistic director. A far cry from years past when he would hold court in the center of the plaza greeting theater lovers and pausing to take photos with them.

"Do you want to come inside?" I asked.

Lance shook his head. "No. I'm not ready to face my public, but swear—swear on your life—that you'll help me."

If I wasn't mistaken I was pretty sure that Lance's eyes were filling with tears. "Juliet, I am *not* having a meltdown. I assure you that I am saner than I've ever been. Someone is setting me up. I saw Antony last night. Where else would I have gotten a bloody dagger?"

I didn't mention the fact that the props department at OSF had dozens of fake swords and daggers on hand.

"You have to find that missing DVD. There must be something incriminating on it. And talk to that puppy

dog of a police officer and the Professor. They'll listen
to you."

"Okay. I promise." I held up my pinkie. "Pinkie
swear."

Lance's shoulders sagged and he let out a halfhearted
chuckle. "Pinkie swear." He wrapped his pinkie around
mine.

"Before I go, let me get you some soup or a muffin
or something."

"I don't think I can eat."

"You should try. Hang on, I'll be right back." I left
him slouched against the tree and hurried inside to pack-
age up a box of comfort food. Mom caught my eye
when I made it to the kitchen and began piling a to-go
box with Lance's favorite baked goods.

"How is he?" she asked.

"Not good." I turned to Sterling, who was frying tortillas at the stove. "Is the soup ready?"

"It should be." He took the pan off the stove and
checked the soup pot. "It smells good. I added the beans
about thirty minutes ago."

"Great. Will you ladle some into a container for
Lance?"

He reached for a container without speaking. I packaged a box of macarons and returned to Lance with a
huge bag of soup and goodies. "Doctor's orders, head
home and make yourself comfortable on the couch. I'll
go talk to the Professor or Thomas. You eat up and stay
put. Got it?"

Lance took the bag from my hands. This time there
was no mistaking the water dripping from his eyes. "Juliet, you are truly the best friend I've ever had." His

sincerity struck a chord. I hugged him tight and sent him on his way.

Once he was out of sight, I decided there was no time like the present and started toward Lithia Park. As Lance had mentioned, the park was swarming with police activity. Police cars and an unmarked black van blocked the end of the street and sidewalk. They must have called in reinforcements from Medford. A perimeter of police tape extended from the bottom of the Shakespeare stairs around the park's entrance and all the way to the parking area on the other side of Lithia Creek. A large pop-up tent had been set up in the grass. I assumed it must be temporary headquarters for the search since two officers with dogs checked in with a uniformed officer holding a clipboard.

I wasn't sure how to get in. There was no sign of Thomas or the Professor near the front, so I continued around the corner. They must have been taking Lance seriously because otherwise why would dozens of officers be searching the park? I wondered if they had found any evidence or a clue to what happened to Antony's body.

The other side of the park was usually packed with families playing on the climbing wall or Southern Oregon University students out for a day hike. Today, it looked like a scene from a police procedural. Crime tape stretched from the bridge across the street to the ice skating rink. My heart rate picked up. I had a feeling they must have found something.

"Jules!" Thomas called. He was standing near the duck pond wearing his standard blue uniform with his iPad in his hand.

I waved and pointed to the tape.

He nodded, which I took as a sign that he had given me his permission to cross the barricade.

"How's it going?" he asked, meeting me halfway with his long stride.

"Not great. I just saw Lance." Big leaf maple trees drank in the sun. The grass was a lush pastoral shade of green, probably from the deluge of rain we had received this winter. Two ducks floated on the pond's surface. The pond was framed in with huge boulders, a few wooden benches, and metal railing that had been painted brown to blend in with the natural landscape. A pressed pebble path connected the pond with a large grassy area on one side and the children's playground on the other.

Thomas checked around us to make sure that none of his colleagues were nearby. "How is he?"

"Pretty freaked out. I've never seen him like this, Thomas." I noticed small yellow markers in a zigzagging line near the duck pond. "How's the investigation coming?" Behind the pond was a gated stairway that led up to the Elizabethan Theater. It was surrounded by dense shrubbery and thick trees. A black sign on the gate warned that access was only granted to authorized personnel. The concrete steps were cracked and hidden under thick moss. It didn't look like anyone had recently used the secret stairwell, but my thoughts went immediately to Lance. He must have a key to the gate.

"Well, we can't find a body, but we can't find Antony, either. We sent a team to his apartment, we've searched the entire OSF complex, and as you can see now we're sweeping the park."

"What are those?" I pointed to the yellow markers.

Thomas hesitated for a moment. "The Professor noticed what he thinks could be drag marks in the dirt and grass."

"So Lance isn't crazy?" I could hear the relief in my voice.

"It's too soon to know. Until we have a physical body every assumption is fair game. The marks could be from kids scootering through the grass, or someone dragging a portable chair behind them."

"What are the odds of a kid scootering around the pond last night?" I couldn't stop staring at the gate. Could Antony's killer have escaped back up to the theater complex that way?

Thomas ran his fingers through his hair. "Jules, cut me some slack. You know how it goes. Until we find a body we can't close any potential door." He followed my gaze. "What are you looking at?"

"Those stairs. Who has access to them?"

"I don't know. OSF staff, probably."

"Did you check the lock?"

Thomas raised his brows. "Seriously?"

"Just checking." I gave him a sheepish smile.

He tapped his iPad. "I do have one piece of news that I can share."

"Really?"

"Don't sound excited. You're not going to like it."

I stared at him, trying to read his blue eyes. "What?"

"The Professor is officially off the case."

"No." I must have spoken too loudly because two ducks paddled off to the opposite side of the pond.

A team with search dogs came toward us. Thomas spoke quickly. "He doesn't want to do anything to jeopardize the investigation, but don't worry. He's doing his own underground work and I'm still on the case. We're getting ready to start searching the ponds and surrounding grounds. The water has been running so high this winter that they're trying to determine what equipment to use."

I looked at the duck pond. It had always been one of my favorite spots in the park with its wooden archways and bridges and peekaboo view of the Elizabethan stage above. Could Antony's body be submerged beneath its waveless surface?

The search team came closer. Thomas wrapped his arm around my shoulder and guided me to the barricade. "You probably shouldn't be here, Jules."

One of the dogs yelped and lunged toward the duck pond. His handler tugged on the leash and sounded a command.

"I better go. I'll check in later." Thomas turned toward the commotion. Both dogs had been released from their leashes and bolted for the duck pond.

My stomach rumbled with butterflies—the sick kind—as I watched the dogs circle the pond and bark. Was this the proof the police were waiting for? I didn't want to wait around to watch.

I headed back the way I came toward the intersection of Main and Main. Brock, Antony's roommate, was loitering about ten feet away from the roped-off area near the Shakespeare stairs. A police officer on the other side of the caution tape pushed him back. "You need to clear the area, son."

Brock kept his gaze focused on the Shakespeare steps

and backed straight into me. "Sorry." He flinched and turned around. "I didn't see you there."

"No problem." I rubbed my shoulder.

He looked completely different from last night in his OSF warm-up jacket and running tights versus his toga. "Hey, didn't I see you at the party last night?"

"Yep. I'm Jules. We did the dessert buffet." I offered him my hand.

"Oh yeah? Those apple tarts were pretty good. Right up there with my grandma's."

"That's high praise." I chuckled. "Stop by Torte anytime. They're on our menu for the spring season."

"Cool." Brock tugged on the strings of his OSF warm-up jacket. "Do you know what's going on around here? The police are swarming everywhere. They're all over my apartment."

"Really?" The sun highlighted the tops of the trees and danced merrily off the yellow caution tape.

"I guess Antony must have had a rough night because he never made it home." His feet were clad in work boots. "That, or he shacked up with one of the actresses."

Had he not heard about Antony?

"The problem is the police won't let me in my own place." He kicked a pinecone on the sidewalk.

"Didn't you hear?"

Shifting his feet from side to side he batted the pinecone like a soccer ball. "Hear what?"

"About Antony," I said, pointing to the park. "He's missing. That's why the police have the park roped off." I didn't mention anything about Lance or that Antony might have come to harm in hopes that I might gauge Brock's reaction to the news.

"What?" The hint of color on Brock's pale face faded. "I thought he was sloshed last night or something. No one said anything to me about him being missing." He twisted one of the strings from his jacket around his finger and stared at the park for a minute. Then he shrugged. "He's probably passed out somewhere, knowing Antony."

"Did you see him after the party last night? I remember you jumped in when he and Lance got into it, but did you see him after that?"

Brock chomped on his fingernail. "Nope. Lance asked me to get him out of there. He didn't want Antony making more of a scene than he already had. Antony likes to drink. He also likes to get in people's faces. It's his thing. He claims that it's because he's a method actor. When he lands a role he never breaks character. In the play Antony is a drinker, courageous on the battlefield, that sort of thing."

"But isn't Antony supposed to be heroic? He's not a villain."

He shrugged. "I don't know. I'm not a Shakespeare guy. I just help on the sets. But I heard Tracy get pretty pissed about Antony ruining the role. She said he's missing the point. *Antony and Cleopatra* is a love story—a tragedy, I guess. They fight all the time. Although I can't blame her. It's stupid that we have to call him Antony. That's not even his name." He kicked the pinecone again and sent it shooting into the grass. "Whatever. You just have to ignore him. He tries to get under your skin. He likes to rile people up and get a reaction. He's been doing it for years. You can't sweat it."

He had succeeded doing that with Lance, I thought. "What is his real name?"

"No idea." He shrugged. "I offered to take Antony home, but as we were about to leave we ran into one of the volunteers and she told me that she would give him a ride home. She said his place was on the way."

"Do you know her name?" I asked.

Brock moved to chewing his thumbnail instead of his index finger. "No. I'm new here. I think she's been around forever. She knows everyone. Kind of plump. Older. Antony was happy to leave with her and to be honest I was glad that I didn't have to deal with him."

Was the volunteer Judy, who had been flirting with Antony last night?

"I should go." With that he took off across the street and past the Merry Windsor. I watched him before continuing to the bakeshop. He had sounded sincere in his surprise that Antony was missing, but then again, I had just met him. He could be lying. The idea of a stagehand killing off the star was so cliché but I couldn't help wondering about Brock's attitude. He hadn't seemed overly concerned that Antony was missing. I wasn't sure if that meant he could be involved in whatever had happened to Antony, but I did know that I was going to try to learn more about him. I had made a promise to Lance that I intended to keep.

Chapter Twelve

When I returned to Torte it was buzzing with the lunch rush. The dining room smelled fantastic. I took in a huge breath of spicy tortilla soup and baking bread. Tables were packed with customers devouring our guacamole wraps. Bethany tapped orders into our sleek new digital system at the pastry counter and boxed up ombré packages of macarons. Thank goodness for the reprieve of the bakeshop. This was my happy place.

I waved to Andy, who was demonstrating how to pour a heart from foam, on my way to the kitchen.

"The soup is a hit, Jules," Sterling said, placing two steaming bowls of soup on a tray along with the guacamole wraps.

"I can tell. It smells amazing and it looks like every table in the front ordered soup." I walked to the sink to wash my hands.

"How was he?" Sterling placed the tray on the island.

"In pretty bad shape, as expected." I squirted repairing beeswax lotion on my hands and rubbed them together. Then I told him about my conversation with Thomas and bumping into Brock.

Sterling listened while he finished off the lunch tray with slices of double chocolate cake, vanilla pudding with blueberry compote, and oatmeal raisin cookies. "Your instincts are right, Jules. It sounds like the police are operating under the assumption that Antony is dead. I don't know what that means for Lance."

"Thanks for the validation." I nodded toward the lunch tray. "Do you want me to take that?"

"I've got it." Sterling lifted the tray with one hand and flexed his arm. Not that I could see his muscles under his hoodie.

"Nice."

Bethany returned to the front counter. "Back to my photo shoot," she said, grabbing a stool and standing on it.

"Be careful up there," I cautioned.

"No worries. I do this all the time." She clicked dozens of shots. When she finished, she jumped off the stool and placed her phone on the edge of the island. "You want to take a look?" She swiped her phone to the photos section.

Each dessert had been plated and shot from above. The pictures were stunning. Bethany certainly had an eye for design. My favorite was the lunch special, which she had shot on the island with recipe cards, bright-colored peppers, and a small bunch of wildflowers. It looked like a photograph from *Sweetened* magazine. No wonder our social media following was growing. "These are incredible," I said to Bethany, handing back her phone.

"You like them?" Her freckles stretched on her cheeks with her smile.

"I love them. Has Mom seen them yet?"

Bethany repositioned a single pale pink rose that she had propped next to Andy's vanilla rose latte along with loose vanilla beans. "Not yet. She's been in high demand."

We both looked to the dining room where Mom was packaging up pastries from the case and our to-go lunch boxes. "When it slows down you have to show her these."

"I will." Bethany smiled and went back to snapping pictures of the creamy latte.

Stephanie was slumped over the counter. I noticed she had inserted the star tip on her pastry bag upside down.

"How's it going?" I asked. The cake she was decorating had a glob of frosting in the middle.

"The pastry bag is broken."

I leaned over her shoulder and took the bag from her hand. "You need to go home. Get some sleep."

Her eyes looked like two swollen purple plums. "No, I'm good," she protested. "I want to learn that spoon thing you did the other day. Can you show me?"

I wondered what my role was in her predicament. Should I force her to leave, or task her with something more manageable like the fluffy retro technique? I decided on the latter and showed her how to create the vintage pillowlike design.

"Keep an eye on her," I whispered to Sterling, as I started on the remaining specialty orders.

"Already on it," he replied in a low tone. "I tried to get her to go, but she won't. You know how stubborn she can be. Women. I tell you." He rolled his brilliant blue eyes, but I could see concern in the way he kept glancing in her direction.

"Let's make a pact to try and lighten her load, but subtly. She can't know."

He spread guacamole on a tortilla. "Done."

By the time I had hand-piped cherry French cream on layers of almond sponge, the dining room had begun to clear out. I had been wanting to make a carrot cake since my conversation with Vera. Sterling and Bethany took on cleanup duty and Mom worked on frosting dozens of cutout cookies for opening night. Lance had ordered theater cutouts for the opening-night cast party a few days ago. The cookies were cut in the shape of playbills and had funny sayings like Break Legs, Happy Opening, OSF Family, Team Antony and Cleopatra. I wondered if the show would go on as planned and whether or not he would be a part of it.

For the carrot cake I rinsed and peeled a bunch of organic carrots. Then I finely grated them into a mixing bowl and set that aside. I creamed butter and sugar in the mixer and slowly incorporated eggs, a splash of buttermilk, the shredded carrots, baking soda, flour, and salt. I like carrot cake that is chock-full of tropical flavors and touches of exotic spices, like fresh ginger. However, ginger can be potent. It's always better to start slow and layer on flavor as you go. A little goes a long way.

I shaved the ginger root and finely diced it before adding it to the batter. Next, I added cinnamon, nutmeg, and a dash of cardamom. I sliced oranges and lemons, squeezed in the juice, and reserved the peel. I planned to zest some of it into the mixture. Finally, I incorporated chopped walnuts and pecans and mixed everything together.

Before pouring the batter into cake pans I gave it a taste with my pinkie. It had a lovely spicy flavor that I knew would develop once it baked. I buttered and dusted baking pans and then spread in the rich, chunky batter. While the cakes baked, I turned my attention to the frosting. Carrot cake deserves a frosting worthy of its zest. In my opinion the tangy cake paired perfectly with a cream cheese frosting.

To avoid a lumpy frosting, it's imperative to start with room-temperature cream cheese and butter. Our microwave had a setting for warming both cream cheese and butter, so I opted to use that to speed the process up. I beat them on high and then added powdered sugar, vanilla, a touch of cardamom, and more fresh-squeezed lemon and orange juice. It whipped into a silky, satin frosting. As Vera had mentioned, the frosting wasn't overly sweet and had a subtle hint of citrus.

Then I used a mandoline to slice thin pieces of the remaining fresh ginger. I planned to candy it and use it as a decoration for the top of the cake. The process of candying is simple. I placed the ginger slices in a saucepan with a quarter cup of water. I would let it simmer on low heat for about a half hour or until the ginger was tender. Then I would strain the ginger and return it to the pan with more water and sugar. Once the sugar and water came to a boil, I would stir it frequently until it thickened into a syrup. At this point, I would continue to cook it until the syrup dried out and evaporated, eventually leaving a gorgeous crystallized-sugar coating on each piece of ginger.

The candied ginger was so delicious it could be eaten as a snack, added to cookies, or in this case used as a decoration for my cake. It would keep for up to two weeks in an airtight container. That was if it would last that long around the bakeshop.

As if reading my mind, Andy appeared behind me. "Are you making candied ginger? You know that's my kryptonite, boss."

I pretended to swat him away. "It has to cool. You don't want to burn your tongue."

"It might be worth it for candied ginger." He threw his hand over his chest and batted his eyelashes. "I have to figure out how to create a coffee drink with candied ginger." His phone buzzed in the back pocket of his faded jeans. "And I have to get to class. See you tomorrow."

Andy and Stephanie both attended Southern Oregon University in addition to working for us. Mom and I never had a problem rearranging their schedules if they had to study for finals or had a class that interfered with their shift. Having Bethany join the team had given us even more flexibility. She and Sterling started their shifts later and stayed later so that Andy and Stephanie could leave for afternoon classes. Thus far it had been working, but I was concerned about our staffing levels once the basement renovation was complete, especially with Mom scaling back. We were likely going to have to hire additional help, but that meant more time training new staff and increasing our payroll. While I stirred the ginger I tried to calm the doubt rising in me. An expansion didn't come without risk. We knew that going into the project, but as it became more of a reality it was hard not to think about the worst-case scenarios.

My dad used to tease me about getting lost in my own head. "Juliet, give those brain cells a rest, darling," he would say and pull up a stool at the island for me. I spent my afternoons and weekends in Torte's cheery kitchen watching my parents work in unison. It was like watching a choreographed dance. They would pass each other with a tray of scones or pot of beef stew. There was a palpable spark between them. I remembered wishing that one day I would find a love like theirs. Their love wasn't flashy. From the outside it might have appeared common and predictable. But that's exactly what made them special.

It was different with Carlos and me. The heat between us was undeniable, but I wasn't sure that we were destined for something lasting like my parents.

The bubbling ginger splattered and hit me on the wrist. I winced, turned down the heat, and ran to immerse my hand in cold water. A red welt the size of a pimple erupted on my wrist. It could have been worse. Good thing I had quick reflexes, but yet another reason to get out of my head and focus on what was right in front of me.

The burn stung. Pain pulsed in my hand as icy water cascaded from the tap. I had been trained in first aid in culinary school. The kitchen can be a dangerous place. Knowing how to react and reacting quickly, like getting water on a burn immediately, is a head chef's duty.

"Are you okay, honey?" Mom returned to the kitchen with empty soup bowls and plates. She started to put them in the sink, but stopped when she saw me running my arm under cold water.

"Just a little burn."

She set the dirty dishes on the counter and reached under the stream of water to assess my injury. "Does it hurt?"

"No, it's fine." I turned off the water and dried my arm.

Mom frowned. "Are you sure?"

"Promise." I went to check on the ginger. "I should have been paying better attention. Rookie mistake."

A faraway look crossed her face. "You are your father's daughter. My daydreamers."

We shared an unspoken memory. It was as if I could feel his presence in the kitchen. His hearty laugh, his meticulous care when piping a cake or cutting out sugar cookies. He lived on at Torte in everything we touched. I knew that he was watching over us and would be thrilled that we were expanding the bakeshop and happy that Mom had found love a second time.

She rubbed her arms and then inhaled. I caught her eye. We didn't need to speak. I knew that we had both been thinking of him. "Are you still up for coming to take a look at flowers with me?"

I'd forgotten all about her wedding flowers. "Of course. When should we head over?"

Mom glanced at the clock on the far wall. "Five minutes?"

"No problem. Let me get this ginger drying and check on my cakes." I lined the island with waxed paper. Using tongs, I removed the shimmery ginger pieces and left them to cool. When I opened the oven a blast of heat and the heavenly scent of cinnamon and nutmeg filled the kitchen.

"That's not fair, Jules," Sterling said as he loaded dishes into the dishwasher. "That smells crazy good."

I laughed. "Maybe that's what we should call it—Crazy Good Carrot Cake. It has a certain ring to it, doesn't it?"

"Call it whatever you want. Just make sure I get a slice once it's ready."

"Deal." I set the deep golden cakes on cooling racks and ran a butter knife around the edge of the pans. "Will you and Bethany be okay to finish cleaning up? Mom and I have an appointment at A Rose by Any Other Name."

"We got this." Sterling turned toward the dining room. A student who had been nursing a cup of coffee had his head buried in his laptop, but otherwise the bakeshop was empty. Torte was typically busy from the time we opened in the morning through the lunch rush, but things died off in the afternoon. That wouldn't be true once the season picked up at OSF. All the more reason to embrace the calm, knowing that it was temporary.

"You know where to find us if you need anything." A Rose by Any Other Name, Ashland's premier flower shop owned by Thomas's parents, was two doors down from Torte. I'd spent many of my childhood hours in the floral boutique.

Mom nudged Sterling's waist. "Don't get lost. It's pretty far."

"Right." He winked.

We left arm in arm. "Have you given any thought to flowers?" I asked Mom, pointing to the spring tulips in the planter boxes. "Something simple like tulips or maybe daisies?"

Mom gave the spring flowers a wistful look. "If it were up to me, yes, but you know Doug. He's such a fan of Shakespeare." She paused and twisted her engagement ring. "I've had an idea percolating that I want to get your take on."

"Sure. Shoot." A dusting of pink blossoms fell like snow as we passed under a cherry tree.

"As you know, we're flexible on the date. If we can find a venue then anytime this summer will work for us. I was looking at the calendar and June 20th jumped out at me. What do you think about doing a Midsummer Night's Eve wedding? Doug be over the moon if I could pull off a surprise."

"That's a great idea." I stopped in mid-stride. "Wait, you want to surprise him?"

The corner of her eyes crinkled. "That's what I was thinking. Is it crazy?"

"No. Not at all. It's romantic." I put my hand over my heart. "He would love that."

A smile spread across her face. "He would, wouldn't he?"

"Yes, he would. And I'm here to help make it happen." I secured my arm tighter and we entered the flower shop.

Thomas's mom greeted us both with a warm hug. "Helen, I'm so thrilled for you! Everyone in town is delighted. It's the main topic of conversation these days."

"Thanks, Janet." Mom's bronze cheeks blushed. "I have to admit that I feel like I'm twenty again. I never imagined I would be planning another wedding in my fifties."

"A surprise wedding," I interjected.

"Surprise?" Janet frowned. "But didn't Doug propose?"

Mom explained her idea about throwing a Midsummer Night's Eve wedding.

"That's uncanny." Janet motioned for us to join her at the back counter. She laid out an assortment of loose bouquets and floral headbands with long silky ribbons. "I don't know why, but I had the sense you might be drawn to a bohemian style. I was inspired by this clipping I saw in one of my industry magazines." She slid a cutout of a Midsummer Night's Dream wedding across the countertop.

Mom and I shared a knowing look. The stars were aligning.

Janet continued. "The couple went with a starry and celestial theme. I used this backdrop for inspiration. What about something like this?" She placed whimsical arrangements and floral headpieces in soft pastels and bright jewel tones along with hints of chocolate on the counter.

"It's like you read my mind." Mom bent over to smell the dark lilies.

"Have you picked a venue yet?" Janet asked.

"Sadly, no. Thus far we haven't been able to find anything big enough."

"That doesn't surprise me. I think everyone is expecting an invite." She handed Mom one of the flower headpieces. "If you end up going with an outdoor venue then I thought we could use trees. They are nature's cathedrals after all. I could take this same design and create long flower garlands that we could string from the trees along with paper moons, stars, and twinkle lights."

Mom stroked the delicate headpiece. "I love it. What do you think, Juliet?"

I nodded. "Agreed. It's gorgeous."

Janet reached under the counter and retrieved two large binders. "I don't want to force you into this. There are thousands of other ideas. We can go with a more traditional look like this." She thumbed through the binder and pointed to a picture of a bouquet of simple red roses and then to one of wildflowers.

"No. I don't need to see anything else," Mom insisted. "Don't get me wrong, these other designs are lovely, but what you've put together reflects Doug and me."

"This is the easiest and fastest bridal consultation I've ever done." Janet returned the binders beneath the counter.

"I've always believed that when things don't come easy, it usually means we're trying to force our own agendas," Mom said, as she tried on the headpiece. The dainty pink roses and chocolaty willow twigs blended in beautifully with her hair.

Her words made me think of Lance. Had forcing his agenda caused him to snap? I wanted to believe that he was telling me the truth, but a seed of doubt lingered.

"Shall we talk about colors and if there are any specific flowers you want me to use?" Janet reached for a sketch pad and Sharpie.

I took that as my cue to leave. "It looks like you're in good hands," I said to Mom. "I can't wait to see what you come up with."

Mom held her index finger to her lips. "Remember, this our little secret."

Janet nodded solemnly. "A florist never dishes the dirt."

I laughed and waved. "My lips are sealed."

Part of me wanted to swing by Lithia Park before returning to Torte. I wondered if the search team had found anything yet. Before I could make up my mind I spotted Judy Faulkner, the volunteer who had been flirting with Antony, heading straight for me.

Was it my imagination or did she seem slightly agitated? She brushed past Puck's Pub and had her attention focused on the flower shop.

"Oh, hello," she said without enthusiasm when she saw me. She was quite attractive with silver haircut in an angular bob that framed her face. Feather earrings hung from her lobes.

"Are you in the market for flowers?" I asked, nodding toward the shop.

She tapped a yellow legal notepad. "I'm here on official business for OSF."

"Really?"

"Tonight is opening night. We always honor our leads and the director with bouquets. It's tradition." Deep lines on the corners of her mouth and eyes gave away her age as she pursed her lips. "I've been tasked with hand-delivering the bouquets."

"Of course." I wondered how to broach the subject of Antony, and quickly decided to be direct. "Is the show going on, as they say? I heard that Antony is missing."

Judy massaged the bridge of her nose. "He is. I can't believe it. I saw him last night. When I heard that he was missing I couldn't believe it. He would never miss a show. Something terrible must have happened to him."

"When did you see him last?" I wondered if her story would match up with Brock's.

"Last night. After the party. You were there when he and Lance had that little tiff, weren't you?"

Two barefoot guys with guitars flashed a peace sign as they walked by. A cloud of patchouli made me cough. "I was there," I said to Judy.

She was unfazed by the scent. "Antony is a consummate professional. He must have had too much to drink. I told him that he had to show Lance more respect. Even if Lance was being unreasonable."

"Unreasonable how?"

Judy stared at her well-worn Birkenstocks. In Ashland when it came to fashion there were no rules, more like a few distinct camps. Judy, along with many longtime residents, embraced a laid-back style tending toward peasant skirts, Birkenstocks, clogs, and cable-knit sweaters. Tourists who came to town predominantly for the theater dressed in more sophisticated outfits with coordinated accessories, silk scarves, and pearl earrings. Ashland's college students and actors knew no limits. Not a day went by when I didn't bump into someone wearing a pirate costume or a hand-stitched skirt made from recycled plastic bottles. I loved the fact that our community embraced such a free-spirited attitude and that the distinct groups mingled together despite outward appearances.

I got the sense that someone was watching me. The weighty stare of someone's gaze made the tiny blond hairs on my arm stand at attention. Looking up, my eyes met Richard Lord's. He motioned with his index finger for me to come join him on the porch of the Merry Windsor. What did he want? I couldn't imagine anything good. Probably to berate me about our renovation plans or try to force-feed me a taste of his gastronomic menu. No, thanks.

"Hey, can we go sit for a minute?" I asked Judy, pointing to a bench on the far side of the plaza behind the information kiosk and out of Richard's line of sight. "Lance and I have been friends for a while and I want to get your take on how you think he's doing."

"You want to talk about Lance?" Judy looked from her legal pad to the flower shop. "I only have a couple of minutes. The bouquets need to be backstage and ready for tonight's performance."

"No problem." I ignored Richard Lord's glare and hurried to the bench. We sat down, but Judy didn't speak. She clicked chunky turquoise bracelets on her wrist and stared at a preschooler trying to drink from the Lithia fountains. He let out a screech when his mom held him close to the sulfur bubbler. "Gross!"

"Is something bothering you?" I asked Judy.

She sighed and she scooted closer to me. "You and Lance are good friends?"

"Yes, we're friends."

"Then you must have noticed that he's not himself. Has he mentioned anything to you about OSF and what's going on with the company?"

I wasn't sure how much I should reveal to Judy. "He's seemed pretty preoccupied."

Judy linked her fingers together then she cracked her knuckles. Her body language reminded me of the fidgety kid near the fountain. "I've been holding on to some information about him and it's making me crazy. I feel like I can trust you. Lance needs an ally right now."

My pulse quickened. "Of course. Whatever you tell me will be in confidence."

She exhaled and lowered her voice. "The board has been talking about letting him go."

"What?" The news wasn't unexpected, and yet I guess a part of me had thought Lance was being overly dramatic about his status with the theater.

"It's not everyone. The board is split in half. There's been one vocal member who has decided that it's time for a change. They claim that it's in the best interest of OSF's future to bring in new blood. Apparently, this sort of thing happens all the time. Lance has been artistic director for over a decade, and there are people who think his time is up."

"But Lance is a fixture here. He *is* OSF."

Judy nodded. She had stopped fidgeting and her eyes were sharper. "I know. There are a number of people who agree with that point of view. Firing Lance would cause an uproar in the company."

A man in a black suit and a woman in a black cocktail dress strolled past us. They each wore VIP tickets around their necks. I figured they were probably heading to the preshow cocktail reception that Lance hosted every year for top donors. Was Lance in any shape to host the party? And if not who would step in and fill his role?

"Do you really think they'll fire him?" I asked Judy once the couple was out of earshot.

She crossed her legs, causing her ankle bracelets to jingle. "Oh, I don't know. The entire board is in disarray. Lance hasn't been able to silence his doubters, but he does have a contingent of support both with the board and, of course, with our volunteer group and the company."

"Not everyone in the company," I said, without thinking.

Judy uncrossed her legs and clasped her hands together again. "What do you mean? The company adores Lance."

"We were just talking about one particular member who certainly isn't a fan of Lance's."

She tapped the tips of her fingers together as her foot bounced on the cement. "You mean Antony?"

Why the sudden shift? At A Rose by Any Other Name Judy had been the one who brought up Lance and Antony's argument last night, now she was acting as if she was completely unaware of the tension between them.

"Yes. Could he be planting a seed of doubt about Lance with some of the board members?"

"Oh no." Judy sucked in a huge breath through her nose. "My goodness. I never considered that. Would Antony do such a thing?" She didn't appear to be talking to me any longer. "I never should have agreed to lie for him."

Chapter Thirteen

Judy's words threw me off. What did she mean, lie for him? I waited for her to elaborate, but she threw her head into her hands and rocked back and forth on the bench.

"Are you okay?" I asked, placing my hand on her back.

She sat up but kept half of her face covered. "I don't know. I think I'm mixed up in the middle of this battle between Lance and Antony and I never meant to be."

I thought she might say more but instead she shook her head and sighed.

"Can you fill me in? Maybe I can help?"

A look of relief crossed her face. She dropped her hands and nodded. "Maybe you can." Her fingers drummed on her wavy ankle-length skirt. "Antony asked me to keep a secret for him. At the time, I didn't think much about it, and to be honest I was flattered by his attention. I guess I got swept up in being friends with one of OSF's rising stars. I've been a volunteer for five years now. When I moved to Ashland from Northern California after I retired from teaching, I wanted a way to meet new people and be able to see shows on a retired teacher's salary, and one of my neighbors told me about the many options for volunteering."

She shifted on the bench. "The show goes on because of us. Did you know there are over seven hundred volunteers throughout the season?"

I did. The sheer scale of performances at OSF required more manpower than paid staff could manage. Volunteers served as ticket takers and ushers, provided assistance for hearing-impaired patrons, staffed information and welcome booths, helped in the costume department, and did a variety of other tasks from handing out chocolates to even taking a four-legged cast member, Sparky the dog, for bathroom breaks at intermission. Around town the volunteers are called penguins due to the fact that they dress in matching white shirts and black pants and skirts. In return for their service OSF offers volunteers free tickets, puts on special performances, and throws an annual "Labor of Love" party to celebrate and honor their contributions.

"I read an article a while back that said volunteers put in over thirty thousand hours last season," I said to Judy.

She nodded. "My favorite thing to do has been to hand out the blankets for the outdoor show in the summer. It's such fun and the energy at the Elizabethan stage is so wonderful. Me and a group of my friends volunteer every night. Last summer I saw every show at least twenty times. You know, there's something slightly different about each performance, too. That's the beauty of live theater."

I agreed with her, but wanted to nudge her back onto the topic of Antony's secret.

"Sometimes it's a prop that fails or a brief look exchanged between the actors that can change the performance. That's the thrill—the exhilaration—of theater." Her voice became animated as she spoke. There was no doubt that she loved the theater.

"That's when it happened," she continued. "It was the end of the season. Late September and I was working the blanket booth. It's very popular that time of year. You know how chilly fall evenings can be?"

I nodded.

"One of our regular volunteers was ill so a college student from SOU filled in and the booth was a disaster at the end of the performance. I sent the student home and stayed to clean up. I swear I wasn't trying to be sneaky. I was simply doing my job. I didn't even realize how late it was because I was busy folding and stacking blankets and sorting through the money in the cash register."

As Judy stretched out the story with extra details about the bright blue pillows and blankets that the local Soroptimist's club loaned to patrons and the process of washing and drying them and where the funds raised from the booth went, I found myself ready to beg her to get to the point.

"How does this tie in with Antony?" I finally asked, trying to get her back on topic.

"Oh, right. Well, I was on the floor in the blanket booth sorting through the pile to be washed when I heard two men talking right next to the booth."

My foot started to quake with anticipation. I pressed my hand in my thigh.

"I recognized Antony's voice right away, but I couldn't recognize the other voice. It was a man though,

I'm sure of that." She twiddled her fingers. "I didn't mean to eavesdrop. I was about to stand up and announce myself but then they started yelling at each other. I didn't know what to do. If I told them that I was there they would think I was spying on them, so I stayed low and listened. The man kept mentioning John Duncan."

"John?" I puzzled out loud.

"Yes, John Duncan. That made Antony furious. He told the man never to mention that name again."

I interrupted. "Or else what?"

Judy shrugged. "I don't know. He didn't expand, but he made it extremely clear that he didn't want anything to do with John Duncan. The other man kept telling him that John was the least of his worries. He was going to reveal many more ugly secrets." Her voice cracked. "I didn't believe it. Antony was OSF's star. How could he have any ugly secrets?"

She didn't wait for me to respond.

"I think that the man was trying to get something out of Antony. Antony told him that he was going to have control of the board soon and that if the man played his cards right good things would come to him."

What did that mean? I tried to stay in the moment with Judy, but questions formed at a rapid pace in my brain. Who was John Duncan, and what was his connection with Antony? Could Antony have actually managed to turn the board against Lance? And if so, how? He was an up-and-coming actor in the company, but I couldn't imagine why the board would take his input into consideration. And who was the mystery man Judy had overheard? Was there a chance that John Duncan was Antony's real name? I thought about that for a minute. It could be a possibility, but Judy made it sound as if Antony and the other man were talking about a third person. If Antony's real name was John why wouldn't the man have addressed him as such?

"The man took off, and I thought the coast was clear," Judy continued, staring at her feet. "I waited for a few minutes but when I stood up Antony was leaning against the side of the blanket booth. He was as surprised to see me as I was to see him. I apologized and explained that I wasn't trying to be sneaky. He believed me, and he asked that we keep what I had heard between us. I told him that was fine. I didn't want to get in the middle of it."

"You never said anything? Not even to Lance?" I asked.

She shook her head. "No and now I feel terrible. Antony didn't owe me anything but after I heard him that night he started paying extra attention to me. I should have realized that he was trying to keep me silent, but I was flattered by the attention." She paused and studied me for a moment. "You're a gorgeous young woman. You wouldn't understand, but when you get to be my age men don't notice you anymore. They don't flirt. It's like being invisible. Antony invited me to cast parties and gave me a tour of his dressing room. He treated me like a friend. I liked not being invisible. But then the rumors started about dissension on the board. Lance has always been good to me and our volunteer group. I felt guilty. I should have told him. I should have mentioned what I heard Antony say about gaining power with the board, but I didn't. I kept quiet and now everything is ruined."

I empathized with her. She wasn't alone in her

adoration for the actors in the company. There were a number of theater groupies who frequented Torte during the season in hopes of catching a glimpse or snapping a selfie with one of the actors. For Ashland residents the OSF cast and crew were friends and neighbors, but for tourists they were like royalty.

"Did Antony ever mention anything more about John Duncan?"

"No. I never brought it up. It didn't seem right, especially because Antony had gone out of his way to do so many special things for me."

"I understand."

"You don't think I'm a terrible person?" Judy said, wringing her hands again.

"No. I get it." I patted her shoulder. "I just wish I knew who Antony had been arguing with. You know the company better than me. There's no one by the name of John Duncan at OSF, is there?"

She shook her head. "Not that I know of. Maybe there was before I started volunteering?"

That was a possibility. I couldn't wait to find Lance and ask him if he knew John Duncan or if the name had any significance. "You said that you saw Antony after the party night?"

Judy ran her thumb on the edge of the yellow notepad. "I did. You're going to think I'm terrible, though."

"I won't. I promise, and this might be important to the case."

"He offered to give me box seats, backstage passes, and put me on the guest list for the cast party for tonight. After he and Lance had their fight he told me to meet him in his dressing room. I did and he gave me the tickets and passes."

"Have you talked to the police yet?" The plaza and sidewalk along Main Street had begun to fill with people. A group of penguins waved to Judy and then disappeared inside the Green Goblin. They were probably getting a quick bite before reporting for duty.

She lowered her voice. "No, why?"

"You might have been the last person to see him alive."

Judy's face went white. "Do you think he's dead?"

"I don't know, but regardless the police are searching for him right now. If you were the last person to see him last night they need to know that."

"But I wasn't. He gave me the tickets and we talked for a few minutes. He even invited me to join him and some of the other members of the cast for a drink. They were going to go out after the party, but we got interrupted."

"By who?"

"Vera, the costume designer. She stormed into Antony's dressing room and said that they needed to talk—alone. She made it very clear that I wasn't welcome, so I left. I waited around outside the Bowman Theater for a while. I thought maybe he would come out and we would still go get a drink, but he never came out."

"How long did you wait?"

"I don't know, maybe twenty or thirty minutes? It was cold and late so I decided to go home, especially because he had gotten me on the list for the party tonight."

I couldn't believe that Judy had been so forthcoming.

Thomas needed to be filled in and I wanted to talk to Lance.

Judy tapped the crumpled list. "I should go. I need to get these bouquets for the show."

"You're going to tell the police about last night and John Duncan, though, right?"

She nodded and stood. "I will. I'll do that as soon as I pick up the flower arrangements. Thanks for letting me get that off my chest. It's been bothering me for a while and I feel lighter."

I smiled. I wished I felt lighter. Judy's news made me more confused, but also more convinced that Lance wasn't having a breakdown or midlife crisis. Antony had been trying to influence and turn the board against Lance. I wasn't sure why, but I was going to do everything in my power to figure it out. I was also curious about Vera. Why had she barged into Antony's dressing room last night, and did that mean that she had been the last person to see him alive?

There was only one way to find out. I would have to talk to her directly and I had a perfect excuse to stop by the costume department. I needed to return my dress from last night and I would bring along a hefty slice of my carrot cake to sweeten her up.

Chapter Fourteen

Sterling and Bethany had finished cleanup when I returned to Torte. The dining room was sparkling and the kitchen was spotless.

"Hey, Jules," Sterling said, turning on the dishwasher. "We were just about to take off, but before you go, you had a couple of visitors."

Everyone in town would be attending opening night at OSF so we had decided to close early. "Who?"

"Your architect. He wanted to warn us that we're probably going to feel some rumbling with demo going on."

That was to be expected. "Okay, and the other visitor?"

Bethany stuck out her tongue. "Richard Lord."

Shocker. "What did he want?"

Sterling tossed his apron on the island. "I'm not sure. He wants 'a word' but didn't elaborate."

"Get this." Bethany took off her apron as well. She wore yet another baking T-shirt. This one was white with red lettering and the words BAKERS GONNA BAKE. "He's starting an Instagram page and wants my help."

Classic. I tried not to let my irritation show. "That could be a good side project for you."

She looked at Sterling and they both laughed. "No way. I don't want to be within ten feet of the Merry Windsor's kitchen. That place scares me. Plus, I'm good, but I'm not *that* good."

"Thanks for the solidarity. I'll deal with Richard tomorrow. You guys should take off." I sent them both home with boxes of leftover pastries and told them to be ready for a busy day tomorrow. Then I got to work on assembling my carrot cake.

The candied ginger had cooled nicely. I popped a piece into my mouth. The crystallized sugar gave the pungent, chewy treat a sweet finish. No wonder these were a staff favorite. I set the ginger aside and sliced the cooled cake into four thin layers. Then, I slathered on generous amounts of the whipped cream cheese frosting. I added bits of the candied ginger between each layer and arranged the remaining candy in a circular pattern on the top. The cake looked decadent and creamy. I couldn't wait to slice into it.

I found a to-go box and cut a thick piece for Vera. But as I told my young staff, a chef must taste before she delivers, so I cut myself a tiny piece. The combination of moist carrot cake, tangy frosting, and zing of ginger brought an immediate grin to my face. The cake was rich without feeling heavy and the intense spice flavor left a warm finish in my mouth. Hopefully, a slice would butter up Vera and get her to talk to me.

Since Mom and I had tickets to opening night, I washed the frosting bowl and flat spatula that I had used to ice the cake and then I closed up the kitchen. Often, I would work late in the evening after we closed. I liked to bake solo in the calm of a quiet kitchen. I used that time to test new recipes and catch up on paperwork. After last night's party, being awoken by Lance in the middle of the night, and going to the premiere of *Antony and Cleopatra* tonight, I knew that there was no way I was going to want to come back later.

I grabbed my dress and the box of carrot cake for Vera and headed for the OSF complex. I was tempted to take a detour to Lithia Park, but I knew that my window for catching Vera before the show was tight. Plus, that way if she shared any new information with me I could pass all of it—what I might learn from her and what I had learned from Judy—on to Thomas and the Professor.

The bricks were packed with theatergoers who had already begun to gather despite the fact the curtain wouldn't rise for another three hours. Eager anticipation pulsed through the dapper crowd. Ashland had put on its Sunday best for the occasion. Women in flowy flower-print dresses and men in tailored suits discussed the playbill, debating whether *Cinderella* or *Love's Labor Lost* would be the most popular outdoor show. The air smelled of cherry blossoms and fresh cut grass. It was hard not to get caught up in the energy. Opening night of the new season meant that spring was finally upon us.

I navigated through the crowd, stopping once to wait while a group of twenty schoolteachers posed for a selfie with an actor dressed as Julius Caesar who stood as still as a statue. They were wearing matching T-shirts with the words I PREFER MY PUNS INTENDED on the front and DRAMA TEACHERS RULE on the back.

A snake keeper with a boa constrictor draped around his neck watched over his cage of snakes as people gawked and snapped pictures. Were the snakes part of the show or a preshow art installation? It had been a while seen I had seen *Antony and Cleopatra,* but if memory served me correctly, Cleopatra's suicide was brought on by a venomous snake.

I shuddered at the thought and made a beeline for the Bowmer Theater. Getting past the ticket booth volunteer took some finagling.

"Show doesn't start until seven-thirty, miss. We'll be opening the doors at seven."

"This is for Vera, in the costume department." I held up my silky party dress. "I catered the party last night and am supposed to return it to her."

He scowled. "I'm not supposed to let anyone in. I guess I can take it for you."

I clutched the dress. "No, Vera will have my head. She specifically instructed each of us to return our costumes directly to her."

He hesitated. I knew that I had him. "Okay, but make it quick."

"Will do." I scooted past him before he had a chance to change his mind.

The costume department was a blur of activity. Actors wearing yoga pants and sweatshirts in full stage makeup posed for last-minute alterations. Portable fans had been placed throughout the room. They spun on high in a futile attempt to bring the temperature down. The basement tended to run high with humidity, particularly on a night like this. I spotted Vera directing a seamstress to take in the hem on one Cleopatra's servants' costume. It took a minute to work my way in her direction. When she spotted me she pointed at a pincushion resting on a messy workstation. I managed to catch it with my free hand. "What's this?"

"What does it look like? A pincushion. Do you know how to sew? She dabbed her forehead with a swatch of purple cotton.

"A bit, but I'm not a professional."

She pushed her oversized glasses to the bridge of her nose. "I don't care. I'll take all the help I can get."

"I came to bring back my dress and give you this." I offered the box of carrot cake. "It's our carrot cake made especially for you."

Vera held a tape measure across a sheath of velvet fabric. "Thanks, thanks. Set it over there for laundering. I can't talk right now. The show must go on and we've had to refit all of Antony's costumes today."

An actor with a five-inch rip down the front of his skintight pants squeezed in next to us. "Vera, you have to fix this. I'm due on stage for final dress rehearsal in ten minutes."

"Jules." Vera nodded to the pincushion in my hand.

"Me?"

"You." She reached into the pocket of her apron and pulled out a pair of silver shears and began cutting the velvet fabric.

I turned to the actor. "I'll give it my best shot, but I have to warn you that the last time I sewed anything was in Home Ec class in high school."

"I don't care. Just get me sewed up enough to get out on stage."

I placed my dress and the box of cake on one of the large green drafting tables nearby. Actors flew in and out of changing stations. Sewing machines sung. A flurry of colorful fabrics danced around the room. The painstaking detail that went into making each costume come to life was evident in the hectic pace.

Here goes nothing, I thought as I threaded a sewing needle with black thread and started to mend the tear. It was easier than I imagined. The actor had ripped his pants on the seam. With a few stiches, it was like new.

"I'm not sure how long that is going to hold," I cautioned.

The actor gave me a bow of thanks. "Not to worry. It only needs to hold for final dress rehearsal. Thanks."

A bell sounded overhead and the lights flashed. "That's my cue." The actor, along with everyone else in costume, left in a mass exodus for the stage.

This was my chance to talk to Vera. I found her with her head bent over a sewing machine, fastening gold strings onto a belt.

"I had forgotten how wild things are before the show."

She looked up from her work and stared at me as if she had forgotten I was here. "Yep. This is the calm before the next storm."

I handed her the pincushion. "I fixed the pants."

"Excellent." Vera removed her glasses and rubbed one eye. "I can't see straight. I've been sewing since we got word late this morning that Antony's understudy is going on for him tonight."

"Have you seen him?"

"Who? Antony?"

"Yeah." I picked up a ball of twine that had fallen on the floor.

"No, not since last night. They say that he's missing, but who knows. There's always something going on around here." She mopped sweat from her brow with the four-inch square of cotton.

She didn't sound particularly worried that Antony was missing.

"I heard that you were the last person to see him last night."

"What?" Her head snapped to the left and then to the right. She put her glasses back on and stood up. "Who told you that?"

"I'm not sure where I heard it, to tell you the truth," I lied.

Vera peered at me from behind her glasses. Her beady eyes made me take a step backward. I got the sense she was trying to gauge whether or not I was lying. "Someone had to have told you that. Who was it?"

"Honestly, I don't know. Rumors are swirling around Ashland like crazy. Antony's disappearance is the only thing that people were talking about at the bakeshop today."

My words appeared to appease Vera. She noticed the box of carrot cake that I had left on the workstation and picked it up. "Come with me," she commanded. "Let's talk in my office."

A brief warning alarm flashed in my head. Why did Vera want to talk in private? Then again, what could she possibly do to me? There were people everywhere and she was half my size and twice my age.

I followed her to her office. The walls in the messy room were plastered with artistic sketches of period costumes. There was a set of creamy white angel wings hanging from the ceiling and stacks of magazines and catalogs in every corner of the small space. Her oak desk was cluttered with jewelry, tiaras, and even a few pairs of shoes. Piles of fabric rested on the floor and on top of bookcases.

"Sit." She pushed a sketch pad off a chair and walked behind her desk. "Juliet, your mother is one of Ashland's most respected residents. I'm well aware of her ability to be discreet and not fan the flames of the rumor mill."

I nodded, wondering where the conversation was headed. Not that I didn't agree with her assessment of Mom.

She picked up a forest-green pencil from one of the many containers of pencils, chalk, paintbrushes, and pens on her desk. "Then I trust that you have inherited the same abilities?"

How was I supposed to respond to that?

Vera gnawed on the pencil and stared behind me. "Here's the thing. The rumor you heard is true. I had to talk to Antony last night—in private. That's why I asked him here."

"Okay."

She held up her hand. Years spent running the costume department had taken a toll on her hands. Band-Aids were wrapped around the tips of two of her puffy fingers. Scratches and scars zigzagged across the top of her hands, and she wore a wrist brace on her left arm. "Costume designers know everyone's secrets. I think the same is true for bakers. That's why I'm telling you this."

"I thought it was just pastry that made our customers spill their secrets," I said with a laugh.

Vera didn't return the laugh. She removed the well-chewed pencil from the side of her jaw and tapped the gnarly end on her desktop. "It comes with the territory.

I know the actors who are starving themselves and the ones who are consuming too many pastries. I know when an actor is pregnant. I know before their spouses or partners know.

There was something slightly smug about her tone.

"Do you know what his real name is by chance?"

"No. He refused to tell anyone his name. Method actors are the *worst*." She flicked the edge of the pencil. "In any event, I had to speak to Antony last night about something very delicate."

My mind tried to make the connection. "Antony is starving himself?"

Vera rolled her eyes. "No. Nor is he partaking of too many sweets."

"Well, he certainly isn't pregnant."

"No, *he* isn't." Vera leaned back in her chair and waited for it to sink in.

"Antony isn't pregnant, but someone else in the cast is?"

"You got it."

I thought about getting my dress fitted yesterday and how Vera had complained about the fact that she had to take Tracy's costume out again. "Tracy?" I asked.

Vera tapped the pencil on the desk so hard I thought it might snap. "Yes, Tracy." She sighed and shook her head. "I told her to be careful, but she didn't listen."

"What does this have to do with Antony?"

Before Vera could respond another bell sounded and the lights flashed three times. Vera jumped up. "Must go. Thanks for the cake."

No! I wanted to scream. I was so close to a major clue. I watched her leave and sat for a moment trying to let the information sink in. Tracy was pregnant and Vera knew. Who else might know? And why had Vera needed to tell Antony? Could he be the father? Or did Vera know more that she hadn't told me?

After running the possibilities through my mind, I decided there wasn't much more I could do for now. Vera would be busy for the remainder of the evening and I needed to get home and change for opening night. And I needed to find a way to talk to Tracy. If she was pregnant with Antony's baby, that changed everything.

Chapter Fifteen

After my conversation with Vera, I reconvened with Mom, the Professor, and Thomas in front of the theater.

"You look nice, Jules," Thomas said quietly so only I could hear.

I willed the warmth in my cheeks to stop. Unlike last night's princessworthy costume, I had opted for a simple black skirt and soft cashmere sweater. I had tied my hair into a low braid and splurged by inserting my favorite pair of silver dangling earrings. "Thanks. You clean up pretty nicely, yourself." I hoped that my playful banter would send the right message.

He brushed off his suit jacket. "Not bad, huh?" The charcoal-gray coat with a smart blue tie brought out the color in his eyes.

Mom and the Professor were like magnets. People surrounded them, asked to see the ring, and peppered them with questions about the wedding. I took the opportunity to fill Thomas in on what I had learned from Vera and Judy. When I finished, he let out a low whistle. "Geez, Jules. You want me to see if I can convince the Professor to give you a badge? How did you learn so much in one afternoon?"

"It's Torte. Pastry chef by day, sleuth extraordinaire by night."

"Jules, you bake almost every night."

"True." I buttoned the top button on my sweater. The sun had fallen, giving the evening a slight chill.

"You can joke all you want, but it's you." His gaze made my cheeks blaze with heat. "People want to open up to you. It's as natural as breathing."

"I don't know about that." His piercing eyes made my throat tighten. I changed the subject. "If what Vera told me is true and Tracy, aka Cleopatra, is pregnant, then do you think Antony could have been the father? I'm not sure about Judy's story, either. She seemed genuinely upset, but then again, she was basically blackmailing Antony for special theater favors. I know that there's a chance that Lance is lying, but the more I learn the more I believe him."

Thomas checked to make sure no one was listening. "We found him."

"You found Antony?" I tried not to blurt it out, but I couldn't believe that wasn't the first thing he had told me. Why had he let me go on and on with my conversations?

"In the duck pond."

"You sound pretty casual about it." My hands tingled. I wasn't sure if it was from the dropping temperature or the fact that the police had found Antony's body.

"Finding a body is never a casual thing, Jules." Thomas frowned. I saw the angst on his face. "It wasn't casual, more like expected."

"Sorry." I reached for his hand. "I didn't mean it like that."

"I know you didn't." He massaged my hand. His touch sent an unexpected shiver up my spine. "The Professor was fairly confident that we would find the body. The drag marks, the vicinity of the pond, everything lined up, but until we actually recovered the body he wanted to make sure that we covered any other possible trail or lead."

"So someone dragged him into the pond after he was already dead?"

Thomas nodded. "It looks that way. The coroner is preparing the official statement, but at the scene he noted that Antony had suffered a major wound to the abdomen."

Exactly as Lance had said.

"What does this mean for Lance?" I asked. Come to think about it, where was Lance? I hadn't seen him earlier when I visited the costume department and typically he would be out on the bricks mingling and hobnobbing with theater patrons before the opening show.

"He's not here," Thomas said as I stood on my tiptoes to get a glimpse of the outdoor stage.

"Where is he?"

"In custody."

"You mean jail?" I shouted. A few heads turned in our direction. Thankfully, the snake charmer had begun his act for a special opening-night Green Show. Flute sounds drew the crowd toward the outdoor stage. The Green Show offered theatergoers free entertainment on the bricks throughout the summer months. Percussionists, dancers, lecturers, and performers of all types would take the stage to amuse the crowd before the main show.

Thomas pulled me over to an alcove with ivy snaking up toward the roof. Climbing roses formed an arch above us. The vines had yet to bud, but I knew that sweet, red blossoms would soon burst open. "The Professor didn't have a choice. It's not his call, but he's doing everything he can. He made a solid case for keeping Lance at the station here on the plaza. Neither of us want to believe that Lance is a killer, but he made it clear to me that we have to follow protocol. In fact, it's even more important that we follow protocol given the personal connections to the suspect."

"Suspect? You mean Lance—our friend?"

"Look, Jules, this is a delicate situation. When word gets out that we have Lance in custody it's going to be mayhem around here." He nudged his head in the direction of the crowd gasping as the boa constrictor slithered up his master's neck. "Lance is a fixture at OSF. He's probably the most recognized person in Ashland. There's going to be some serious fallout. The Professor is worried about what the news might do to ticket sales. Think of all of the businesses that will be impacted. This isn't just Ashland news. This will be national news. Can't you see the headline now?"

He had a point. There had been quite a few news vans at Lithia Park earlier. Lance's arrest would definitely make for sensational headlines, but in my experience things like this tended to bring gawkers to town. If anything, Ashland might be inundated with people coming to steal a peek of the drama.

"So no one knows?" I asked.

"Not yet. It's dicey. That's why he pressed to have Lance placed in custody at our office on the plaza. If Lance gets booked at the main precinct and the media get wind of it this place will be swarming with press The Professor is working his connections on the down low. The Medford detective who is replacing him is very Type A. She isn't even sure that I should stay on the investigation. Basically, she's treating me like her lackey for the moment. That's fine. I'll run errands as long as she doesn't pull me from the team. Hopefully, we'll have the forensics report by morning. We're holding Lance on circumstantial evidence at the moment. Best-case scenario, the report clears him and we let him go before anyone is the wiser."

"And if not?"

"If not, your friend is going to need a good lawyer."

The doors opened to the theater and a throng of people pushed toward us. Thomas grabbed my hand and we joined the line. There were so many more things I wanted to ask, but we were ushered to our seats. I leaned over to Mom and mouthed, "Did you hear about Lance?"

Her eyes darted to the Professor who sat with his arm draped around her shoulder. She nodded and mouthed, "We'll talk after the show."

In seasons past, Lance would take the stage to introduce the show, cast, and director. He relished the opportunity to welcome everyone to his gleaming town and award-winning theater. I hadn't been around for one of his opening-night performances, but from what I had heard, they were legendary. He would give a synopsis of each upcoming show along with a long-winded soliloquy about the company's commitment to the "work" and the "craft." Mom told me that one year his opening speech ran longer than the actual show.

Tonight, instead of Lance, the director of *Antony and Cleopatra,* a woman about Mom's age with long curly hair down to her waist, came out to the center stage. A single spotlight illuminated her. "Sorry to disappoint. I know many of you make plans months in advance to be here for opening night and to hear our esteemed artistic director, Lance Rousseau, give you a rundown of the upcoming season, but unfortunately he has taken ill and can't be with us tonight."

A collective gasp sounded in the audience.

"I know. I know. You're stuck with me." She waved both of her arms to the side and right on cue the spotlight expanded to fill the stage. The entire company stood behind her. "And these guys," she added with a laugh.

This garnered a huge cheer and applause from the audience.

"Meet your cast for this season," the director continued. "We're thrilled to be bringing you world-class performances of some of Shakespeare's classics like tonight's performance of *Antony and Cleopatra* along with some incredible modern shows and two musicals. Here in Ashland, Oregon, just north of the California border, you're going to dance with *Cinderella* under the stars this summer and we're taking you on a wild ride into space later this season with *Exoplanet,* which was written by one of our very own actor/directors."

The woman seated next to me riffled through the pages of her playbill. "That's this one." She placed the paper on the armrest between us and pointed to a synopsis of the forthcoming show. "It's supposed to be amazing. Dystopian meets *Star Trek*."

"Sounds great," I replied.

She flipped to the front of the playbill where there was a headshot of Lance and his welcome letter. "Can you believe he's sick? My friends and I come up from Northern California every year and Lance is always here. He's signed every one of my playbills. I don't know what I should do? Do I have the director sign it or wait for him? He's got to be around this weekend, don't you think?"

"I'm sure." Maybe Thomas was right. What would Lance's adoring fans do if they learned that he was behind bars?

The show started a few minutes later. I had a hard time concentrating on the performance because I was intent on watching Tracy and Antony's understudy to see if there was anything strange between the two of them. They were both professionals and if news of Lance's arrest and finding Antony's body had made it to the cast they didn't show any signs. Tracy moving her body in rhythm with her fellow actor had me believing that they really were star-crossed lovers. The play reminded me of an adult version of *Romeo and Juliet*. Only instead of the anguish of two lovesick teenagers, *Antony and Cleopatra* captured the angst and aching that go along with mature love. My thoughts strayed to Carlos. Our time together had been magical, but maybe like Shakespeare's ill-fated romance we weren't destined to last.

When the performance finished, the audience jumped to its feet and showered the cast with thunderous applause, delighted hollers, and two extra encore bows.

"That was wonderful, wasn't it?" Mom asked, standing and wrapping her pashmina shawl around her shoulders.

"Indeed, no one writes a romantic tragedy like the Bard," the Professor seconded.

I drifted away from the conversation momentarily as Brock and Thad appeared at the side of the entrance to the Elizabethan stage. Brock was fixing a broken light stand. Thad held a screwdriver in one hand and was motioning with it. Had something gone wrong with the set or were they fighting?

The Professor cleared his throat, jolting me back. "Might I interest you young ones in a bite to eat or a nightcap? We have much to discuss, I do believe." He raised one brow and gave me a knowing look.

"I'm always game." Thomas waited while I gathered my purse. "As long as there's food involved."

Mom nudged him in the waist. "You have never changed on the food front. I remember your mother constantly lamenting about not being able to keep you fed, especially when you were playing football."

"That's still true today, Mrs. Capshaw." Thomas grinned.

I rolled my eyes.

"Don't give him that look, young lady. You were no better. We called her the bottomless pit," she said to the Professor.

"Well, in that case I daresay we must find these poor starving creatures nourishment immediately." The Professor had abandoned his usual tweed jacket in favor of a more refined classic sport coat and slacks. His tie revealed his true nature with tiny busts of Shakespeare and the words "Love all, trust a few, do no wrong." The quote summed up the Professor's approach to life and felt especially true this evening. Who should I trust? Everyone associated with Antony had been lying about something.

"Shall we?" He bowed to Mom. She chuckled. "Oh, Doug, sometimes you're too much."

I appreciated his attempt to keep the mood light, especially while we left the theater. There was no point in bemoaning Lance's situation until we could talk in private. Moonlight cast a hazy glow on the bricks as we headed down Pioneer Street. I was glad that I had worn a cashmere sweater and found myself rubbing my shoulders to stay warm.

Thomas took off his jacket and wrapped it around my shoulders.

"Thanks. You didn't have to do that." It was true, however, that my numbing fingertips appreciated the gesture.

"What, and face the wrath of the Professor? Or worse, my mom—if we happen to bump into her? I've been well trained in my gentlemanly duties."

I put on his coat and laughed. "I seem to remember you scarfing down cookies by the handful in the high school cafeteria and getting in trouble from the lunch lady for your slovenly ways."

"Me? Never." Thomas kicked a pebble off the sidewalk.

His coat was still warm from his body heat and smelled of his cologne, which had a hint of menthol. When we dated, I kept one of his sweatshirts under my pillow. The familiar scent took me back to being seventeen.

We had had many fun times as well as our fair share of sad days intermixed. Thomas had been by my side after my dad died, and I could never repay him for his kindness during the darkest hours of my life. I liked the fact that he knew the seventeen-year-old version of me with chipped red fingernail polish and intentionally ripped jeans. We shared a past. He knew me when my father was alive, and for that fact alone he would always hold a special piece of my heart. There's something about people who know our history. Thomas had seen me on my knees sobbing with grief. He knew the girl with puffy eyes and a runny nose who missed her father so desperately that it hurt to breathe sometimes. He also knew the girl who could eat a hot dog in two bites and danced spontaneously in the Lithia fountains at midnight. We had spent countless hours dreaming about our future on the benches next to the duck pond. Thomas had always wanted to work in law enforcement. Only back in those days, he envisioned working a beat in a big city like Chicago or New York. Ironically, I had been the one who left. While Thomas fantasized about life outside of Ashland, I actually experienced it, and on such a grander scale than I ever could have imagined as a teenager.

I liked that we each held memories of one another that no one else could share. But I also knew that he wanted more. He had said that he would wait, but I didn't want him to put his dreams on hold for me.

"Jules?" Thomas's voice shook me from my thoughts.

"Huh?"

"The door. Are you coming inside?"

I looked up to see him holding open the heavy

wooden door to Puck's Pub for me. Mom and the Professor were already chatting with the owner. "Yeah, right. Sorry."

"Your mom is right about some things—some people never change."

"What's that supposed to mean?" I stepped inside.

He closed the door behind him. "You. Ms. Day-dreamer."

Before I could come up with a smart retort the owner showed us to a table near the back of the warm and cheery pub. The owner went over the daily specials and suggested we sample a taste of the new beer recently tapped—the Bard's Best—a chocolate stout brewed by a new microbrewery in town in honor of the new theater season.

We agreed to a taste. The owner left to pour us samples and Thomas handed out menus. "The special stew sounds good."

I couldn't think about food. I wanted to talk about Lance, what the Professor knew, and how I could help my friend, but the owner returned with a tray of tasting glasses. We each took one. I held mine up to the light. The beer was black as night and tasted of chocolate and a hint of something spicy. I wondered if it was the hops they'd used. A while back, I had met a female brewer from Leavenworth who had shared some insider tips on brewing and how to judge whether a beer was good. The Bard's Best had a hearty flavor and smooth finish.

The Professor toasted with his tasting glass. "Shall I order a round for the table?"

"Yes," Mom said. "I really like this and I don't usually like dark beers."

"I agree." I finished my taster and set it on the table. The old-English pub was filled with the after-theater crowd. Mouthwatering smells of garlic and onions wafted from the kitchen. A minstrel group, much like the band that had performed at Lance's party, warmed up on the wooden stage. Beer flowed from oak taps behind the bar as the steady hum of chatter grew louder and louder.

Once we put in our order for beer and food, the Professor leaned his elbow on the table and met my eyes. "I sense that you are ready to get to the matter at hand, am I correct?"

Was I that obvious? "I'm worried about Lance."

He stroked his beard with one hand. "Yes, I believe that we all share your concerns."

"Thomas said that he's in custody?" My hands were finally starting to thaw, but I kept them in Thomas's jacket pockets anyway.

"Yes, correct again, but I assure you that that is as much for his protection as for anything else."

I looked to Mom. "For his protection?"

She shook her head.

The Professor nodded. "As you know Lance is Ashland's closest thing to a celebrity."

"Not according to Richard Lord," Mom chimed in as our drinks arrived.

"True, my dear." A slow smile spread across the Professor's stubbly face. "Aside from our resident Lord, Lance is one of the most popular figures in town. Keeping him in custody should help ensure that there will be no chance of it looking like he's being given preferential treatment, and as precaution for the fallout that could occur should news spread of his detainment. Due to potential conflicts of interest, I've also removed myself from the investigation."

"That's what Thomas said." I sipped my frothy beer and filled Mom and the Professor in on what I had learned thus far from both Vera and Judy. "I just can't picture either of them having the strength to drag Antony's body into the pond. Vera was furious with Antony and she was the last person to see him alive. Judy had traded her silence for special treatment. They both could have done it, I suppose, and then there's Tracy. What would her motive be for killing him? To keep her pregnancy quiet?" I asked when I finished.

The Professor considered this for a minute. "My, you have not had idle hands today, have you?" His hand gently stroked Mom's shoulder. "Remember, rage can do strange things to our human limitations. It's possible that one of these women could have moved his body. Although that still leaves us with the question of why. And, of course, there is always the possibility that one of them was working with an accomplice."

"Or that Lance was the accomplice," Thomas added in.

I wanted to kick him under the table. Instead, I gave him my best glare. Thomas threw his hands up. "Hey, don't shoot the messenger. I'm just saying it's an avenue we have to explore."

"Exactly," the Professor agreed. "Do not fret, Juliet. I understand your concerns and I share them."

As always, the Professor's astute ability to read me and those around him was clear. I had often wondered if it was an innate trait. Had he been drawn to his line of work because of skill and ease with people or was it the result of years on the police force? Probably a combination of the two.

"What about Thad and Brock?" I asked. "They both have the physical strength, but what motive?"

The Professor's eyes twinkled as he waited for me to continue.

"I mean motives aside, they were each definitely strong enough, right? And as set designer and stagehand one of them might have keys to the secret stairs leading to the duck pond, right? Not to mention John Duncan? Who is he and what's his connection to Antony?" I could hear my voice becoming shriller as I regurgitated the questions that had been assaulting my brain. "And the DVD? Why was there an empty DVD case next to Antony's body? What if whatever is on the DVD implicates the killer?"

Mom sighed. "Doug, look what you've encouraged. My sweet daughter obsessing over a murder investigation."

He placed his hand over his heart. "My dearest, I do apologize, but we can agree on the fact that she has a certain knack for my line of work, doesn't she? Question everything. That's the first rule I teach our young men and women in blue."

Mom gave me her best "mom" face. "That may be true, but I don't want you to stress about this or put yourself in harm's way."

"Don't worry, Mrs. Capshaw—I'll never let Jules come to harm." Thomas's voice was husky. Fortunately, the food arrived at that moment. Thomas dug right into his stew.

"What's going to happen next?" I picked at the hummus plate I had ordered. Mom caught my eye and gave me a look of concern.

The Professor removed his arm from Mom's shoulder and tucked his napkin into his shirt. "It will depend on the lab results. Detective Kerry should have them in the next few days. Until then, I'm going to check in with my sources. The missing DVD is most intriguing to me as well. I think a visit to headquarters after dinner would be advised. Thomas, would you escort Jules to meet with Detective Kerry tonight?"

Mom made a clucking sound. "Hmm."

"I think sharing this information with Detective Kerry will help you release stress, yes?" The Professor looked to me for confirmation. I nodded. Then he squeezed Mom's shoulder. "As the Bard says, 'Come what come may, Time and the hour runs through the roughest day.'"

I didn't stay much longer. The hummus plate tasted dull and lifeless. I knew it wasn't because of the food. Puck's Pub had some of the best pub fare in town, but until I figured out a way to clear Lance I couldn't concentrate on anything.

Chapter Sixteen

"Do you want your jacket back?" I asked Thomas as he held the door open for me and waited for me to step outside.

"No, keep it."

It was a short walk to the police station, but I was happy to have an extra layer of warmth. Nighttime temperatures still dipped into the thirties. It wouldn't be until after Easter or maybe closer to Mother's Day when the steady evening warming would begin. "What's Detective Kerry like?" I asked as we passed a sleeping Torte.

"I've only worked with her for a day, but like I said earlier, she's all business. She likes doughnuts, though."

"Well, she can't be that bad, then." I laughed.

"Just wait." Between the light from the nearly full moon and the glow from the antique street lamps lining the sidewalk I could see his eyes roll.

I stopped on the corner and took a quick peek at the basement property. A piece of plywood had been put up as a temporary door and the stairs had been blocked off with two plastic sawhorses. Good. At least I didn't have to worry about vandals—or more likely Richard

Lord—sneaking into the space while renovations were going on.

"Hey, before we head into the station, I wanted to ask a favor earlier but got so caught up in the case that I forgot."

Thomas waited at the crosswalk. "Shoot."

"Mom is thinking of surprising the Professor with a Midsummer Night's Eve wedding. Do you think you could feel him out? Subtly ask his thoughts on being involved in all the wedding details. Mom and I are both pretty confident that he's game for anything, but she would hate to leave him out if he's really excited about the planning."

"Aw, that's a cool idea. I think as long as the plans end with him marrying your mom, he'll be fine, but yeah, I'll see what I can get out of him."

"Thanks." We crossed to the police station, which looked dark. "Are you sure Detective Kerry is here?"

"Yeah, she wanted to take the graveyard shift. Someone has to be here," Thomas said. "Lance can't be left alone. State and federal regulations."

"It looks dark, though." I peered through the front window.

Thomas knocked on the door. "I know. I have my keys, but let's see if she answers first."

Light immediately flooded through the window. A woman, much younger than I anticipated, opened the door. She was dressed in a tight navy pencil skirt with a crisp white blouse and stylish navy heels. She was quite pretty with long auburn hair and bright green eyes.

"Officer Adams," she addressed Thomas. I had to suppress a giggle. I'd never heard anyone call Thomas "officer."

"Hey." Thomas gave her a nod. "This is Juliet Capshaw; she owns the bakeshop across the street and has some information about the investigation for you."

Detective Kerry studied me for a minute, taking careful note of Thomas's jacket that was still around my shoulders. "All right, come on back."

I felt my cheeks start to warm. It's not like I had anything to be embarrassed about, but the way Detective Kerry stared at me made me feel like a teenager who had just been caught trying to sneak in after curfew. I took off the jacket and handed it back to Thomas. "Thanks for this."

"I'm going to catch up on some paperwork." Thomas took his jacket and left us.

"This way." Detective Kerry pointed to the Professor's office. Unlike police stations I had seen on television, the Professor's office paid homage to his love of Shakespeare. Playbills, posters from past performances, and photos of him on the stage dotted his walls. His desk housed a coffee mug designed to look like the bard's bust. A tweed jacket hung on a wooden coat rack near the window. I wondered if he kept a backup jacket on hand or if he had simply forgotten it here.

Detective Kerry sat in the Professor's chair and crossed her legs. "What do you have for me?" She clicked a ballpoint pen and waited for me to speak.

I felt strangely protective of the Professor's space, and wanted to ask her not to touch anything. Instead, I explained in full detail everything the four of us had discussed at dinner, from Tracy's secret pregnancy and Judy's blackmail.

She gave no indication of interest while I spoke.

Every once in a while, she asked for brief clarification, but otherwise she jotted down notes and said "uh-huh" a lot.

"Got anything else for me?" she asked when I finished.

"Can I see Lance?" I asked, noticing an empty doughnut box in the trash can.

"Lance? Why?"

"He's my friend, and I just want to make sure he's okay."

She sat up and gave me a severe look. "He's in custody."

"I understand. That's why I was hoping to have a minute with him."

"You're a pastry chef? Did I misunderstand what Officer Adams said?"

"Yes, I'm a pastry chef."

She stood. "Not a lawyer?"

"No."

Straightening her narrow skirt, she moved toward the door. I could guess what she was about to say, but Thomas opened the door at the same moment and knocked her off balance. "Sorry. I didn't see you there." He offered his hand to help. Was it my imagination or had the faintest of smiles passed her lips?

She brushed off her spotless blouse. "I'm fine. I was about to see your friend out."

"I assume that means I can't see Lance?" I asked, picking up a framed photo of Mom and the Professor from the cruise. The photo was from the night they got engaged. It reminded me of a photo of Carlos and me with our arms entwined smiling under an apricot sunset.

Only the difference was that Carlos was my past and the Professor was Mom's future.

"It's fine," Thomas said to Detective Kerry. "The Professor—uh—Detective Curtis is going to be her stepfather. He would want Jules to have a minute with Lance."

She scowled and stared at the picture I was holding. "This is highly unusual. Like I told you and Detective Curtis earlier, keeping a murder suspect in a glorified office is extremely irregular and goes against all protocol."

"This is how we do things in Ashland," Thomas countered. "We're family here. The Professor knows every resident by name. So do I, because this is a small town. I went to school with a lot of the people here, and sure, maybe we don't have motor pools or divisions for fraud. Our property room is a locked closet with old shelving from my parents' flower shop." He nodded toward the hallway. "Sometimes if the garage is busy, I'll change the oil in our squad car. If we're short staffed then our 'dispatch department' turns into two sweet little old ladies who knit while they answer the phones. But you know what the best difference about working in a small town is? The Professor stops by Mrs. Jenkins's house every day with a loaf of bread and cup of soup because he knows that otherwise she might forget to eat. He told me on my first day wearing the badge that I only needed to know one thing to be successful in this job. And that is that police work is always personal."

His impassioned plea impressed me. I wasn't so sure about Detective Kerry. She listened to Thomas with her arms tightly wrapped around her chest and watched him through the narrowed slits of her eyes. I thought she was going to refuse, but she tapped her wrist. "Fine. Two minutes."

"Thanks," Thomas said with sincerity and then turned to me. "I'll take you back, Jules."

I didn't hesitate, afraid that Detective Kerry might change her mind. "Wow, that was quite the speech," I said as he led me to the locked office where they were keeping Lance.

"It's true. You know, big-city cops have this impression that us small-town guys are a bunch of bumbling idiots. Murder is murder. We treat it with the same respect."

"I think what you said made an impression."

He shrugged as we arrived at the holding room. "Did you know that the New York City police department has a staff of fifty thousand? That's more than double Ashland's entire population. But I wouldn't change working here for anything. I've learned from the best, and just because the Professor is off the case doesn't mean we suddenly have to change the way we do things."

"You're right." I put my arm on his shoulder. "Honestly, I loved what you said to Detective Kerry. I guess I've never thought about how hard you and the Professor have worked to earn and maintain everyone's trust."

Thomas smiled and then found the right key. "Two minutes, Jules." He winked and unlocked the door.

I took in a breath at the sight of Lance as I stepped inside. He was slumped on a temporary cot under a window. His hair was disheveled and he wore the same sweatpant outfit I'd seen him in earlier. Unlike the Professor's office, this room was obviously used for storage. The walls had been painted a stark white and housed a calendar and bulletin board with flyers for community events and safety procedures. There was a desk, a portable safe, and black industrial shelving with stacks of orange construction cones, boxes of plastic gloves, trash bags, cleaning supplies, and a megaphone. The top shelf was lined with kids' bike helmets in bright colors. I knew that Thomas and the Professor handed out free helmets on school visits or to anyone who couldn't afford one.

Lance looked up at me and gave me a feeble smile. They must not have considered him a danger or flight risk, I thought as I moved closer to him. He could easily use the mop and bucket propped near the shelves to break through the window or attack his captors. "How are you holding up?" I sat next to him on the squeaky cot.

"Ruined." His bloodshot eyes looked like something from a horror flick. "I've been crying for hours."

"I'm sure." I meant my words to be comforting but he recoiled and let out a howl.

"I'm hideous, aren't I?" He didn't comment on my outfit or ask about opening night. That was a bad sign.

"No, I didn't mean it like that." I scooted closer so that our knees touched. "Look at me, Lance."

He sniffled. "What?"

"You're going to be okay. We're all working on this—Thomas, Mom, the Professor."

"I thought he had been removed from his duties?" Thomas wiped his nose on the back of his baggy sleeve.

"No. He took himself off the case to protect you." I looked at the shut door, wondering if Detective Kerry had been serious about two minutes. "I don't have much time, let me fill you in on what I've learned."

Lance mopped his face on his snot-stained sweatshirt and continued to fight for control over his emotions. I didn't get far. I told him that Antony's body had been found in the duck pond, how the Professor was checking with some of his contacts, and my suspicions that the killer had used the authorized-personnel stairs to make his or her escape.

"Wait, stop there." Lance sounded more stable. "You said the stairwell was locked?"

"Uh, I think so. I couldn't exactly see, but it looked like there was a chain around the fence. I wasn't close enough to tell if it was locked." I thought back to my conversation with Thomas by the duck pond. "I'm pretty sure that Thomas said it was."

Lance sat up. "No. It's never been locked. The sign has been enough to deter people. We keep it unlocked because some of my actors and crew like to sneak out between rehearsals to get a bit of fresh air in the park. It's an easy way to duck out without running the risk of bumping into an adoring fan on the bricks."

"Really? Do the stairs get used for anything else, like deliveries? The steps looked pretty mossy."

"No. In fact, I asked the grounds crew not to pressure-wash the steps. I don't want them to get more use." Lance drummed his long fingers on his sweatpants. "Juliet, you may have discovered a critical clue. You have to go investigate. If there's a lock and chain on the gate Antony's murderer must have put it there."

I started to reply, but Thomas opened the door. Detective Kerry stood behind him with a scowl that made her otherwise attractive face look long and misshapen.

"Sorry, Lance, but I've got to send Jules home," Thomas said.

Lance normally would have protested, but his dejected sigh was the only response he could muster. I hugged him and whispered, "Don't worry."

"Get up to the park," he hissed in response.

There was so much more I wanted to tell him. We had barely scratched the surface, but I knew from the slow burn emanating from Detective Kerry's green eyes that I had to get moving. "See you soon." I kissed Lance's cheek and left the room.

Thomas walked me to the front with Detective Kerry at our heels. "You want me to walk you home?"

I wanted to tell him about my conversation with Lance, but I could almost feel Detective Kerry's breath. She stood two inches away from Thomas wearing the same look of displeasure on her face. "No, I'm good. It's only a block," I replied, and then smiled at Detective Kerry. "Nice to meet you. Thanks for letting me see Lance."

She offered a curt nod.

A blast of cool air hit my face as I exited the police station. Tiny droplets of dew gleamed in the moonlight. Soon they would turn to frost and blanket the plaza like a thin layer of buttercream. I rubbed my cashmere sweater and hurried across the street. The cold wasn't going to deter me. I had a singular mission. I would stop by my apartment and put on warmer clothes and then I was heading straight for Lithia Park.

Chapter Seventeen

I quickly changed out of my skirt and into a pair of jeans, a fleece sweatshirt, and tennis shoes. Then I found the flashlight that Mom had left at my apartment in case the power ever went out. Before I had returned to Ashland, Mom had stocked my kitchen with baking supplies and my medicine cabinet with toothpaste and Tylenol. It was a thoughtful and practical gesture, especially since I had left the ship in such a hurry that things like food and toiletries never crossed my mind.

Along with the flashlight and my phone, I also stuck a pink canister of pepper spray into my pocket. Thomas had insisted I keep the self-defense product on hand after a recent altercation at the Chocolate Festival. He had stopped by my apartment with a three-inch pink canister that could be attached to a purse or key chain, or tucked into a pocket. "This will impair any attacker for forty-five minutes," he had explained, showing me how to use the flip-top safety feature that prevented the pepper spray from accidentally misfiring and demonstrating how to use the finger grip to spray any would-be assailant directly in the eyes.

At the time, I had assured him that I was fine, but tonight I appreciated having a defensive weapon secured in my pocket, just in case. I pulled a ski cap over my braid and put on my winter coat before heading to the park. Nervous excitement pulsed through me as I descended the stairs past Elevation. The after-theater crowds were still going strong at the restaurants along the plaza. The sound of live music and jovial chatter made my nerves calm a bit. There were people wandering about the plaza and packed into the pubs. It was after eleven but Ashland was wide awake with the thrill of a new season.

I would hurry over to the duck pond on my mission for Lance and be back in a flash. Should I happen upon anyone who appeared dangerous I had my Mace and a healthy set of lungs. One loud scream should send people running.

"Right, or you're simply trying to justify being reckless," I told myself as I passed the Green Goblin and crossed East Main Street. My breath formed pockets of fog with each exhalation. Every hair on my neck and forearms tingled. I zipped my parka all the way to my chin and followed the spotlight from my flashlight along the pressed pebble path that wound from the Shakespeare stairs along the tree line toward the pond.

A symphony of croaking frogs reverberated, welcoming me to their forest and making me feel less alone.

Was this a bad idea? I shivered from the cold and my returning nerves. Maybe I should turn around and come back in the morning.

I stopped at the base of an ancient redwood tree. The duck pond was only another two or three hundred feet down the path. It wouldn't take more than a couple minutes to check out the gate and take a few pictures of the lock.

You can do this, Jules. I gave myself a little pep talk. If I waited until morning that would give the killer time to return. If the lock had been put on the gate by the killer, it could still have their fingerprints—hard evidence to clear Lance.

I inhaled a deep breath of frosty air and pushed on. Aside from the frogs, the park was eerily quiet. My every step seemed to echo, and I was acutely aware of the sound of my heartbeat pulsing in my head. I quickened my pace to a steady jog. The sooner I got this done, the sooner I could be home and safely tucked in my bed.

The duck pond came into view as I passed through a break in the trees. There was no sign of policy activity, but the area remained off limits with caution tape.

Okay. I sighed with relief, pressing my fingers together to try and steady my breathing.

Out of the corner of my eye I saw a flash of movement. A wave of adrenaline pulsed through my body. I whipped my flashlight in the direction of the movement and reached for my Mace. A duck let out a warning quack, flapping its wings and levitating over the pond.

It's just a duck, Jules.

I exhaled again and bent under the police tape. Suddenly, I was overcome by thoughts of the police dragging Antony's body from the pond and Lance finding him dead. Thomas was right, this was personal. Someone had disturbed our idyllic lifestyle and if there was even the slightest chance that I could help bring them to justice, I had to push through my fear.

"Go back to sleep, ducks," I said aloud, for my own

benefit. Then I walked around the benches to the secret set of stairs. The lock was still there. Thank goodness.

I removed my phone from my pocket and took a dozen photos of the chain and black combination lock. Why had the killer locked the gate? I tried to put myself in their head.

Lance had found Antony's body about four or five hundred feet away at the base of the heavily used Shakespeare stairs. He had panicked and fled the scene of the crime. Perhaps he interrupted the killer. Maybe the killer had hidden behind one of the nearby trees and waited for Lance to leave. Then they came back for Antony's body. It would have been late and dark, much like now.

The killer probably realized they didn't have much time. They assumed that Lance had gone for help and the police would soon follow. They must have had to act quickly. If I were in that position I would have taken the path of least resistance and dragged the body to the closest place I could find to dump it—the duck pond. Hence the drag marks in the grass.

But then what? The killer couldn't return to the park entrance, knowing the police were on their way. They had two choices. Run deeper into the Lithia forest, or take the secret stairs up to the theater complex. The stairs were unlocked. Had they known that? Was Antony's murder premeditated? Or could the killer have made his or her escape in a rush and then returned with the lock later? What if the lock had been put there in an attempt to keep the police from sweeping the area?

I sighed. Did that mean that the killer had to be connected to OSF? Who else would have known that the stairs were unlocked?

The sound of crunching leaves nearby put my body on high alert. I froze.

For a moment, the park was deadly calm, other than the sound of harmonizing frogs and the slight wind fluttering through the trees.

Then another crunch and the sound of heavy footsteps thudding toward me.

I yanked the Mace out of my pocket, and fumbled for the safety switch. What had Thomas said? Was I supposed to hold it all the way down or press it once and wait for it to click into place?

My heart rate pounded so rapidly that my breath couldn't keep pace. Every sound came into sharp focus. It was as if my body had shut down every other function and given me superhearing.

I held my flashlight high and aimed it in the direction of the footsteps. A figure, wearing all black, darted behind a tree.

"I have pepper spray," I shouted. "I'm not afraid to use it." I knew from past experience and from the Professor and Thomas that it was critical to be as loud as possible in a situation like this.

I tried to stay as calm as possible as my breath came in quick, shallow bursts. What should I do? I could hold my ground and confront whoever was in the woods, or I could make a run for it. I wasn't the fastest runner but my legs were long and my adrenaline was pulsing on high. If I stuck to the main path, which was dimly lit by antique lights, I figured I had a pretty good shot of making it back to the plaza unharmed.

But running came with risk. What if whoever was out there was faster than me? They could overtake me from behind. My pepper spray would do no good if they tackled me to the ground.

Whoever was out there raced from one tree to another a few feet away. It felt like a dangerous game of chess, and I was the pawn. They were strategically moving closer, managing to stay out of my line of sight.

I couldn't wait around and risk them sneaking around from the other side of the duck pond. Once they made it to the pond they could easily run around the back side without any chance of being seen and come at me from behind. My best bet was to make a break for it. I shined the flashlight in a zigzagging pattern from tree to tree.

The person remained cloaked in darkness.

It's now or never, Jules, I told myself. Then I grasped the Mace as tightly as I could, but in my haste my flashlight fell on the ground. I hesitated for a second. The flashlight could serve as a weapon, but there was no time. I left it glowing on the sidewalk, and ran quickly toward the police tape.

Chapter Eighteen

I hurdled the tape. There was no time to try and duck under it. For all I knew my attacker could be at my heels.

Run, Jules! I commanded my feet to fly. My breath burned in my lungs as my toes barely touched the pavement.

Was whoever had been hiding in the trees following me? Or had they run off, too? They wouldn't dare risk attacking me in the plaza, would they?

I glanced behind me. It was too dark to see anything. Keep moving!

The landscape blurred. My chest tightened, and a dull ache spread beneath my rib cage. The park entrance had to be close. Why did it feel like I had been running for miles?

I sucked chilly air in through my nose and ran on. Finally, the hazy lights of downtown came into view. I didn't stop, though. I sprinted straight to my apartment, took the stairs two steps at a time, and raced inside.

I slid down the back of my locked door and collapsed on the floor. The ache in my side radiated down my back and into the top of my thigh. My breath came in shallow pants and sweat poured from my face. I wiped it on the back of my coat. That was close. Really close.

Now what? Who had been at the duck pond? Was it Antony's killer? Maybe they had come back to remove the lock, or had they stashed evidence nearby? I poked two fingers underneath my rib cage, trying to massage the nagging pain. Had it all been a figment of my imagination? Maybe Lance's flair for the dramatic had rubbed off on me. It could have been nothing more than one of the many black-tailed deer that live in the park.

After my breathing returned to a semi-normal pace, I stood and went to the kitchen to douse my blazing cheeks with cold water. Regardless of whether my eyes had been playing tricks on me, I knew that I had to call Thomas and let him know what had happened. I dabbed my face with a dish towel and pulled my cell phone from my pocket.

"Long time no see," Thomas said after picking up on the second ring.

"I was just chased out of Lithia Park," I panted into the phone.

"What?" Thomas sounded incredulous. "Hang on a second. I'm going to step outside."

Based on the sound of muffled footsteps I figured he was getting out of earshot of Detective Kerry. "What did you say, Jules? You were chased?"

"Just now. I went to the park to look at the lock." I told him about my conversation with Lance, and how Lance had insisted that the gate had never been locked before.

"Whoa. Slow down. Breathe."

I knew I must sound crazy. "Someone was out there, Thomas. I know it."

"Okay, I'll go check it out now." He sighed. "Jules, stay put. In fact, go to bed."

My pulse still pumped through my neck. "There's no way I'm going to be able to sleep, Thomas."

He let out a groan. "Fine. Lock your door. Don't move a muscle and I'll stop by once I survey the scene."

"Thank you." I clicked off the phone and put on a pot of water for tea. If whoever I had seen in the park was Antony's killer, what had they been doing? Could it have something to do with the missing DVD? What if they had dropped the DVD while escaping up the unused stairs? Or maybe they had intentionally hidden it in the brush nearby.

Sleep would be futile until I heard from Thomas, which made me think about Stephanie. I had promised to bring her my old earplugs.

With the kettle warming on the stove, I tugged off my coat and went to look for the earplugs. My belongings were pretty sparse. Life at sea lent itself to prioritizing essentials. Everything I owned fit into two suitcases, which meant that my bedroom housed nothing more than a bed, a dresser, and a small bedside table. Like the rest of my place, I needed to add some personal touches, like a picture, plant, or even splurge on one of the colorful handwoven tapestries that I'd seen at the Artists Market a few weeks ago.

I checked my closet for the earplugs, wondering if perhaps they were still tucked into a suitcase or if I had put them in my dresser. They weren't in either place, so as a last-ditch effort I checked my bedside table. When I had moved back home I had dumped an assortment of miscellaneous items into the drawer, which rarely got opened.

Sure enough, the earplugs were in a box at the back of the drawer along with a mysterious gift from Carlos—a key. My heart caught in my chest at the sight of it. Carlos had given me the key when I left the ship, but I hadn't figured out its cryptic meaning. I had assumed maybe it was a last effort to express his love for me. A symbol of holding the key to his heart, but even for a romantic like Carlos the gesture seemed out of character. Plus, the key was a regular ordinary house key. If Carlos meant the gift to be a token of his affection it was more likely he would have given me an ornate and elegant key. I couldn't shake the feeling that this key actually opened a door. The question was where and what.

I ran my fingers along it and returned it to the drawer. Then I took the plastic box with the earplugs out to the living room and tucked them into my purse to give to Stephanie in the morning. The tea whistled, causing me to start. Obviously, my adrenaline was still running high.

Warm steam enveloped the kitchen. I poured water into a mug and opted for a cup of lemon zinger tea. My thoughts turned to Thomas as I opened the fridge. Had he found anything? Or had I sent him on a wild-goose chase? Since he was always hungry, and because he'd readily dropped whatever he had been working on to go search the park for me, I wanted to offer him a token of my thanks.

I scanned the shelves in the fridge and decided on a grown-up grilled cheese with fontina, basil, tomatoes, and honey on thick-sliced Parmesan bread. I warmed butter in a skillet and spread it on both sides of the fresh bread. Then I cut thin slices of fontina and layered in basil leaves and tomatoes. Once the sandwiches had been stacked, I drizzled a touch of honey on the top and placed the first one in the sizzling skillet.

The lemon tea soothed my nerves as I flipped the first sandwich and drizzled honey on the other side of the bread. Fontina is an Italian cheese made from cow's milk. And not just any cows. The most exquisite fontina is produced in the summer months when the cows are moved to higher elevations to dine on rich alpine grasses. It's a wonderful melting cheese with a creamy texture and woodsy aroma.

A knock sounded on the door as I plated both sandwiches.

"Jules, it's me!" I heard Thomas call.

Perfect timing. I walked to open the door, stopping to place the sandwiches on the small two-person dining table in the corner of the living room.

"What smells so good?" Thomas said, peering over me toward the kitchen.

"I made you a late-night snack. I figured I owed you." I pointed to the table. "You want a cup of tea, too?"

"You don't owe me, Jules. It's my job to serve and protect." He patted the word POLICE on the bulky navy jacket he had on over his suit. "But if you insist, I certainly will never turn down anything you make."

I smiled. "Sit. I'll get your tea and then you have to tell me what you found."

He removed his jacket and hung it by the door. I returned with two mugs of tea and handed one to Thomas. "What is this?" He picked up half of his sandwich. Lovely white fontina cheese stretched like Silly Putty.

"I'm calling it grown-up grilled cheese."

Thomas bit into the sandwich and closed his eyes. He

tilted his head to the ceiling then looked at me. "I'm calling it the best thing I've ever tasted."

"You say that about everything I make," I scoffed, and pulled my gooey sandwich in half.

"That's because it's true." Thomas took another bite. "It's like slightly sweet, too."

"Yeah, that's from the honey." I tasted my sandwich. The nutty fontina merged with the basil and warm tomatoes while the Parmesan crust gave the sandwich a nice sharpness, and the honey a final hint of sweetness.

"I don't know how you do it."

"Do what?"

Thomas held up his partially eaten half. "This. Who puts honey on a grilled cheese sandwich? Honey!" He munched a corner of the golden bread. "Jules. Jules Capshaw does."

"Trust me, lots of chefs pair sweet and salty foods together. It's one of the building blocks of a well-balanced plate."

"Whatever," he said through a final mouthful. "You are a miracle worker and this is forever my new favorite thing."

I grinned and sipped my tea. "So, did you find anything?"

"No." His face turned serious. "Don't look so dejected. That doesn't mean anything. If there was somebody out there with you tonight, the odds of them sticking around are pretty slim. Did you get a good look? Can you give me a description?"

"It was so dark." I paused and tried to concentrate on exactly what I had seen. "I only caught a quick glimpse of whoever it was."

"Male? Female?"

"Honestly, I'm not sure." It could have been anyone. I thought about my current list of suspects—Judy, Brock, Vera, Tracy, and Thad. "I think the person was tall." That made Brock, Judy, and Tracy the most likely. Thad and Vera were both short.

Thomas tucked into the second half of his sandwich. "I'll take another look in the morning. See if there are any footprints around. Or if anything's been disturbed. What's this about the locked gate?"

"Oh, right." I jumped up and went into the kitchen to get my phone. The scent of grilled bread and butter lingered in the tiny space. "I took pictures for you," I said, handing the phone to Thomas and scrolling through the photos I had taken.

"Can you send those to me? I'll share them with Detective Kerry and talk to Lance first thing in the morning." He gave me back the phone.

"You weren't kidding. She's very . . ." I searched for the right word. "Professional."

"That's one way to put it." Thomas polished off his sandwich and washed it down with his tea.

"You don't think that the Professor is planning to hire her on permanently, do you?"

"Who knows." He shrugged. "She's going to have some serious adjustment issues if he does."

"Isn't she from Medford? It's hardly like she's coming from New York or something."

Thomas scowled. "She kind of is, though. I guess she came out from Chicago a couple weeks ago. I'm pretty sure that Medford can't handle her, either. I bet they gladly sent her to us on temporary assignment."

That made much more sense.

He stood. "You should get some sleep, Jules. Be careful, please?"

I picked up our plates. "Bakers' honor."

"Right." Thomas gave me a knowing look. "Thanks for the sandwich. I'll see you tomorrow." He walked to the door. "Lock this behind me and no more park stunts, got it?"

"Got it." My experience in Lithia Park had spooked me. He didn't need to ask twice. I followed his instructions and locked the door behind him. Then I cleaned up and headed for bed. Unfortunately, my brain had other plans. I lay in stillness, considering each suspect.

Vera had been the last person to see Antony alive. She had access to all kinds of props and weapons at OSF as well as keys to everything. But did she have the strength to have dragged his body to the pond? Whoever I had seen in the park was tall. Did that rule Thad out, too? Like Vera, he was short and had keys to every office and building in the theater complex. He was definitely strong. Years of constructing heavy sets had left him with well-defined muscles. What was his motive, though?

Tracy had motive, as did Judy. Both were tall and had been at OSF the night of the murder. Judy could be lying. Perhaps Antony had been giving her more than special perks for her silence. What if she was actually blackmailing him and he had had enough? And Tracy was pregnant. Was Antony the father, or had he been about to out her? What about Brock? What motive could he have for wanting his roommate dead? My thoughts flashed to Stephanie. Could Antony have had an annoying habit that drove Brock to the edge?

The one thought that brought me relief was Lance. If the killer had been lurking in the forest tonight, it couldn't have been Lance. He was miserably snug in Ashland's police office. Which made me even more confident that he couldn't be the killer.

Chapter Nineteen

The next morning, I woke with a throbbing headache. It had been a restless night, even worse than when Lance had stumbled into my apartment with blood on his hands. I found myself waking every thirty minutes with nightmares. Sometime after four I finally gave up, made a strong pot of coffee, and took two Advil.

I figured the headache was from lack of sleep and worry, so I decided my best bet was to dive headfirst into baking. I was resolved to do whatever it took to clear Lance. Once things were up and running at Torte I intended to have my own conversations with Thad, Brock, and Tracy.

Shockingly, Stephanie was already partway through the morning's bread orders when I arrived at the bakeshop. "You're here super early," I said, tying on an apron and joining her in the kitchen where loaves of dough wrapped in plastic sat rising on a portable rack. The ovens had already come to temp, and a carafe of coffee sat on the island.

"Can't sleep, so what else are you going to do?" Her

normally sleek purple hair was frizzed and had a slight curl.

"A gift," I said to Stephanie and tossed her the earplugs. "Hopefully, these will help and, if they don't, I think you should stop by the health center on campus and talk to someone. Maybe they can give you a temporary sleep aid."

She stared at the box. "Thanks."

"I'm serious, Stephanie," I said, moving closer but careful not to touch her. "Days and days without sleep is taking a toll on your health, not to mention your schoolwork and baking."

"Am I in trouble?" Her eyes were nothing more than tiny slits.

"No, no, of course not." I didn't mean to cause her any worry.

"I'll take care of it." She stuffed the earplugs into the back pocket of her black ripped jeans.

"It's not that. It's that we're all worried about you."

"You don't have to be. I said I'll take care of it." She dug her hands into the bread dough. "I'm cool."

I felt terrible. That wasn't the result I had been hoping for. I tried to reassure her once more, but without success. It was probably the lack of sleep. Between her and Lance, it was terrible to watch my friends suffering without knowing what else to do to help. I dropped the subject. Once Stephanie clammed up, no good would come of continuing to prod her.

Nothing about the morning felt routine. I found myself constantly checking over my shoulder, unable to completely shake last night's nerves. Stephanie's negative energy rubbed off on everyone. My staff gave her a wide berth. Sterling kept his head down while simmering tomatoes, garlic, and beef broth for our lunch special—cheeseburger soup. Bethany tried out uniquely shaped macarons, like bunny ears and carrots. She didn't bother to ask Stephanie's input when she set up a photo shoot of her Easter-themed treats. Even Andy cut his usual banter. Anytime he entered the kitchen, he quickly refilled the coffee carafe and made a quick escape. If the earplugs didn't work I was going to have to stage an intervention. There's nothing worse than an unhappy kitchen.

My day brightened a bit when Tracy and Thad came in for lunch. Sterling ladled two heaping bowls of our cheeseburger soup, thick with chunks of potatoes, ground beef, onions, and sprinkled with cheddar cheese. "I'll deliver that order," I said, piling Bethany's orange carrots onto a plate. She had trimmed the cookies with lime licorice tops, and using edible pens, she had hand-decorated pink bunnies with black whiskers.

What were Tracy and Thad doing together? I thought as I balanced the tray on one hand and walked to the booth where they were sitting. "Delivery," I announced with a smile.

Tracy's eyes went straight to the plate of macarons. "Oh my goodness, those are the cutest ever." She looked different without her stage makeup. Her hair was indeed dark, but unlike her performance as Cleopatra last night, she wore it twisted up in a bun. Her porcelain skin didn't need any extra enhancement.

I set the tray on the table. "You mentioned how much you liked them the other day so I thought I would let you be the first to sample our latest creation—Easter macarons."

Her doelike deep brown eyes lit up. "They're too cute to eat, though. Don't you think, Thad?"

Thad sat across from her. His bald head was covered with a carpenter's hat. His suspension tool belt looked lighter than it had before. I wondered if he'd taken out some of his tools to lessen the load on his shoulders. "Sure."

She rolled her eyes at him and shot me a look of exasperation. "Men."

I wondered how to barge into their lunch, but didn't have to think long.

"Sit with us for a minute." Tracy patted the booth. "I want to talk to you about a special order. Don't you think something like these would be perfect, Thad?"

Thad stared at her and gave her a look I couldn't read.

She ignored him and dug into her soup. "This actually tastes like I'm eating a juicy cheeseburger."

"That's what we love to hear. I'll be sure to pass your praise on to our sous chef." I watched Thad, who kept his gaze focused on Tracy as she ate. "What's the occasion for your special order?"

Tracy's pale skin flamed with color. "Uh, um—well." She looked to Thad.

He yanked up the shoulder straps on his tool harness. They shared another look, then he changed the subject. "Have you talked to Lance?"

Did he know about Tracy's pregnancy? Something was going on between the two of them. I got the sense that Thad didn't want Tracy to tell me more.

"Yeah, I saw him last night," I replied.

Tracy slurped her soup. "It was so weird to open a show without him. The whole night felt strange, didn't it?"

Thad removed a flat pencil from his tool belt and moved it to a different pocket. "Yeah. It was a different vibe backstage for sure."

"It's just so sad." Tracy stirred the melting cheddar into her soup.

"You mean Antony's murder?" I asked.

"Well, yeah, I mean everything, though. Running a production without Lance is like . . ." She paused, bit her bottom lip, and pointed to the plate of cookies. "Like eating a macaron without filling."

"I heard that Lance was having challenges with the board," I said.

Thad still hadn't touched his soup. "Lance made his own bed."

What did that mean? I started to ask him, but Tracy cut me off. "That's not true. How would you deal with someone like Antony? Why am I still calling him Antony?" She threw her head back.

"Did you two get along?" I asked. "You and Antony."

"His name wasn't Antony," Thad said under his breath.

"I don't know. It's always hard when you're cast in a role like Cleopatra, especially with a *method actor*," she said in disgust.

Thad cleared his throat. Tracy glanced at him. "So, tell me about these adorable macarons. How did you make them into shapes like this? And what flavors are they?"

I knew that I had been dismissed. "The carrots are orange with a sweet cream filling, and the bunnies are cherry with almond."

"Yum." Tracy reached for a carrot.

Thad finally tasted his soup.

"I should get back to the kitchen," I said. "Before I go, do either of you know whether the back stairway from the Elizabethan theater is usually locked?"

Tracy shrugged. "No idea."

Thad took a minute to respond. "Why do you ask?"

"Lance mentioned it. That's all." I tried to keep my tone casual.

"No one uses those stairs. They're crumbling and not safe." He gave Tracy a hard look. "You shouldn't use them."

She crunched the carrot-shaped cookie. "I don't. They creep me out with the woods on either side." She shuddered.

"Good." He looked relieved. "They should be locked. I've told Lance that at least a dozen times. They're dangerous and no one needs access from the park. We're inviting vagrants to come up into the complex."

"Yeah, I wondered the same thing when I was looking at them yesterday," I said, instantly regretting the words as they escaped my lips.

"You were there?" Thad's hand went to his tool belt.

"Oh, I was just walking through the park and noticed them. We're doing a renovation downstairs and our steps are in the same shape." I stood. "I'll let you two finish your lunch. Just holler if you want to talk about your special order."

Tracy nodded. Thad kept his hand wrapped around a chisel and watched me leave. I wasn't sure what was going on between them, but he obviously didn't want her talking. Why? Had I been mistaken about the height of the person hiding in the woods last night? Could it have been Thad? He wanted the steps locked. Or was that a convenient excuse? Maybe he had been the person who put the lock on the gate.

I returned to the kitchen feeling more confused. Tracy seemed sincere, but I couldn't forget the fact that she was a talented actress. She could easily be fooling me. Or were they working together?

"Hey, boss," Andy whispered as I passed the espresso bar. I was so deep in thought that it took me a minute to register.

"Sorry, what?" I shook off my conversation with Tracy and Thad and concentrated.

"We have to do something about you know who." He tilted his head in the direction of the kitchen.

"Steph?" I mouthed.

Andy acted out a pantomime of what I assumed meant that Stephanie was killing him by the way he clutched his neck and pretended to gag. "She's killing you?" I asked.

"She's killing the coffee vibe in here." He massaged the top of the shiny espresso machine. "This baby needs good energy to churn and burn."

"Churn and burn?" I raised my brow.

"Cut me some slack. We're all walking on eggshells around here. I can't even come up with any good jokes."

"I know. I talked to her this morning and I gave her a pair of really good earplugs. Hopefully, they'll do the trick," I assured him.

"And if they don't?"

I tucked the empty tray under my arm and patted his shoulder. "Don't worry. I have a plan."

"Good." He reached for a latte resting on the bar. "In the meantime, you want to give her this. It's my newest latte art, Ode to Stephanie."

I picked up the cup, which had a grumpy but shockingly accurate portrait of Stephanie's profile crafted in foam. "Andy, this is terrible. True. Talented. But terrible."

He grinned. "We have to lighten it up somehow."

I laughed. "Fair enough. But you're taking your own life in your hands if you give her that."

"Don't I know it." With that he snatched the cup out of my hands and gulped down the grumpy face of foam.

Andy was right. Torte was supposed to be our happy place. If the earplugs didn't work, then maybe it was time to force Stephanie to take a break.

Chapter Twenty

Things didn't improve the next day. The tension was thicker than the new vat of chili Sterling had made. "How's everything going?" I asked, returning from delivering a custom cake order.

"Can you tell Andy to turn down his tunes?" Stephanie plugged her ears. "It's giving me a headache."

I hadn't noticed the music. I paused and listened for a minute. Light classical music was barely audible above the chatter of customers and the hum of the espresso machine. "That's loud?"

Stephanie stuck her fingers deeper in her ears and nodded. Bethany caught my eye from across the counter where she was whipping a batch of buttercream. She dipped her pinkie into sky-blue frosting. "Is there even music on?"

Stephanie rubbed her eyes, leaving a smear of cake batter on her face. "I'm a freak. I swear, listening to the *Oklahoma!* sound track nonstop has given me superhuman hearing or something."

"Did you try the earplugs?" I asked.

"I tried them last night. I think they helped, but honestly, it's all I hear in my head. I'm not even sure what's real and what's not anymore." She clutched the counter.

Sterling slid behind her to support her. "Steph, you should sit down. You don't look very steady." He looked to me.

"Yeah, he's right," I agreed. "Have you been eating? I've seen you guzzling coffee for the past few days, but have you eaten anything?"

She shrugged. I noticed that she didn't push Sterling away. "Let's get her a sandwich," I said to Bethany. "Sterling, take her up front."

Stephanie didn't resist. She let Sterling place his arm around her shoulder and lead her to the dining room. "Hey, Andy," I called. "Can you do me a favor and kill the music?"

He stared at me as if I was speaking a foreign language. "Huh?"

"The music is bothering Stephanie." I nodded to the front.

Andy scowled and pointed to a speaker mounted on the wall. "This? It's *Bach*."

"I know," I mouthed.

He left the espresso counter and came closer to us. "Steph usually throws down with her punk beats. If Bach is bugging her, she really needs to see a doctor." His boyish eyes were full of concern.

"I know," I repeated. The question was, how could I convince her to go? I knew that as her employer I couldn't force her to see a doctor, but as her friend and mentor I was genuinely worried about her mental health.

I had always thrived on little sleep. It was a hazard of working in the bakery industry. Fortunately, genetics played a huge role for me. As long as I had a few hours of solid sleep I was completely functional. But I understood that wasn't true for everyone. Stephanie's lack of sleep had clearly gotten out of control.

Bethany made a turkey sandwich that I paired with a fruit salad, green salad, and chips. I took it to the front. "Eat something, then I want you to take the rest of the day off. Do me a favor and just drop by the student health center and ask them if there's something they can give you. Melatonin, or a sleeping pill."

Sterling's cornflower-blue eyes were filled with worry. "I told her to come stay at my place tonight."

"It's a good idea."

Stephanie picked at the sandwich. "You guys are freaking out. I'm fine."

"You almost collapsed back there." Sterling's voice was firm. "You need to eat, like Jules said, and then I'm taking you to the health center."

She started to complain, but he fixed his piercing eyes on her.

"Fine," she snarled.

"Good. I'll check in with you later." I touched her bony shoulder. "We all care about you, Stephanie."

Sterling caught my eye to say thanks as I walked away. Hopefully, the health center would have something to ease her sleeping angst. I felt relieved knowing that she was at least going to see a doctor.

"Everything cool, boss?" Andy spoke in code since there were two regulars waiting for iced caramel lattes at the bar.

I flashed him a thumbs-up, and went to check in with

Bethany. "Sterling is going to take her to the health center," I said.

"Thank goodness." Bethany scooped fluffy buttercream into a pastry bag. "She's getting worse every day."

"Yeah. I'm going to call Mom and see if she can come help cover."

Bethany stood on her tiptoes. "It's not too bad up there. We can handle it."

"True, but I know she likes to be needed, and we could use an extra set of hands to get us through the lunch rush. Previews start tonight for two new shows so I was planning to close early anyway." I went to call Mom who immediately agreed to come help.

"Juliet, why didn't you tell me about this? I'm putting on my clogs as we speak and I'll be there in ten minutes." She didn't give me a chance to explain.

Not even ten minutes later Mom had an apron wrapped around her white capris and cable-knit cardigan. Bethany and I explained that Stephanie had gotten progressively worse while she took over the chili Sterling had been working on.

"Mrs. C.'s in the house!" Andy shuffled in with a lavender honey latte. "Made this one special. Just for you."

"Look!" Mom waved us over to the stove to show us Andy's creation—a three-tier wedding cake in foam. "We have to enter him in competitions," she said to me. Then she blew Andy a kiss. "You have outdone yourself, young man. I'm serious. We are signing up for the barista competition in Seattle, and Torte will foot the bill."

"Sweet." He cracked his knuckles. "My steaming pitcher is going to get a workout."

"Wait." Bethany held up her index finger. "Can I borrow you and the drink for some quick pics?"

Mom carefully handed her the latte so as not to disturb Andy's artwork. "Hold the cup like that," Bethany directed, having Andy pose for a couple of pictures and then taking close-ups of the foamy cake.

"We have to send him up to Seattle to compete," Mom said to me. She cracked ground pepper into the chili. "You should go with him. It would be a great networking opportunity, especially with the expansion."

"I'll look into it," I agreed. Barista competitions attracted highly skilled coffee connoisseurs to showcase everything from latte art to roasting methods, along with a barista throwdown, where participants had mere minutes to make and serve a perfect cup of espresso, latte, and signature drink while being scrutinized by judges on technique. Not only were regional, national, and world competitions a feast for the senses, they brought big prize money for the winners. Andy could win thousands of dollars to put toward his tuition or save for after graduation. It had been years since I had attended a competition, but I was fairly confident that Andy had a good shot at making it at least past the first round. Plus, it would be a chance for him to learn new skills and meet coffee artists from different corners of the world.

"How's the Professor doing?" I asked Mom after Andy returned to the front.

She tasted the chili before adding another grind of pepper and a sprinkling of salt. "He went up to Medford again. He's doing everything he can behind the scenes." Pausing, she pursed her lips. "How are you doing? That was quite the speech you made last night."

"Sorry. I'm just upset about Lance." I opted not to mention anything about my adventure in Lithia Park. "By the way, I met Detective Kerry."

"And?" Mom tasted the chili with a soup spoon.

"She's, er, serious?"

"That's exactly how Doug describes her." She savored the chili for a minute and then reached for the cumin and chili powder. "Although he says that she's very talented. She comes highly recommended."

I thought about Thomas's perspective—that Medford was more than happy to send her our way.

"He thinks that having someone without an attachment or history in Ashland might be good for the department. He's always hired from within, and said it might be time to bring in some fresh eyes."

I hoped that didn't mean that the Professor was thinking about offering Detective Kerry a permanent position. Detective Kerry was much too serious for Ashland.

We got off the topic because Sterling returned with an update on Stephanie. "She's at the health center," he said, tugging on the strings of his black hoodie. "But she wouldn't let me stay."

"At least she's there," Mom assured him. "Good work convincing her to go."

"I guess." He didn't sound convinced.

At least the mood in the kitchen lightened. With Mom beside me rolling out sheets of pie crust and fielding gossip about Lance and why the Professor wasn't on the case, I felt more centered. I plunged into piping royal icing on our sugar cookies. My thoughts continued to stray to Lance, but the steady stream of customers forced me to stay in the moment. By late afternoon the crowd had dissipated, as everyone headed to previews. OSF ran a week of previews before the official opening of a new show. It was a chance to work out any last-minute kinks and generate buzz.

Andy had already left for class, Sterling to check on Stephanie, and Mom offered to stay for a while and play around with macaron designs with Bethany. I opted to do some more digging. Under the guise of delivering boxes of cookies to the theater, I went off in search of Judy. I wanted to get a better sense of whether she was lying. Had she only gotten favors like an invite to Lance's party from Antony, or had she been blackmailing him for cold, hard cash? And the missing DVD was nagging at me. If Judy had really been close with him maybe she knew something about it.

I loaded two boxes with our signature sugar cookies cut in the shape of tiaras and glass slippers in honor of the preview of *Cinderella*.

As I crossed Main Street, I heard Richard Lord's booming baritone. "Juliet, a word!"

Just my luck.

He was on the porch of the Merry Windsor with a lit cigar clenched in his jowls.

"What's up, Richard?" The smell of the cigar made me nauseous. Not that I had any intention of hanging around for long, but I didn't want my sugar cookies to soak in the scent of the musty tobacco.

"You've been avoiding me." His yellow teeth gripped the base of the cigar as he spoke.

"No. I've been working." I lifted the box of cookies.

"Have you talked to your friend?" He tipped his cigar in a greeting to a guest leaving the decrepit hotel.

"Who?"

"You know who—Lance."

"No," I lied, shifting the boxes in my arms. There was no way I was divulging anything to Richard.

"We need to talk." His belly squished over the top of his plaid slacks. "Soon."

I wondered if he knew that Lance was in custody. "About what?"

"You know." He chewed on the cigar.

"I don't."

"Tell Lance I want a meeting with both of you. This week!" Richard turned on his stubby legs and padded inside, still puffing on his cigar.

Could he know something about Antony's murder? What Richard Lord knew was always a mystery to me. The thought of spending more than two minutes with him was about as appealing as a root canal. Whatever Richard wanted could wait. I repositioned the cookie boxes and continued on to the OSF complex.

I was hedging my bets that Judy would be around for previews, and sure enough she was sitting at a table on the bricks handing out preview programs. I hurried to drop off the cookies at the box office and then returned as the bell dinged, signaling that the first preview was about to start.

Her hair was wrapped in a paisley scarf and her

forearms were covered in bangles. "Hey, Judy," I said, coming up to the table.

"Jules, are you here for previews?" She thrust a program at me. "You better hurry."

"Actually, I was hoping to talk with you for a minute."

"Yes, of course." She motioned to the empty folding chair next to her. "What do you need?"

"It's about Antony. Did you ever see him with a DVD?" I said, taking a seat.

A flicker of something—fear—crossed her face. Then she swept the programs into a stack. "A DVD? What kind of DVD?"

"I'm not sure."

She flipped through the glossy pages of one of the programs. "Oh, wait, I did see him with a DVD."

"You did?" I tried to temper my excitement.

"Come to think of it I saw him with a DVD a few times. Lance films each dress rehearsal. He gives the actors critiques. Notes on blocking, vocal quality, and diction. They take the DVDs home to review. It's like football coaches having their players watch film of other teams. Lance does that sometimes, too. He'll send an actor home with a performance tape from a past season to give them inspiration."

Could that be what was on the missing DVD? What would the killer want with a film of a dress rehearsal? Unless it didn't have anything to do with the dress rehearsal. Maybe something else—something offstage— had been captured on the DVD.

"Jules?" Judy patted my wrist.

"Sorry. I got lost in thought for a minute." I blinked

and shifted in my chair. "All of the actors get copies of dress rehearsal?"

Judy wrapped a rubber band around the stack of programs. "I think so." She placed the stack in a cardboard box. "I have to get inside. I'm supposed to help pass out cookies at intermission."

"I just delivered the cookies." I stood. "Thanks for your help."

She hoisted the box, making her dangling bracelets reverberate against each other. "Does this have to do with the investigation?"

"I'm not sure, but I think it might."

I walked down Pioneer Street, feeling one tiny step closer to learning why Antony had been killed. As I rounded the corner onto Main Street, past the Shakespeare Education Center where gorgeous, jeweled Tudor costumes were on display, I spotted Detective Kerry. She had one foot propped up against the door to the Education Center. She had a jelly-filled doughnut in one hand and was deep in conversation with Thad, who stood on a step stool, wearing coveralls.

I thought about stopping but decided against it when I heard her sharp tone and barrage of questions. Did she think that Thad was the killer? I wasn't sure but I was happy to see that she was questioning other suspects. Now, if I could only find that missing DVD.

Chapter Twenty-one

The rest of the evening passed without incident. I filled Thomas in on what I had learned from Judy, called Sterling to see if he had had a chance to talk to Stephanie, and stopped by to check in with Lance. Unfortunately, the station was locked when I dropped by. Nightfall had left Ashland quiet and still. I considered returning to Torte for some late-night baking, but after the whirlwind of emotions I had experienced the past few days I decided to turn in early.

I must have crashed because I awoke the next morning feeling refreshed, with a bright idea. Thomas had mentioned that Detective Kerry was a fan of jelly doughnuts and I had seen her munching on one while interrogating Thad. I also knew that Lance had a sweet spot for doughnuts. Perhaps I could sweeten the new detective up and get a chance to talk to my friend.

I dressed quickly in a pair of jeans and a long-sleeved V-neck shirt. I pulled my hair into a ponytail and moisturized my face. My skin appeared pale and splotchy. Lance's arrest had impacted me physically. In some ways that shouldn't have come as a surprise. He and I had grown closer the longer I had been in Ashland, yet it wasn't until now that I realized how much I relied on his friendship. I missed his playful banter and snarky comments and I felt responsible for proving his innocence. He was the first real friend that I had had in years. On the ship, I'd had plenty of acquaintances and crewmates whom I hung out with, but that lifestyle wasn't conducive to building long-term relationships. Friends came and went. Not so with Lance. Despite his teasing and tendency toward melodrama he'd been by my side and cheering me on with every endeavor. Why had it taken a tragedy to make me understand how much I had come to care about him?

The plaza was plunged into a peaceful slumber as I made my way to the bakeshop. No one would suspect that our tranquil village had recently experienced a gruesome murder.

Stop, Jules, I told myself as I unlocked Torte's front door and quickly locked it behind me. I wasn't taking any chances this morning.

The staff weren't due to arrive for almost forty-five minutes, so I used the silence to try and clear my head and think strategically through my current list of suspects. There's no meditation or escape better than baking and the smell of rising yeast.

We don't make doughnuts daily at Torte. There was a fabulous family-owned doughnut shop located near the Southern Oregon University campus. Most of the time we sent customers looking for a maple-bar or apple-fritter fix up to their shop, but every once in a while, we would make the time to produce a batch of the deep-fried doughy treats. I started by combining yeast, warm milk, and a touch of sugar. While the yeast began to ferment, I sifted cake flour into a large mixing bowl. Then I created a well in the center and added egg yolks, salt, butter, and more sugar. I worked it into a sticky dough and sprinkled flour onto the island. Once the yeast had doubled in size and began to foam I incorporated it into the mixture and plopped the ball on the counter.

My muscles flexed as I kneaded the springy dough. The physical exertion was a relief. Pounding the dough with my fists released some of the tension I had been holding in my body. I thought about everything that Lance had done for me as I stretched and massaged the dough. Not only had he saved me from a crazed killer, but he had ensured that Mom and I got approved for the basement property and even helped secure a grant. He had listened knowingly to my struggles with Carlos and had been the one who first pointed out that Thomas still had feelings for me. He had hired Torte for every party and event that OSF had hosted, and made sure to purchase weekly boxes of pastries and cakes for his staff.

I owed him a favor or two. The dough became pliable in my hands. I returned it to the bowl and covered it with a towel. It would need to rise and double in size. In the meantime, I filled a pastry bag with our homemade raspberry jelly and placed vegetable oil in a fryer to get it warming on the stove. Doughnuts can be tricky. The type of oil used to fry them and the heat can be the difference between a light and fluffy doughnut and one that is dense and greasy. By the time the dough had doubled my oil was bubbling at 370 degrees. I rolled out the dough on the island and used a two-inch circular doughnut cutter to create perfect circles.

Using a slotted spoon, I cautiously submerged the round circles into the hot oil. It only took about thirty seconds on each side for the doughnuts to puff up and turn golden brown. I scooped them out with the slotted spoon and placed them on cooling racks lined with paper towels. After they cooled I used a wooden skewer to make a tiny hole in the side of the doughnuts and then piped them with the raspberry jam. For the final touch, I dusted them with powdered sugar and placed a half-dozen of them into a box for Detective Kerry and two in a paper bag for Lance. The remaining doughnuts would go in the pastry case. I had a feeling we would sell out of them before the morning rush hit.

I knew Lance was probably desperate for good coffee so I brewed a pot of French press. The strong scent of coffee and the yeasty doughnuts permeated the bakeshop along with the loaves of bread that I had baking. I whipped up a batch of our standard cookie dough and muffin mix and placed them in the walk-in, so we'd have a head start on the morning prep. I left Andy and Bethany a note, in case they showed up before I got back, and poured a cup of the French press into a paper mug.

The police station's charm was undeniable with its navy blue awnings and arched windows trimmed in matching blue. It was more adorable than intimidating with its window boxes and welcoming benches. Short of steering panhandlers out of the plaza and dealing with the occasional shoplifter the police station rarely saw much action. I wondered how Detective Kerry was adjusting.

I knocked on the door, carefully balancing the doughnuts and coffee.

Detective Kerry opened the door with a suspicious frown. "Oh, it's you."

"Morning," I said, offering her the box.

She scowled. "What's in here?" She wore another trim skirt and a tailored black blouse. Her features were angular and striking. If she ever smiled she would be quite beautiful.

"Jelly doughnuts." I lifted the lid of the box to show her the neat row of droolworthy sweets. "Can I come in?" I held the box out for her.

She took it and moved to the side to allow me entry. "They told me things were different in Ashland, but doughnut deliveries weren't on the list."

I almost thought she was making a joke. "It's one of the perks of being across the street from a bakeshop. I wasn't sure if you were a coffee drinker. I brought a cup of French press for Lance, but we have an open-door policy at Torte. Stop by anytime for coffee or a pastry."

Her narrow face softened. "Thanks."

"How's the investigation coming?" I asked.

"I can't discuss an ongoing investigation." Her sharp jawline tightened.

"Can I have a minute with Lance?" I held up the coffee and bag of doughnuts.

"It's going to take a while to get used to this place," she mumbled, but headed for the back. When we reached the office, she stopped. "I'm going to need to see what's in the bag."

"This?" I offered her the paper bag. "Doughnuts."

She examined the bag with a frown, and then unlocked the door. "Okay, ten minutes."

The room was humid and stagnant. Lance was curled up on the cot under a thin blanket. "Juliet." He sighed and tossed off the blanket.

"I brought you a pick-me-up." I held up the doughnuts and coffee.

He managed a weak smile. "You are too kind."

Detective Kerry shut the door and locked me in with him. "Ten minutes."

I walked over to place the doughnuts and coffee on a small side table near the cot. "How are you doing?"

Lance rubbed his temples and reached for the coffee. He took a long whiff. "Oh, dear Lord, you are a savior. You wouldn't believe the sludge she tried to give me earlier." He crossed his legs and patted the empty spot on the end of the cot. "Sit. Sit."

"Do you want a doughnut? I made your favorite— jelly filled."

Lance shook his head. "Thank you, darling, but no. Coffee is all I need for the moment."

I sat on the edge of the cot. "How are you doing?"

"How do I look?"

"You look fine," I lied. He had changed out of his sweatpants into a pair of jeans and fleece OSF jacket. At least the outfit wasn't three sizes too big, but I noticed that his face was drawn and his nails had been gnawed in jagged edges.

"Please, Juliet. You are the worst liar. I'm a disaster. Don't try to make me feel better. Join me in my pity." He clutched the coffee as if it was a lifeline. "Do tell. What's the news? I've been stuck in this cell without even so much as a newspaper."

"This isn't exactly a cell," I pointed out.

Lance scoffed. "Am I locked in a room in the police station?"

"Yes, but—"

He cut me off. "Juliet, I'm nothing more than a common prisoner at the moment. What have you learned and what are we going to do to get me out of here?"

I felt bad for him. Lance was used to being lavished with praise and surrounded by art and beautiful things. I told him about my list of suspects and explained that Mom and I were both sure of his innocence and that the Professor was working underground. "Richard Lord stopped me yesterday. He said that the three of us need to talk. Do you have any idea what that's about? Could he know something about Antony?"

Lance waved me off. "No, no. Richard can wait. He's nothing. What else have you learned?"

None of my information fazed Lance. He sipped the coffee and nodded. "Lance, can you think of anything else from that night that might be important? Anything you saw? Anything?"

He tapped the top of the plastic lid. "Nothing. I've had nothing but time to think in here. I've replayed the ghastly scene again and again and there's nothing. The only thing that I've come up with is the DVD. Why was there an empty case next to Antony's body? It can't be a coincidence, can it?"

"No, it can't. I talked to Judy Faulkner and she said she thought it might be from one of the dress rehearsals." I paused for a moment. "What if something else was caught on film? Maybe a fight?"

"It's possible." He drummed his wrecked nails on his chin.

I went on to explain everything that I had learned from my conversation with Vera. Lance perked up when I mentioned Tracy's pregnancy.

"Wait, what? My leading lady is knocked up?" Lance sipped the coffee and stared off at the white wall with the bulletin board.

"According to Vera, yes."

"She would know. Costume designers know everyone's secrets, darling."

"That's what she told me. Do you think it could be Antony's? Maybe they had a lover's spat? Maybe he refused to acknowledge that the baby was his?"

Lance set the coffee cup on the side table. "No. No, no, no. There's no chance that the baby is Antony's."

"How can you be so sure?"

"Those two hated each other. They couldn't stand to be in the same room together."

"Really? But they seemed so chummy when I saw them at the party."

Lance rolled his eyes. "Acting, darling. Acting." His jaw softened and he reached for a doughnut. "This is news. Well done, my fair Juliet."

"But what does it mean? Tracy's pregnant. She and Antony didn't get along, but why would she kill him? Maybe Antony threatened to reveal her secret?" I offered.

Lance bit into the doughnut. Red jam spilled onto his chin, making him look like an evil villain. He wiped it away with one hand and smiled. "Or perhaps Tracy's paramour killed to keep their love child secret."

"Huh?"

"Darling, this doughnut is to die for." Lance licked the jelly from his hand. His demeanor had shifted. "Do scurry up to the theater. You have some more sleuthing to do. I think we have our first real lead."

"I'm not following you."

He tapped his chin with his free hand. "Chin up, darling. Costume designers might get the good gossip, but I assure you as artistic director I'm privy to everyone's secrets, including Tracy's."

Now he was enjoying the moment. He was intentionally stringing me along.

A knock sounded on the door. "Time's up," Kerry said in a harsh tone.

I heard her turning the key. "Lance, what do you know? You have to tell me. She's going to kick me out."

Lance swallowed a bite of doughnut. "Go have a little chat with Thad. Let's just say that I've caught him and Tracy with their lips locked in some unusual places."

"Really?"

He shot me a wink. "Really, darling."

Kerry thrust open the door and tapped her wrist. "Time's up."

"I was just leaving," I said, standing up. "Take care of yourself, Lance. Mom and everyone at Torte will be happy to hear that you're in good spirits."

"I am now." He waved his fingers. "Ta-ta!"

Kerry scowled. "Let's go."

"Oh, Jules," Lance called after me as Kerry escorted me out of the room. "I'd spend some time in the props department if I were you."

I was going to respond, but Kerry pointed to the front.

What did Lance know about the props department? I wasn't sure, but I would keep my promise and find out later. For the moment, I was relieved to see a little glimmer of my old friend. I took that as a promising sign along with the news that Tracy and Thad were having an affair. I couldn't imagine her dragging Antony's body to the duck pond, but Thad had the strength, and if he had killed to protect his pregnant girlfriend then that changed everything.

Chapter Twenty-two

I returned to Torte with new resolve. We had to be getting closer to figuring out who had killed Antony and I was sure that Lance would be exonerated soon. Sure enough, the entire team—even Stephanie—was fast at work in the humming kitchen. I paused to take in the mingling scents of coffee, doughnuts, and baking bread. Food is a sensory experience. The texture of a chewy crust, the taste of a zesty lemon scone, the scent of hot rolls straight from the oven, and the smell of brewing arabica beans. Mom and I often joked that we should find a way to pipe the bakery scents onto the plaza. We would probably double our customer base instantaneously.

"Morning," I called to the crew.

Andy steamed foamy milk behind the espresso machine. "Hey, boss. You need a morning fix?"

I smiled. "I'm fine for the moment, thanks."

He shrugged. "Okay, but if you change your mind you better let me know soon because the smell of fried doughnuts is thick in here and I think we're going to run out of coffee the minute we open the doors."

I stopped in front of the pastry case and breathed in the scent again. "It's true. Deep-frying sends little droplets of oil into the air. We're going to smell like a doughnut shop all day."

"You know what pairs well with doughnuts?" Andy shifted the stainless-steel pitcher of milk into his left hand and held up a shot of espresso with the other. "Coffee."

"Also true." I glanced at the pastry case, which held two trays of my raspberry-filled doughnuts on the top shelf.

"You know what I need to create next?" Andy said almost to himself. "A doughnut latte. I wonder how I can make that without it being too sweet?"

I continued past the espresso bar and turned toward the kitchen. "That sounds like the perfect challenge for you."

Andy poured the shot into a ceramic mug and swirled hot milk over the top. "I'm on it. Don't you worry."

Bethany and Steph were huddled around the island with an assortment of plates, platters, and cake stands along with stacks of rainbow-colored macarons. I didn't want to get my hopes up, but Stephanie's hair was pulled into two tight braids and the bags under her eyes looked lighter.

"Hey, Jules," Bethany said, looking up from the display she was working on. "We're trying to figure out how to get the best shot. We want to hashtag this #TasteTheRainbow, but we can't decide if we should line them in a row on a plate or stack them on a cake stand. What do you think?"

I picked up a pink macaron and examined it. They

had followed my instructions to the letter. The round airy cookies were symmetrical and crispy. I bit into it and was immediately transported to a summer strawberry patch. The macaron was chewy and the texture smooth. The strawberry cream filling was light, silky, and tasted like the strawberries had been picked fresh this morning. The ratio of cookie to filling was just right. If you spread the filling on too thin you miss the balance of the creamy center and crunchy cookie, but no one wants a blob of filling that oozes out the sides, either.

"These are amazing," I said as I finished off the sandwich cookie. "The strawberry cream is some of the best I've ever had."

Bethany's face swelled with pride.

"How are you feeling?" I asked Stephanie quietly.

"Better. The earplugs helped." She didn't meet my eyes.

"What did the health center say?" I licked strawberry cream from my finger.

She shrugged. "Nothing. Said I have sleep exhaustion. Gave me a couple sleeping pills."

"Did you take one?"

"Yeah, but the doctor said that sleep loss is cumulative. She said it's going to take a few days to feel normal." Her hand shook as she spread a layer of peanut butter between two grape macarons.

"Take it easy. Let me know if you want a break or need to leave early, okay?"

She nodded. I changed the subject. "What other flavors did you bake?"

"Blackberry, banana, key lime, orange, cherry, peanut butter and jelly, and Fruity Pebbles." Bethany pointed to each colorful macaron, ending her tour of the rainbow cookies with one that looked like a sprinkle-covered Easter egg.

Stephanie tucked her violet braids behind her ears and held the entire stack in one hand. Her black nails served as end caps for the festive cookies. "Can you get a shot like this with depth effect? Focus on the macarons and have the kitchen fuzzy in the background?"

Bethany grabbed her phone. "Yes! That's it." She snapped a few pictures, stopping to have Stephanie reposition the stack and move her hand to the left and right. When they finished Bethany quickly tweaked the photos with editing tools built into her phone and showed us the results. The photo looked like a professional shot and showcased the macarons and Torte's cheery kitchen.

"Should we go with this?" Bethany scrolled through each picture and landed on the last one.

"I love it," I said. It was true. I was beyond impressed with the initiative the two of them had taken and their creativity.

Stephanie went back and forth between the photos. "I think I like the first one the best. See how the stove almost has a halo effect?"

Bethany leaned over and studied the photo with Steph. "You're right. Let's do this one. Is it too cheesy to use the hashtag #TasteTheRainbow?"

I shrugged. "I'm leaving that to you two. You are the social media experts."

Sterling, who had been gathering soup ingredients in the walk-in, came into the kitchen with a basket full of fresh veggies.

"Is #TasteTheRainbow super cheesy?" Bethany asked him.

"What?" He looked at Stephanie. They shared a stolen glance.

"For our macarons, is it stupid?"

Sterling placed the basket on the edge of island and helped himself to one of the Fruity Pebbles cookies. "No, it's funny."

Bethany smiled and started typing at a lightning pace with her thumbs. "Awesome. I'm posting this right now. Anyone who uses the hashtag in the next hour gets a free Fruity Pebbles, cool?"

"Cool," Sterling agreed. I caught him nodding at Steph. They were both alternative and, one might even say, cooler than Bethany, which made me all the more appreciative that they embraced Bethany's enthusiasm. It proved that appearances can be deceiving. When I'd first met Steph, I had wrongfully assumed that her goth style and reserved attitude meant that she thought she was superior. The same was true for my first impression of Sterling. His skater look and pensive stare had made me consider him a suspect for a murder that took place in the bakeshop. Little did I know at the time that nothing could be further from the truth. Sterling was one of the kindest and most self-aware men that I had ever met. He had become like a younger brother to me, and Stephanie like a younger, albeit much edgier, sister.

I was more like Bethany. I had always admired classmates who were free spirits and able to express themselves artistically, but it wasn't until I went to culinary school that I really found my place and calling—in the kitchen.

Steph stocked the pastry case while Bethany boxed up the rainbow macarons.

"You want me to get a soup on?" Sterling asked.

"That would be great." I noticed that he already had the recipe I had left on the counter. I joined him at the stove and dropped my voice. Sterling had become a confidant and I appreciated his perspective. He'd only been in Ashland for the past year, which gave him different insight than the rest of the team. "I talked to Lance," I said, pouring olive oil into the stockpot.

"What did he say?" Sterling reviewed the recipe.

"He wants me to talk to Thad."

"Really?" He tapped the index card with the recipe written in Mom's beautiful cursive on the counter.

"Yeah, but he was very Lance-like about it." I opened a nearby cupboard and retrieved a big mixing bowl. "Want me to peel the onions for you?"

Sterling placed the recipe in a holder next to the stove. "You bet. So, how was he?"

"To be honest, I was worried when I saw him. He was not his usual self. He even turned down my jelly doughnuts at first."

"Oh, that's bad." Sterling ran cold water in the sink. "One day he polished off three of those in about ten minutes."

I told him about what I had learned last night and my conversation with Lance while he scrubbed veggies and I peeled onions. "What do you think?" I asked, tossing the last of the peel into our compost bin. "If Thad killed Antony to keep Tracy's pregnancy secret that would give him a motive, and he has the physical strength to have dragged the body into the pond. He had the opportunity, too. As one of OSF's most senior set designers he would have access to every building in the complex. Maybe he hid somewhere and waited for Antony."

"But didn't you say that Lance found Antony's body at the bottom of the stairs?"

"Yes. The Elizabethan theater has two entrances. He could have camped out and waited until Antony passed by and then followed him down the stairs with the dagger."

"That sounds like something out of a Shakespeare play." Sterling gave the veggies a final rinse and placed them on a cutting board.

"True. Lance hinted that he'd spotted Tracy and Thad making out in the theater before. What if Antony caught them?" I paused as a thought formed in my mind. "Maybe that's what is on the DVD. What if they were making out on the side stage when dress rehearsal was being filmed?"

Sterling pushed up the sleeves of his charcoal hoodie. "Antony realized it when he watched the footage." He lined up a row of carrots and began to chop them. "Maybe Thad was trying to get the DVD back from Antony when he killed him."

"Right. So that means he's probably in possession of the DVD. Lance said something about the props department. We got cut off, but do you think he could know about the DVD? Maybe Thad hid it somewhere among the props."

I watched as Sterling cut the carrots lengthwise and then in half. His knife skills had dramatically improved, thanks in part to Carlos. Carlos had showed him how to protect his thumb while holding the knife and educated him on how every knife had its own purpose and should be used accordingly.

"Could be. Why would Tracy's pregnancy be such a huge secret, though?" Sterling asked, sliding the chopped carrots into the soup pan on the stove. "It's hardly like this is the 1950s or something. It's Ashland, and as long as they were both consenting adults why would it matter?"

"Good question. I thought about that, too. Lance would never fire her. I guess she would potentially lose her lead once she starts to show. But Vera and the costume department would be able to find a way to adjust her costume at least for a while."

Sterling stirred the carrots in the olive oil and then began to quarter the onions I had peeled. "Would a pregnancy make her contract vulnerable?"

"I don't know. I'd have to ask Lance." For this soup, we would rough-chop the veggies and let them simmer for twenty minutes to marry the flavors. "I must be missing something. What other motives could there be for killing Antony?"

"Lance's motive is pretty clear." Sterling tossed the quartered onions into the pot.

"Exactly, but he's the one suspect who can't have done it."

Sterling brushed a strand of jet-black hair from his eye. "Probably, but you can't rule him out just because he's your friend."

"You sound like Thomas."

"Geez, Jules, are you trying to kill me? Don't say that." He winked.

"Sorry, but you're right. I know there's an outside possibility that Lance could have snapped. I'm choosing to believe him, though. What about Vera?"

"The costume designer?"

I handed Sterling a bunch of celery. "Yeah. She had the opportunity. She was the last person to see him alive. Judy admitted that she was basically blackmailing him. I haven't figured out who John Duncan is, and what motive Brock could have had." I sighed. "There are just so many options to consider."

"Whoa, slow down." Sterling motioned for a time-out. "You're really wrapped up in this one."

"I know. I guess it's never been this personal before."

"Sure. I get that, but you're not going to help Lance by running around in circles. How much sleep have *you* had?"

"Not a lot," I admitted.

"Maybe you should take a break this morning. I know you have a lot on your plate with the renovations and your mom's wedding."

"Those are good stresses."

Sterling set the knife on the cutting board and placed his hand on my wrist. His voice was thick with emotion. "You don't have to try to hold it all together for me. I know about loss, too. Remember?"

"What do you mean?" I bit the inside of my cheek.

The tenderness in his tone struck a nerve. "Your mom. The wedding. I know that you're happy for her, but it has to be a little bittersweet, right?"

Tears welled. I fought them back. Sterling gripped me tighter. "It's cool. It's normal, and I think she feels it, too.

Your dad was her first and longest love. That doesn't go away."

Salty tears pooled in my eyes. Until this very moment, I had never considered that I was anything but happy for Mom. Then I thought about how many memories of my dad had been surfacing lately. I hadn't made the connection to the wedding. I thought it was because of the expansion and the fact that I had finally made a decision to stay in Ashland for good. Sterling's words hit me.

I wiped a tear from beneath my eye. "Is it that obvious?"

He gave my arm a final squeeze and shook his head. "Only to me. Remember, I've been where you are. The thought of my dad remarrying sent me into a really dark place."

"Right." I saw the pain in his clenched jaw and rigid posture.

"Except she turned out to be a raging nightmare who was only out for his money." He laughed, but it wasn't a happy laugh. "You don't have to worry about that with the Professor. He adores your mom. She's going to be in good hands, you're not going to lose her, and you are going to be fine. It might be kind of tender for a while. It's weird how it sneaks up on you, grief. I think it's because the people who leave us leave pieces of themselves behind." He ran his hand along the hummingbird tattoo on his forearm, a dedication to his mom.

"Seriously, how did you get this wise, and how did I get so lucky to have you stumble into the bakeshop?"

"Maybe your dad and my mom recognized that we're

kindred spirits and needed to meet. Don't underestimate the power of divine intervention."

I leaned on his shoulder and gave him a side hug. "Thanks, Sterling. I needed to hear that." His words had had a calming effect on me. Was that part of the reason I'd been so consumed by the investigation into Antony's death? Had I been worried at some level that I was losing Mom to the Professor? She had been gone more often and I hadn't realized that I missed her.

"That's what I'm here for. Well, that and soup." He picked up the knife and returned to chopping.

"I'm going to take you up on your offer and take a break. I don't think I can sleep but I'll take a quick walk through Lithia Park and clear my head."

"Take your time," Sterling said.

I left with a small smile. Once I stepped outside I power walked to Lithia Park, found a secluded bench, and let the tears spill.

Chapter Twenty-three

The revelation that Mom's wedding had triggered memories and a longing for my dad was strangely comforting. When he died, the grief felt unsurmountable, like it would be with me forever. Now it felt like an old friend. In a way, missing him made me feel closer to him than I had in years. The crisp morning air, scent of blossoming lilacs, and the sound of chirping birds flitting between the deciduous trees enveloped me as I sobbed on the bench. Lithia Park had been a touchpoint and one of my favorite escapes after my dad died. It felt familiar to let go of my other worries and sink into sadness. I lost my sense of time as tears flowed and I opened myself up to memories of my dad twirling me in the grassy area nearby. I could almost feel his firm grip on my wrists and the feeling of freedom as we spun in a circle faster and faster until my feet hit the air. We were a happy and carefree threesome, Dad, Mom, and me. They invited me into their love, encouraging me to ask questions and pursue my passions. I'm sure they must have had stresses with starting a bakeshop and raising a young daughter, but they never let it show. Torte and my child-hood were idyllic and filled with affection and plenty of comforting treats.

In the first few years without him the bakeshop felt empty, but not anymore. Mom had kneaded, rolled, pressed, and baked her way through loss. She had created a space of comfort and warmth and now it was my turn to carry on our family legacy.

I exhaled and brushed away tears. Thank goodness for friends like Sterling. His insight had given me a fresh perspective that I didn't even know I needed. Releasing the sadness I had been holding deep in my heart made me feel lighter. I stood, craned my neck, and drank in the gently bowing branches of the redwoods above me. These trees had stood, rooted into the ground, for decades. I was ready to do the same.

The plaza was showing the first signs of life as I walked by the Green Goblin, one of the businesses on our morning bread delivery route. The owner of the magic shop swept the sidewalk and gave me a hearty wave. "Morning! It's going to be a magical day!"

I waved in return and continued. Hopefully, it would be a magical day and hopefully some of the magic would wear off on Lance. I wondered if the Professor had received the forensics report and whether Lance had been released yet. The minute I looked down the street I knew that the team had already opened for the day because a line, six people deep, had formed in front of Torte. Time to get moving, Jules. I picked up my pace and scooted past the small crowd waiting at the front door.

"Doughnuts do it every time, boss," Andy said with

a nod to the pastry case where Sterling was packaging up boxes of the raspberry-filled delights.

"Can you blame them?" Doughnuts were one of my weaknesses. Maybe it was because they weren't in our daily rotation of pastries. For the moment, I had to get downstairs. Andy handed me a coffee. "Here you go, boss. You look like you could use a latte."

"You are a mind reader, thanks." I grabbed the drink. "Be back in a few." As I turned the corner toward the basement steps I bumped into Richard Lord.

"Well, well, if it isn't Ashland's pastry queen," he sneered. As usual he was dressed in golf attire. I wasn't sure if he ever spent any time on the links or just liked the look. Today's outfit included pink and green plaid shorts, shockingly white golf shoes, a pale pink Polo shirt, and a matching cap.

"Morning, Richard." Richard wasn't usually an early riser. He liked to make an appearance on the porch of the Merry Windsor later in the day when there was the best chance of being seen by the most people.

"It is a good morning, isn't it?" He glanced at me and then whipped his head in the direction of police head-quarters. "Did you speak with Lance?"

What did he know? Did this have anything to do with why Lance had been hanging around in Medford? I clutched my coffee. Richard had a way of getting under my skin just by being him.

"Where are you off to this early?" Richard stared at me with his beady eyes.

"It's none of your business, but I happen to have a meeting." Richard tried to make everything and every-one in Ashland his business.

"A meeting with who? Your friend Lance? Because I hear that he's . . . hmmm . . . how shall I put it? Unavailable."

"I have no idea what you're talking about, Richard."

"Oh, but I think you do, Juliet Capshaw. I think you do." He tipped his cap.

I sighed. "I need to get downstairs."

"Downstairs?" His lips turned into a thin hard line. "You're not still really thinking of going forward with your silly expansion project, are you? Take my advice, it's a terrible business decision."

"Right. And I'm sure if Mom and I canceled our contract you wouldn't take on such a terrible investment, either?"

He tossed his head to one side and let out a half snort. "Ha. As I've told your dear mother a thousand times, you should leave the business decisions up to those of us who actually know business."

I wanted to punch him. The man was vile and such a chauvinistic pig.

"Thanks for the advice," I said through my clenched teeth.

"Let me offer you another nugget of wisdom, Juliet Montague Capshaw. I know about your plans and I'm not having some flaky pastry chef try to outdo me. You're in over your head. Managing one tiny coffee shop has obviously taken its toll." He paused and ran his grubby eyes over me from head to toe. "Get out now while you still can. You can't handle three businesses, and let me tell you, I won't stand for it and neither will Ashland."

He brushed past me, intentionally bumping my shoulder and nearly knocking me off balance. The man was an oaf. I knew he was trying to rattle me. Unfortunately, it worked. Richard had tapped into my fears. What if I was taking on too much? What if I was in over my head? And what did he mean by three businesses?

Chapter Twenty-four

"Juliet, is everything okay?" Mom asked when I huffed down the stairs.

"I'm fine. I just bumped into Richard Lord." I shuddered.

"That would explain it." She squeezed my hand. "Do you need a minute or are you ready to look at the flooring?"

"Richard Lord is not going to stop me from enjoying this process. I'm good. Let's go." I returned the squeeze and dropped her hand.

Robert updated us on progress. I couldn't believe the difference with the walls torn out. The basement property had been brought down to the studs. The space appeared huge and to the delight of both of us things were progressing even quicker than planned. The redesigned walls would be framed in and Sheetrocked in the next few days. Once the walls were complete the electrical and plumbing work would start. If things continued at this pace we would easily meet our July deadline.

"I can't believe how much they've already completed," Mom said as we returned up the stairs. "I've heard so many horror stories from other business owners about contractors dragging their feet and it taking weeks and months longer than anticipated."

"Me, too," I agreed.

She grinned. "We must have good construction karma."

When we reached the top of the stairs we stopped on the corner to debrief for a moment. "Have you heard anything about Lance this morning?" I asked, glancing across the street to the police headquarters. There wasn't any sign of press gathered outside.

"No. Doug is in Medford again this morning."

"When I bumped into Richard he hinted that he knew something. Do you think he could?"

"Really?" Mom frowned. "I don't think so, but Doug has been incredibly tight-lipped."

"It's Richard. He probably bulldozed his way in there and demanded answers." I paused. "By the way, have you met Detective Kerry yet?"

Mom shook her head. "No, I'm still waiting to meet her. Although I have the sense that Doug thinks she's doing a good job. Maybe his retirement plans will get bumped up sooner than we expected."

"You haven't talked about it?" This news surprised me.

"Oh, no. You know that Doug has been talking about retiring for quite some time now. It's been an ongoing discussion for us. I think he wants to take his time to find the right person to replace him. It's one of the reasons he's been back and forth between here and Medford lately. I have the sense that this is the first test."

"What about Thomas?"

Mom nodded. "Thomas will certainly be considered.

Doug has been grooming him for the role, but he's not sure that Thomas wants or is ready for the next level of responsibility."

I believed that. Thomas relied on the Professor's wisdom and expertise. That didn't mean that he wasn't an intelligent and instinctive cop, but I could imagine that Thomas wouldn't be thrilled to hear that the Professor was considering retirement.

"Doug is committed to finding the right fit for Ashland. It's not exactly a cookie cutter assignment. He said he might need to get creative. Maybe he'll pair Thomas with someone new and they can team up."

"That makes sense." I thought about the Professor's gentle yet firm approach to investigations. When he finally retired, his presence would be sorely missed.

"It's nothing to worry about yet, dear." Mom patted my hand. "Doug is a planner so he's thinking ahead."

"What about wedding plans? Any new insights after our discussion last night?"

She shook her head. "I wish. There has to be a space big enough to accommodate our guest list out there somewhere, but I have yet to find it. At the moment, I'm leaning toward hopping on a plane and eloping to Vegas."

"Mom, you can't be serious!" That was a one-hundred-eighty-degree shift from inviting the entire town to a potluck in the park.

"Can you imagine Doug and me in Vegas?" She laughed. "But there is something compelling about the idea."

"Can I help?" I felt bad that I hadn't been more involved.

"No, no. It'll be fine. I'm sure we'll figure something

out. I'm having a brief moment of panic, which I'm sure is part of the process." She attempted a smile.

"Mom, is there anything else?" I thought about my conversation with Sterling

She stared wistfully at the cheery front window display and then down at the basement steps. "Your father would have loved this, you know. He would be so proud of the chef and woman you've become." Her voice caught.

I reached for her. "I've been thinking about him a lot lately, too."

"It's funny, isn't it? How something so wonderful can stir up the sadness." Her eyes were moist. "Doug has been wonderful. He has assured me that it's normal to miss your father right now, but I didn't expect to be so . . ." She trailed off.

"Torn?" I offered.

"That's a good word. I'm blissfully happy. Doug is a wonderful man, and I can't wait to embark on new adventures with him, and yet every night when my head hits the pillow I can sense your dad, standing over me."

"He's sending you his blessing."

She smiled and twisted her wedding ring on the chain around her neck. "I don't doubt that. He would certainly approve of Doug. In fact, sometimes I wonder if he brought us together. I've been lonely without him. I'm not lonely with Doug, but I suppose that I thought that missing your father would fade with the loneliness. It's the opposite. I almost miss him more."

"Me, too." I leaned into her. We held each other.

"How do we always end up like this?" Mom said after a minute. "Are we hopeless romantics or emotional messes?"

"I think we're women," I kidded and tried to wink. Instead I felt my top lip contort into what must have been a goofy grin.

"Poor Doug, he has no idea what he's getting into. Yesterday, I teared up watching a Hallmark commercial."

"Well, that's totally understandable. Those commercials are designed to trigger the waterworks."

Mom laughed and tucked her hair behind her ears. She glanced at Torte's steamy front windows. "Now that we've had our cry for the day should we get back to it?"

"You bet." I let her go first.

"Jules! Jules!" someone called after me.

I turned to see Thomas sprinting across the plaza from the police station. "You go ahead," I said to Mom. "I'll catch up."

She nodded and disappeared into the bakeshop.

"Hey, you're just the person I was hoping to see," Thomas said, slightly winded. His iPad was tucked under one arm and he held a sealed envelope in his hand.

"Me, too."

Thomas's boyish face lit up at my comment. I didn't have the heart to tell him that I meant because I wanted to talk to him about the investigation.

"Want to sit?" He nodded at an empty bistro table.

"Sure." I brushed pollen from the wrought-iron table. "Have you learned anything new? Is Lance still in custody?"

Thomas sat and rested his iPad on the table. "Geez, Jules, give me a minute to breathe." He grinned. "Lance is still over there, but I have to find Detective Kerry and give her this." He patted the sealed envelope.

"What is it?" My eyes went to the envelope Thomas clutched in his right hand.

"Not sure. Either lab results from the crime scene or a report on names that we've run through the system." He stared at the envelope for a second and then tucked it into his back pocket.

I blew pollen dust from my hands. The tree above us was heavy with the sticky yellow powder. Soon it would transform into glowing pink blooms. "How are you and Detective Kerry working together by now?"

Thomas leaned his elbows on the table. "I don't know. I really hope that the Professor isn't thinking of giving her a permanent position, because I can totally see her changing everything. She is crazy serious."

"Yeah, I got that impression." I filled him in on my conversation with Lance, making sure to explain Lance's suspicion that Thad and Tracy had been having an affair.

"The balding set guy?" Thomas asked. He removed his elbows from the table. They were covered in pollen.

I brushed it off for him.

"Thanks." He smiled. "I wouldn't have pictured a gorgeous actress going for someone like him. Antony, I would get. It makes sense. You hear about movie stars falling for each other all the time."

"Agreed." I nodded. "Maybe it's the fact that Thad is older?"

A brief look of envy crossed Thomas's face. "Why is it that women always go for older men?"

I knew that he was referring to Carlos, but I ignored the comment. "Have you guys found out anything more about John Duncan?"

Thomas shook his head, but I saw his hand instinctively touch his back pocket where he had stored the envelope. "Nope." He picked up his iPad. "But on that note, I should get going. I don't want to be late to meet the Kerry. Thanks for intel, Jules."

"Anytime." I waved and watched him leave. He obviously knew much more than he was telling me. I couldn't blame him. I wasn't part of law enforcement and I knew that he was being extra careful given the circumstances of this investigation and Detective Kerry's watchful eye. Something was in that envelope. Was it evidence clearing Lance, or was it information about the mysterious John Duncan?

Chapter Twenty-five

I couldn't stop thinking about John Duncan. When I returned to the kitchen and tried to distract myself with baking, even pastry couldn't keep my thoughts from returning to the mystery. When I told the Professor about Judy overhearing the fight between Antony and Brock, he had said that the name John Duncan was common, but if anything came up in their database they would know. Could that be what was in the envelope?

I had been worried about Stephanie's ability to work under the influence of sleep deprivation, but if I was being honest with myself my heart wasn't in the kitchen. After an hour of going through the motions I decided to keep my promise to Lance and go talk to Thad.

For cover, I boxed up an assortment of pastries. If I happened to bump into Detective Kerry I would simply tell her I was delivering an order. She couldn't argue with that. I took the long route around the far side of the plaza to avoid another potential Richard Lord sighting. One Richard interaction was plenty for the day— for the week, for the month, for the year. Forever.

I stopped to admire some of Vera's costumes on

display in the front windows of the Education Center at the base of the hill that led up to the theaters. The amount of work and detail that went into each costume was mind-blowing. One of the ball gowns from *Cinderella* must have had a million tiny beads.

And I thought my hands got tired working bread dough, I thought, as I headed up the hill. I had no idea where I might find Thad and what I was supposed to ask him, other than confronting him about his relationship with Tracy. I wished I had had more time with Lance. He had been cryptic and I hoped he wasn't sending me on a wild-goose chase.

When I arrived at the theater I asked a stagehand if he had seen Thad. He pointed me to the props department. I hurried downstairs before I ran into anyone else. It was amazing what kind of doors a pastry box could open. No one ever declined a box of baked goods. Particularly starving artists.

Thad was kneeling in front of a Grecian column when I stepped into the workroom. Tools lay all around him as he twisted a screwdriver into its base.

"Hi, sorry to bother you," I said, holding out the pastry box as an offering. "I thought you might want a pastry. I brought a bunch for the entire crew."

He finished tightening the screw, stuffed the screwdriver in his tool belt, and stood up. His expression was leery. "You brought everyone pastries?"

"I know that things are stressful around here and thought everyone might want a pick-me-up."

"A pastry pick-me-up?" His lip curled. "What?"

Maybe I had been wrong about a pastry delivery box being a perfect disguise. Thad folded his arms and stared at me with disbelief. I decided to try another tactic. There were a few people working on various props throughout the room, so I lowered my voice. "Actually, I'm here for Lance. He asked me to talk to you about Tracy."

Thad's eyes darted around the room. "Not here." Without another word, he stalked out of the room. I took that as a sign I should follow and ran after him. He trudged down the corridor underneath the theater without turning around. Finally, he came to a door with his name on a gold placard, threw it open, and waited for me to catch up.

His office was nothing like Lance's. For starters, it was half the size, and cluttered with tools, broken parts, and set models that reminded me of my childhood dollhouse. He didn't bother to clear a space for me to sit. Instead, he slammed the door behind us and leaned on it. Was he blocking me from leaving? Should I be worried? Maybe I should have thought this through a bit more.

"What did Lance say?" Thad asked, fiddling with a roll of duct tape on his tool belt.

I wasn't sure where to start.

Thad stared at me. "Well?"

Thad's eyes burned into me. Maybe I should leave it to Detective Kerry. I wavered for a moment. Finally, I said, "I know that Tracy's pregnant."

His hand clamped the tape. "So."

"Lance seems to think that you're the father."

His shoulders sank. "We were so careful." He wasn't exactly talking to me. He stared at a sketch of Cinderella's castle on the far wall.

"Is it true?"

He sighed and moved away from the door. For a minute, I thought he was going to tell me to get out, but instead he walked over to his desk and sat on the edge. He motioned for me to have a seat in his chair. I did and set the pastry box on the desk. "I can't believe Lance knows. Who else knows?"

"I don't think anyone."

"That's good." He grabbed a pencil from his tool belt and stabbed it in his palm.

"I'm probably being naïve, but I don't understand what the big deal is. I mean, of course a pregnancy is a big deal, but why does it matter if anyone knows?"

Thad rubbed his balding head. "We were discreet," he repeated, not answering my question.

"Right. I'm sure you were."

He removed a miniature flashlight from his tool belt and stood. Then he began pacing in front of the desk, flipping the flashlight on and off. "What are we going to do? I need to find Tracy."

"I'd like to help," I offered. "I got the sense that Lance does, too. That's why he asked me to come talk to you." That wasn't entirely true. I was never one hundred percent certain of any of Lance's motives.

"This isn't great." Thad shined the flashlight on the wall.

"Is there something I can do?"

He cleared his throat and seemed to focus. "You're sure no one else knows? Just Lance?"

I paused. Should I tell him about Vera? As far as I knew Vera thought that Antony was the father, but she definitely knew that Tracy was pregnant. "Well, I think there might be another person who knows that Tracy's pregnant," I said. "I don't think they know who the father is, though."

"Vera?" Thad asked.

"How did you know?"

"Tracy was worried that Vera was going to figure it out. Her dresses have been getting tighter. She's had to have them let out. Damn. I thought we were going to get away with it a while longer."

My heart sank. Get away with what? With murder?

Thad looked at me. "No, whoa. Look, I'm talking about keeping her pregnancy a secret."

I exhaled. "Right, but why does it matter?"

"Tracy is starting her career. We're both really happy about the baby, but the timing isn't great. We had talked about trying during the off-season. Neither of us planned that it would happen like this."

Without thinking I said, "Wait, so it wasn't a mistake?" The minute the words left my mouth I wished I hadn't said them.

He looked injured. "What? The pregnancy? No. Tracy and I got married at Christmas. Like I said, we're both thrilled. It's just terrible timing with the show."

"You and Tracy are married?"

His face lit up when he talked about her.

"Why didn't you tell anyone?"

"She wanted to keep it on the down low. Actors get weird about that kind of thing. She thought it would be better to keep it quiet at this stage of her career. Having a leading lady who everyone can fall in love with can help land roles."

"Really?" I found that hard to believe. Lance wouldn't discriminate against anyone for any reason. If an actor was right for the role, I was sure that he would cast them.

"I told her she was overreacting. OSF isn't like that, but she'd had friends who had gotten leads snatched out from under them for stranger things. I'm sure you've heard about the casting couch?"

I nodded.

"Unfortunately, in some places there's rampant sexism still at play. That means actresses will go to great lengths to land a lead even if it means flirting—or more—with the powers that be."

That made sense, and yet nothing could be further from the truth about Lance and the way that he ran OSF.

"The same is true for her pregnancy," Thad continued. "Of course people are going to find out. *Antony and Cleopatra* runs for six months. She's hoping to get at least four months in before she has to hand it off to her understudy."

"And that's why the secrecy?"

"It's a big deal to have to leave a show halfway through, and she's worried about her contract. She's slotted for the school tours and wants to get a new contract next year after the baby is born."

"Got it." Is this why Lance wanted me to come talk to Thad?

"Now if it's out and public she's going to freak out. She's convinced that they'll pull her from the show."

"Will they?"

Thad shrugged and stuffed the flashlight back into his tool belt. "I don't know. I know that Lance wouldn't fire her, and I don't think we need to keep our marriage a secret, but they might decide to give the role to her understudy now and not have to worry about things like constantly having to adjust her costume."

"Right."

He glanced at the clock. "Look, I need to get back to the set and go find Tracy."

"Of course." I slid the box of pastries toward him. "You should give her these."

"She'll love them. It's pretty funny to watch her eat. Usually, she's counting every single calorie." He smiled. I could tell that he was genuinely pleased that they were having a baby.

We walked to the door together. I paused. "Do you have any idea if this could be connected to Antony's murder?"

He shook his head. "I don't think so. Why?"

"The police found an empty DVD case by Antony's body. I wondered if maybe someone could have caught you and Tracy together."

"You mean and recorded it?"

I nodded.

"No way. We were careful." He yanked the straps on his tool belt.

I considered telling him that they weren't careful enough not to have been spotted by Lance.

"You mean you think that someone was blackmailing us with the DVD?" Thad scratched his head. "Wait, you think one of us killed Antony?"

"No. I'm trying to figure out how the DVD factors into Antony's death."

"I promise you that neither Tracy nor I had anything to do with Antony. We couldn't stand the guy. He was a pompous jerk, but why would we kill him?"

To keep him quiet, I thought.

"I don't know anything about a DVD, but I assure you that it doesn't have anything to do with me and Tracy. If someone caught us making out we would have admitted it. We wouldn't have killed over it."

He sounded sincere. I believed him. The only problem was that if he was telling the truth, that crossed him and Tracy off my suspect list.

Chapter Twenty-six

Now what? I asked myself after leaving Thad at the theater. With every new piece of information that I learned I felt like I was more lost than ever. His reaction made sense, but he could have been lying. If he was really worried that Tracy's pregnancy would have an impact on her ability to re-sign with OSF, or keep her leading role, maybe he killed Antony to protect her. I stopped in front of the outdoor stage and took a moment to collect my thoughts and figure out my plan of action.

A handful of tourists emerged from the theater gift shop on the south end of the bricks. They opened up their shopping bags and showed each other their finds—Shakespeare bobbleheads, chewing gum, and insult mints. The market for novelty Shakespeare-related gifts was huge in Ashland. Many retail shops housed vast collections of gag gifts along with high-end items, like silver necklaces etched with famous quotes such as "To Thine Own Self Be True."

I smiled as one of them pulled a pink T-shirt from her bag and put it on. The shirt had a black-and-white picture of Shakespeare's bust and the words WILL

POWER. Was there any other writer—alive or dead—who had garnered such an enthusiastic and enduring fan base? Not in my opinion, but perhaps living in Ashland made me biased.

My thoughts drifted to Antony's murder. Assuming Thad was telling the truth I could scratch him and Tracy off my list. That left Vera, Judy, and Brock. Could either of the women have had the physical strength to move the body? And what motive did Brock have other than wanting an apartment to himself? I was about to let things lie when I heard Lance's familiar, upbeat voice. "Darling! What a pleasant surprise." He strolled up to me and sat so close that our knees touched.

"Lance, what are you doing here?" I threw my arms around his neck.

He stiffened.

"They let you go?" I asked, removing my arms.

His body posture was perfectly erect, yet his eyes gave away a look of relief. "Thankfully, yes."

"What did they say? Did they find something else in the forensics report or figure out who John Duncan is?"

"Easy, easy," Lance said, pushing his index fingers and thumbs together in a meditative pose.

I socked his shoulder. "Stop. You have been Mr. Panic for the last week. You can't seriously try to tell me that you're now a model of calm."

He pursed his lips and bent his head in the direction of the group of tourists waving mini Elizabethan banners and chatting merrily about tonight's show. "I have an image to protect. Not in front of my people."

His people? Classic.

Lance stood and offered me his hand. "Let's go find

someplace more comfortable." Under his breath, he whispered. "And I must find some better clothes."

He offered the tourists a regal wave. It took them a minute to register who he was. I could hear their delighted shouts once they did. "Keep your head down and let's sneak in the back," Lance commanded, leading me to a private door on the side of the outdoor stage. He didn't speak until we made it to his office and he locked the door behind us.

"What an ordeal." He collapsed on the couch.

"What happened?" I sat next to him.

"That woman is humorless."

"Well, in fairness, she is investigating a murder."

Lance recoiled and then tapped both of his cheeks. "Look at this face, Juliet. Take a good look. This is not the face of killer."

"I know, but she has to follow procedure."

"You're siding with my captor? Some friend you are." Lance gave me an exaggerated sigh and crossed his thin legs.

"She's not exactly a captor—" I started to say, but Lance cut me off.

"Did she or did she not imprison me?"

"Technically, yes, but—"

"But nothing." Lance clapped his hands. "She detained me unduly and potentially tarnished my reputation and name. She will be hearing from my lawyers shortly."

I had the sense that Lance might change his tune once things settled down and returned to normal, so I just nodded. "What did you find out, though? Did she say anything when she let you go?"

"Only that new evidence had come in. Then she gave me the usual 'Don't skip town' talk. As if."

"What about the Professor or Thomas? Have you seen either of them?"

He shook his head. "She's not letting the Professor anywhere near her investigation and she has Thomas running around like her personal errand boy."

"I had a chat with Thad like you suggested."

Lance kicked off his shoes. "Do tell."

I explained my conversation and how Thad had appeared to be sincere. "What do you think?" I asked when I finished. "Would Tracy have been in danger of losing her role or contract if you found out she was pregnant?"

"Good Lord, no." Lance stood up and walked over to a closet on the opposite side of the office. He opened it and thumbed through a collection of expensive suits. Leave to it Lance to keep a backup wardrobe on hand. He removed a black tailored suit and crisp white dress shirt. "You don't mind if I freshen up, do you?"

Without waiting for me to respond he went into the attached bathroom and splashed water on his face. Then he shut the door to change, and raised his voice so I could hear him. "No one in my company would ever feel threatened or need to conceal something like that. What a ludicrous idea. I would never fire an actress for being with child. How barbaric."

I heard the buzz of an electric razor. "That's what Thad said."

"Good," he shouted. "I mean don't get me wrong, we'll have to accommodate and shuffle some things around, but my God, I wouldn't throw her out on the streets."

Lance's reaction confirmed everything that Thad had said and made me even more sure that he and Tracy weren't the killers.

The door to the bathroom opened and Lance emerged a new man. Gone was the disheveled hair and overnight shadow. He had shaved his face clean and applied a moisturizer that made his skin glow. His suit fit like a glove and matched his aristocratic posture. "That's more like it." He swept his arms out to both sides and bowed his head. "I'm back, baby."

"You look like your old self," I said, smiling.

"Finally." He sighed. "I hate to admit it but being tossed in jail like ordinary pond scum might have been good for me, but don't you dare tell another soul."

"Never." I laughed. "This morning you were a wreck. What changed?"

"You." His catlike eyes focused on me. "As much as I tease, I have never had a friend like you, Juliet, and for that I'll be forever grateful."

His sincerity was evident. I started to tell him that the same was true for me too, but he continued. "Don't worry, I'll limit my mushiness to those words." He returned to the closet, rummaged through his ties, and tucked an apple-red pocket square into his breast pocket. "As you're well aware I've been, hmmm, how shall I put it? Down in the dumps of late."

"I know."

"That changed today. I'm ready to fight. I'm ready to end this battle with the board, starting right now."

"Wow." I could tell he was serious from his battle stance. "I'm glad that you're feeling like yourself again, but what's your plan?"

"My plan—our plan—is to catch Antony's killer tonight."

"What? How? I don't even have any idea who the killer is."

Lance twined his fingers and gave me a Grinch-like smile. "Not to worry, darling. I do and it's all thanks to your jelly doughnuts."

Chapter Twenty-seven

"What! You know who killed Antony?"

Lance grinned. "I do, and there's no time to waste." He practically leaped behind his desk and slid open the bottom drawer.

"I don't understand." I watched him flip through file folders.

"You will." He didn't look up. His fingers flew as he whipped folder after folder on the hanging rack in the desk drawer.

"Lance, what are you doing?" I stood up and walked over to the desk to get a better look.

"Found it!" He grabbed a thick file folder from the drawer. Then he yanked my arm, pulled me out of his office, dragged me down the hall, and into the Bowmer Theater.

"What are you doing? And why aren't you talking to me?"

He whipped his head around and pressed a finger to his lips. "Silence, darling. You'll see."

How had Lance figured out who the killer was before

me? Had he overheard something at the police station? I wanted answers.

We entered the dark theater and Lance crouched down and pointed to the back row of seats. "This way. Stay low."

He slunk into an empty seat in the middle of the row. "Lance," I whispered. "What is going on?"

He tapped the file folder on his knee. "Patience, Juliet," he hissed. "Stay low and be quiet. You don't want to ruin the reveal."

The reveal? What was Lance talking about? My mind spun and my pulse beat in my neck as we sat in the dark theater.

What was in the file folder?

Lance kept glancing around in the blackness. I'm not sure how long we sat in silence, but it felt like an eternity. Every time I would try to ask Lance any questions he would press his hand over my knee and hush me.

Suddenly, there was a flicker of light from the side of the stage.

My breath caught. "What's that?"

"Silence," Lance whispered almost violently.

Had he lost it? Maybe his return to normal was really just the next evolution of his paranoia. Had I made a serious lapse in judgment? The shift in attitude had come quickly and out of nowhere. Maybe I had read the situation wrong.

Lance wouldn't hurt me, would he?

Doubt invaded my senses. Sweat formed on my brow. My hands felt clammy. I wiped them on my jeans and stared at the light flicking on the left side of the stage.

Why had Lance brought me in here? Alone. In the

dark. What if he hadn't been released by Detective Kerry? What if he snuck out? Maybe this was a setup to kill me. Maybe the light on stage was meant for me.

You sound like a nutjob, Jules, I told myself and tried to relax. The past week had been such a whirlwind of changing personalities from Lance to Stephanie to my own roller coaster of emotions about Mom's wedding. I didn't trust my usually solid intuition.

The light danced across the stage. Someone emerged from the shadows. At the same time, I heard muffled rustling behind us. I whipped my head around to see who was back there, but saw nothing.

"Is someone here?" I mouthed to Lance. It was too dark for him to see.

Again, the sound of shuffling feet made the hairs on my arms stand at attention.

I had a bad feeling about this. My eyes darted back to the stage as the person with the light stood in its center, backlit by the flashlight. It was Brock.

What was he doing here?

I nudged Lance in the waist. He pressed his fingers into the top of my thigh so hard I thought they might leave a mark.

Brock stared out into the darkness. He shined the light across the front row of seats and then along the back. Lance pushed my head down into my lap as the light made its way through the eerily empty seats.

Nothing made sense. What was Brock doing alone onstage with a flashlight and why were we here? "What's he doing?" I whispered to Lance.

"Following my orders, darling," Lance said in a hushed voice.

The light drifted away from our seats so we both cautiously sat up, being sure to keep our heads even with the row in front of us. I had to stretch my legs underneath the seat in front of me.

Brock moved the flashlight underneath his chin and craned his neck backward. The ghostly halo of his lit-up face gave me the creeps. He let out a low, evil laugh. At that moment I knew he must have killed Antony, but I had no idea why or how Lance had figured it out.

I waited in silence. Lance didn't have to tell me to keep quiet. Brock's sinister face was the only warning I needed.

My throat tightened as Brock sat down in the middle of the stage, keeping the flashlight butted up against his chin. He folded his legs and looked as if he could sit like that forever.

I wondered how long this stalemate could go on, and if Brock had any idea that Lance and I were in the theater.

Lance continued to clutch the file folder and hold his position slouched down in his seat. He had been right about the acoustics in the theater. It was so still that I could hear Brock breathing. It sounded shallow and fast. He was nervous. Why?

My hands began to tingle and my feet felt numb. How long had we been here? Time ticked by as we waited. I wished I could adjust my body position. The muscles in my lower back tightened and a steady ache ran up my spine. I knew there was no chance of making a move now. Lance would kill me and Brock would hear it for sure.

Brock reminded me of a statue. He sat with intention. The only thing that gave him away was his breathing.

Suddenly, the door to the theater opened and light from the hallway flooded in. Detective Kerry stormed in. Her heels echoed on the cement floor. Brock jumped to his feet. He looked wobbly and had to catch his balance.

Detective Kerry held up a gun and shouted, "Stay right there, or I will shoot."

Lance sat up and whispered, "Let the games begin."

Chapter Twenty-eight

My eyes tried to adjust to the light and my mind tried to make sense of what was happening. Thomas popped up behind us. I let out a small scream and threw my hand over my mouth.

"It's just me, Jules," he said in a reassuring tone as he pushed down one of the seat backs and stepped over it to join us.

"Now?" Lance asked.

Thomas nodded. "Now."

Lance stood and clapped his hands together. "LIGHTS!"

The entire theater illuminated. Light blinded my eyes. Brock stepped backward and shielded his face from the light. "What is this?"

"ACTION!" Lance shouted again.

A screen slowly came down behind Brock. Detective Kerry moved closer to the stage. Once she got about ten feet away from the orchestra pit she motioned with the gun. "Get down from there and come take a seat."

Brock followed her command. He appeared to be as confused as I was.

Lance sat. The lights dimmed in perfect timing. And a hazy video that looked like it had been shot on a phone camera started to play on the screen.

"Get ready, darling." Lance wrapped his arm around the back of my chair. "This is about to be theater at its best."

The video started with a rally of sorts. A group of people were gathered around a park, holding hand-painted protest signs. They chanted and hollered, and then a young man appeared with a bullhorn. It was Brock.

He was wearing a sleeveless tank top and ripped cut-off shorts. "Hey Idaho, we're here to keep our state clean. No illegals. White power!"

The crowd cheered in response. The camera panned to the crowd. Antony stood among the protesters. I almost didn't recognize him. Gone was his polished look and debonair style. Brock shouted and pointed him out. "I see my bros in the crowd like John Duncan right there!"

"What is this?" I asked Lance.

"This is his past catching up to him."

I watched the video in stunned silence. The hate speech got worse with each minute. This must have been the DVD that was missing at the crime scene. Thad had been right. The missing DVD had nothing to do with a dress rehearsal. I felt sick as I watched Brock rile up the crowd and spew violent language. Antony, or actually John, cheered along with everyone else.

When it was done, the lights came on and the Professor emerged from the side of the stage.

"Everyone knew? Everyone but me?"

Lance patted my knee. "Don't worry, darling. I couldn't have figured it out without you."

Detective Kerry made Brock stand, while Thomas and the Professor surrounded him. They didn't need extra hands. Brock didn't put up a fight.

I watched them escort him from the theater and turned to Lance. "What just happened?"

Lance reached over and tapped my chin. "Close your mouth. It's not the least bit becoming to sit there with that expression on your otherwise gorgeous face."

I glared at him and folded my arms across my chest.

"Fine, fine. I jest." He handed me the file folder he'd been holding. "Here, this will explain it all."

I opened the folder to find headshots of Antony aka John Duncan. Of course. I wanted to kick myself. I had wondered about the connection, but dismissed it because Judy had made it sound like Antony—John—was talking about another person.

John had obviously gone through a major transformation after leaving Idaho. The photos had been professionally shot. His original application for OSF and Lance's notes on his audition were also included. On the application he had used the name John Duncan. Someone had crossed it out and written "Antony Lethello" in purple pen. If I wasn't mistaken it looked like Lance's handwriting.

"Antony was John," I said to Lance, leafing through the papers.

"Yes. It's obvious, isn't it? The minute I heard the name John Duncan I knew who the killer had to be." He pushed my hand away and thumbed to the back of the stack. Then he pulled another application from the pile. "Look."

The application was for Brock. It appeared pretty

standard to me, but Lance tapped his fingers impatiently. "Right here." He pointed to a scribbled note on the bottom right corner that read: "Recommended for hire by Antony."

"Antony recommended him for the company?" I asked.

"Now the lightbulbs are starting to go off." Lance stared at me.

"But how did you figure it out?" To be honest I felt a bit jealous that Lance had put the clues together before me. I thought back to Brock's mention of putting up with Antony for years. I should have picked up on that. Not to mention all the times that someone brought up the fact that Antony wasn't his real name. I had missed so much.

"Your jelly doughnuts."

"Seriously?" I handed him the folder.

He rested it on his lap. "Yes, what a brilliant and deceptive plan to butter up the unsmiling lady cop with your siren sweets."

"I have no idea what you're talking about."

Lance threw his hand on his forehead and tilted it toward the ceiling. "Your pastries make grown men cry. Detective Kerry was no match for your culinary delights."

"Okay, so Detective Kerry ate one of my jelly doughnuts. What does that have to do with Antony's murder?"

"The art of eavesdropping, darling. While I offered to share one of my prized doughnuts with her she happened to get a call. I overheard her conversation. She mentioned the name John Duncan." He paused and snapped his fingers. "I knew immediately that she was talking about Antony."

"You never mentioned John Duncan in our jail cell visits," Lance noted with a hint of a glare.

I thought back to my trips to the police station. He was right. John Duncan had never come up. "It wasn't intentional. I had so much to fill you in on that I guess I forgot."

"Don't worry, darling." Lance patted my back. "It happens to the best of us."

I rolled my eyes.

Lance ignored my response. "What Brock didn't realize is that I knew all about John's past. He confessed everything to me. You should have seen his first audition. I can count on my hands the number of times that I've seen the level of raw emotion that came through. After the audition when I asked him what he had tapped into, it came spilling out. He told me that he had been trapped by his upbringing. Stuck in a world he didn't want to be part of. He left for theater school and left John Duncan behind. I think that's something we can understand, isn't it?" Lance dabbed the corner of his eye. "John's story rang true for me. I've been trying to outrun my past for years."

"You have?"

Lance waved me off. "That is a story for another day."

I wanted to press him, but his demeanor shifted. "Back to John Duncan; I made a mistake. I had a soft spot for him and then he turned into a monster. The attention went to his head. It felt like a slap in the face after I gave him a shot, knowing what he'd come from. Our company is diverse and diversity has to include *all*, right? Even someone like John who had made a mistake in his past."

I nodded. "Why was Brock sitting alone on the stage? I don't get it."

"For dramatics, of course. If I had to be locked up in a stuffy broom closet I figured Brock owed me. Why not add a touch of flair to the big reveal?" Lance let out a small chuckle. "I told him to meet me on the stage with nothing more than a flashlight. Then I tempted him with the promise of a huge payout. Detective Kerry and I crafted our plot carefully. And I'll have you know it was all my idea—I lured him to the stage under the guise of a cash reward for info on his old pal. Little did he know that he was the payout."

Classic Lance. "How did you find the DVD and how did you convince Detective Kerry, Thomas, and the Professor to meet you here?"

"That was easy. The Professor found the DVD in the park. Apparently, thanks to you. Word is you had a late-night escape that led him to the search area. Once he found it, he deduced that Brock had planned to destroy it, but must have gotten spooked. Probably by a white-tailed deer." He laughed. "That would be justice, wouldn't it?"

"The Professor wasn't allowed to be part of the investigation, though."

"I know. That didn't stop him from sleuthing. It's in his blood. It's like pastry for you."

"Where did he find it?" Thomas must have called him that night. I wondered if they had gone back to the duck pond later.

Lance shrugged. "No idea."

I thought about the Professor saying he was working "underground." Had one of his sources come through? "So I'm still not entirely clear why Brock killed Antony. He didn't want anyone to see what was on the DVD?"

"Apparently, and he might have had a fair point."

"What?" I looked at him in shock.

"No, I don't mean in killing him, but he had fair reason to be concerned. We have a strict policy on discrimination at OSF. It's one of the guiding principles of the theater. Everyone is welcome onstage, backstage, in the cheap seats, and the box seats. I pride myself and this company on our ability to be inclusive. While I wouldn't have fired Tracy for getting pregnant, I would most certainly have fired Brock for that hateful language."

I shuddered to think about the terrible language we heard on the video and that Brock had felt the need to take the most drastic measure to silence it. I almost felt sorry for him. Had he realized his mistake, too? I have always chosen to believe the best about people. Perhaps they were simply a product of their environment.

That had been one of the most amazing gifts of my time at sea. My horizons had literally and figuratively expanded. Connecting with my colleagues from every corner of the globe had made our spinning planet feel smaller.

"Would you have fired him for sure?" I asked. "What if he changed?"

"People don't change, Juliet."

"That's not fair. Of course they do. Everyone changes. We all learn and grow."

Lance huffed. "Oh, to be so naïve."

I socked him in the shoulder.

He rubbed his arm in mock pain. "Darling, let's not fight. Maybe you're right. Maybe people can change, but trust me, Brock's intention to murder John had nothing to do with OSF. He came here intentionally, I think to blackmail John, but John must have turned the tables on him. John came clean with me, but Brock didn't know that. So John used that against him. He blackmailed Brock, and Brock must have had enough. Ah, the irony."

I had to admit that made more sense than Brock being worried about getting fired.

Lance stood. "What's done is done." He reached for my hand and pulled me up. "And the most important news of the day is that yours truly is back and all is right with the world again."

We left the theater. Lance returned to his office and I went in search of Thomas and the Professor. I was glad that Antony's killer had been caught and happy that Lance was free, but I felt unsettled about how things had ended. Antony had been killed over words. There had to be another way, and unlike Lance, I refused to believe that people couldn't change.

Chapter Twenty-nine

We reconvened later at Torte. Twinkle lights and antique street lamps glowed in the otherwise dark plaza. Mom brought a platter of sandwiches and pot of coffee to the dining room. We pushed two tables together and gathered around for a late-evening snack and to hash out everything that had happened.

The Professor and Thomas looked relieved.

Mom poured cups of coffee and passed around cream and sugar. "Don't be shy. I made too many sandwiches because I wasn't sure how hungry you would be and whether Detective Kerry or Lance might join us."

Thomas reached for a salami and provolone sandwich with thinly sliced pickles and marinated peppers. "I'm starving."

"Exactly," Mom said with a smile. "I figured you might eat the entire tray."

"Leave it to me, Mrs. Capshaw. I'm at your service."

The Professor took a roasted turkey with dill Havarti. "I don't know if Detective Kerry will join us, but I did extend the offer."

"Are you back on the case?" Mom asked.

"Yes. Well, technically, no. She'll close the investigation, but thankfully with Antony's killer apprehended, she's able to share information freely"

"I can't believe Brock killed him over an old video."

"That was pretty inflammatory language, Jules." Thomas chomped his sandwich. "And, don't forget money. Money makes people do crazy things."

"I know. I agree. Absolutely, but it makes me sad, all the same."

"Ah, yes." The Professor removed his glasses and tucked them in the breast pocket of his tweed jacket. "But you, Juliet, see the world in color and varying shades of gray. I've learned through my years of observing people and behaviors that those who see in black-and-white—like Brock—are much less likely to understand that their choices are infinite."

"Yeah." I nodded and helped myself to a turkey sandwich. "What's going to happen to him?"

"We'll know more as the case unfolds," the Professor said. "He'll get a fair trial."

"Do you think he planned to kill Antony—sorry—John?"

"No. I would say with certainty that wasn't his plan. My guess is that he felt threatened. We know that John was blackmailing him, and have the bank statements to prove it. I believe that Brock tired of it and refused to keep paying him, but John wouldn't let it go."

"Wouldn't the video have damaged John's career, too?" Mom asked.

The Professor stirred cream into his coffee. "Yes, but

John's stock had risen so high within OSF that he decided it was worth the risk. And our friend Lance already knew about his blemished past."

"Lance was right all along," Mom interjected.

"Indeed. This might be a case of John's ego inflating to the point that he believed himself infallible. You know what the Bard says: 'What's past is prologue.' "

"I wonder whether Lance's frustrations and challenges at OSF are really due to John?" Mom said aloud.

"That remains a mystery," the Professor replied, pausing to take a bite of sandwich. "It could be that John thought that even though the video was unflattering, he could smooth-talk his way out of it should any of the board members have ever found out."

That made sense. "Do you think that John was responsible for the board turning on Lance?" I asked.

"I find it more than coincidental that John's ascent paralleled Lance's decline."

Thomas grabbed another sandwich. "You know, for a while there I wasn't sure if Lance was telling the truth or was completely off his rocker."

I held my coffee up to him in a toast. "You and me both."

The Professor topped off his coffee.

"How do you think Brock did it?" I asked.

"Do you mean how he killed John?"

I nodded. I wasn't sure I wanted to hear the Professor's theory and yet I needed closure.

"This is speculation, of course, but I think that John tracked down Brock on the night of the party in hopes of upping his payment or maybe requesting a new favor.

Maybe Brock brought the DVD with him as collateral. I suspect that they fought and Brock stabbed him."

"With the dagger?" I interrupted.

"Ah, no." The Professor pressed his hands together. "Thank you for reminding me. As a matter of fact, the dagger found in his abdomen was nothing more than a prop."

I thought about Brock's costume and the fake dagger strapped on his gold belt.

"John was killed with a much smaller blade. A hunting knife."

"Lance always talks about keeping the drama on the stage, but I don't think he was successful this time. John was blackmailing Brock, Judy was using her knowledge about the fight she overheard to gain favors from John, and then there was a secret pregnancy and marriage." I rubbed my temples.

"The Bard would be envious," the Professor joked.

Mom encouraged us to finish off the sandwiches. "I made chocolate cream pie with my special crunchy cookie crust. Eat up."

"Hey, what's the scoop with wedding plans?" Thomas asked, changing the subject.

I was glad for the shift in tone.

The Professor and Mom shared a look. "Who knows," they said in unison and then laughed.

"That doesn't sound good." Thomas caught my eye.

"No, no. It's nothing between us. We're happier than we've ever been, aren't we, Doug?" Mom's eyes lit up as she reached across the table for his hand.

"Yes, my dear Helen. I now understand why Shakespeare wrote so many sonnets."

"What's the problem then?" Thomas took the last sandwich on the platter.

"The problem is finding a venue big enough for the entire town." Mom stood and picked up the empty platter. "I think it's going to have to be Lithia Park."

A small shiver ran up my spine. As much as I loved the park I couldn't erase the memory of watching Thomas, the Professor, and the search team sweep the area for John's body. I wondered if they were thinking the same thing from the way Thomas focused on his sandwich and the Professor's brow furrowed ever so slightly.

"Let me grab the pie," Mom said, and turned toward the kitchen.

"Are you thinking what I'm thinking?" I asked softly, although I doubted she could hear me.

The Professor gave me a quick nod. "The park feels, how shall I put it? Tainted? However, I do not want to ruin your mother's wishes and dreams. Therefore, should we be unable to secure another venue, let's all make a pact that we shall never speak of this again."

We each put our hands in the middle of the table and shook.

"Right," Thomas added. "The park is already back to normal. It's not like John's spirit is going to hang around and haunt it or anything."

"Thomas." I kicked him under the table.

"What?"

"Now I'm going to think about a ghost every time I walk by the duck pond."

"You don't believe in ghosts, Jules."

"I do now." I scowled.

The Professor grinned. "Truce, you two." He lifted

his head. "Your mother is about to return. What do you think of the idea of surprising her?"

I nearly choked on my coffee. "What?"

He glanced in the direction of the kitchen and lowered his voice. "You know that summer solstice falls in June. What if we planned a surprise Midsummer Night's Eve wedding in the park?"

Thomas eyes bulged. Had he said something to the Professor about Mom's idea?

He caught my eye and shook his head.

I chose my words carefully. "I like the idea, but I think she has her heart set on finding a venue and planning the food and flowers and everything."

"You don't think she'd want a surprise?" He sounded disappointed.

"It's not that. It's just." I tried to think about how to frame it. What were the odds that each of them wanted to surprise the other?

Thomas came to my rescue. "Jules is trying to say that it's a woman's domain."

I twisted my ponytail. "Kind of?"

The Professor's lips thinned. His gaze drifted toward the espresso bar where Mom balanced her chocolate crunch pie and a stack of plates. "You're saying that maybe I should leave it to her."

I hated making him feel bad. "Well, not exactly."

He smiled. "Then I shall put on my thinking cap."

Fortunately, Mom's creamy dark chocolate pie with shaved chocolate, mounds of whipped cream, and crunchy cookie crust distracted us from the topic. We devoured the pie and the conversation shifted to the basement renovations, and whether or not the Professor was seriously considering bringing Detective Kerry on permanently.

I could see Thomas's body stiffen at the mention of her name.

The Professor was noncommittal, which wasn't like him. He was usually direct and straightforward. It made me wonder if he had already extended her an offer and if Thomas was about to get a new partner.

Chapter Thirty

The next morning there was a steady stream of customers waiting for Andy's coffee special—the jelly doughnut—and for the gossip about Antony's murder. I barely had a free moment to catch my breath, let alone catch up with the team. I gave them a brief update before we opened to customers, but otherwise they got the news along with the rest of town.

Once the lunch rush was complete and the dining room was basically empty we all gathered around the island. Andy offered us each one of his signature drinks while Sterling passed around bacon and cheddar biscuits.

"What do you think, boss?" Andy asked with an expectant grin. "I added a hint of raspberry syrup to go along with your filled doughnuts. It's not too sweet, is it?"

I took a sip of the latte. The doughnut flavor definitely came through. I tasted notes of cinnamon and the sweet touch of bright raspberry. "It's fantastic," I said, taking another sip.

"You think?"

Bethany agreed. "It's great. What else did you add? White chocolate?"

Andy nodded. "Yep. A teaspoon of white chocolate, cinnamon, vanilla, and raspberry syrup plus dark espresso and milk."

Sterling placed the extra biscuits in the middle of the island and picked up his coffee. "This tastes like a doughnut, man. You are the master." He reached across the workstation and gave Andy a fist bump.

Andy swelled with pride as we raved about his latest creation. Stephanie nibbled on a biscuit. For the first time in a week her skin had color and her eyes a healthy brightness.

"Did you finally sleep?" I asked.

She twisted a strand of purple hair around her finger. "Yeah, thanks."

"How's *Oklahoma!*?" Andy asked and then ducked away from the island as if anticipating Stephanie's wrath.

"Well, there's good news." She unwound her hair. "Jules's earplugs worked, but on top of that, my dorm-mate is on to a new soundtrack."

"Really. What?" I asked.

Stephanie almost smiled. *"Hamilton."*

"Dude, I love that soundtrack," Andy said. "We should play it now. I have it on my phone." He looked to me for approval.

"Go for it," I said. "As long as it's cool with you, Stephanie."

She shrugged. "Whatever. I only heard it last night. I'm sure I'm going to be sick of it soon, but anything is better than *Oklahoma!* and *Hamilton* is actually pretty cool."

Andy ran to plug his phone into the speaker. Soon music pulsed in the kitchen as we chatted about the case, next steps for the basement project, and made plans for the next few weeks. With the new season of OSF officially under way there wouldn't be much downtime for months to come. I knew that my team could handle it, but I also knew with Mom's wedding right around the corner we were going to have to stay on task and organized.

I looped them in on Mom's idea to throw a surprise wedding. They were excited about the idea and Steph and Bethany began sketching out table displays and summer flavors of macarons. "We could stencil each macaron with a monogram and their initials," Bethany suggested, showing me a rough sketch they'd done on paper.

"I love it." Now if we could only figure out a venue the wedding would come together without a hitch.

I lost myself in baking for the remainder of the afternoon. I had my own surprise in store—the wedding cake.

A cake is the centerpiece of the entire wedding and I wanted Mom's to be spectacular. She had always loved strawberry shortcake, so I wanted to test a variety of recipes over the next few weeks to find the perfect one for her wedding cake. Once the team left for the afternoon, I got to work on my first test. Strawberry shortcake is almost more like a shortbread meets cornbread. I didn't want something too dry for the wedding cake, but I also wanted a cake that would have enough structure to hold up with multiple layers, especially because I planned to layer it with tons of vanilla whipped cream and fresh strawberries.

To start I creamed butter and sugar together in the mixer until they were a lovely pale yellow. Next, I incorporated eggs, vanilla, and a splash of buttermilk. In a separate bowl, I sifted flour, salt, baking soda, and two tablespoons of cornmeal. Hopefully, the addition of the cornmeal would give the vanilla cake the flavor profile of shortcake without making it crumbly or too dense.

Once I added the dry ingredients and folded them into the batter, I coated two nonstick pans with butter and more cornmeal. Then I spread the batter evenly and put them in a hot oven. While the cakes baked, I sliced strawberries and whipped cream. I thought about what a wild week it had been. Despite the drama, things were good at the bakeshop. Really good.

I couldn't believe how lucky I was and how happy I was for Mom. I could almost hear my dad's hearty laugh as I sliced the cakes in thin layers and piled on strawberries and fluffy whipped cream.

Now, if only I had someone to taste this with, I thought, cutting a slice. As if on cue, I heard a rap on the front door. Lance!

I hurried to open the door for him.

He breezed in wearing a pale blue suit and carrying a bundle of spring daisies. "For you, darling." He thrust the bouquet into my hands.

"Thanks, but what are these for?"

"For saving my life, of course."

"I didn't save your life. You saved your own."

He waved me off. "Details. Details."

"You're just in time," I said, shutting the door behind him. "I'm testing wedding cakes."

"Oh." He clapped. "You know how much I adore weddings."

I stopped at the sink to fill a vase with water and added the daisies. "These remind me of spring."

"Good. We could all use a little spring around here."

"How are you doing?" I set the bright yellow vase of flowers in the center of the island and sliced him a piece of cake.

"The shock has worn off, and now the real battle begins."

"What do you mean?"

He studied the cake. "This is dainty and sweet. Like a slice of summer on a plate. Or better yet, like your mother. She'll adore this."

"Right, but don't tell. I want to surprise her with the cake."

"Your secret is safe with me."

I knew that was true. "What's your plan with the board now?" I asked, taking a bite of the cake. The flavor was just as I had hoped. The cornmeal gave it a hint of grit, but the cake itself was light and moist. Strawberries weren't quite in season yet. These had been shipped from California. Even so the delicate berry and vanilla cream paired perfectly with the cake. Maybe I wasn't going to have to do weeks of testing after all.

"Well, darling, as you know, Antony tried to ruin me, but he did not succeed. The board sent me this." He reached into his sport jacket and removed a handwritten letter.

It was a formal apology.

"That's nice." I slid the letter back to Lance.

He stabbed his cake. "Ha! Nice. We're well past nice."

"What?"

"I intend to use the board's lapse in judgment as a negotiating tool."

"How so?"

He tasted the cake and inhaled deeply. "Divine, darling. Absolutely divine."

"It's pretty good, don't you think?"

"It reminds me of strawberry shortcake. The quintessential summer dessert."

I smiled. "That's exactly what I was going for."

"Why do you sound surprised? You're a revered pastry chef."

"I don't know about revered, but even professional chefs have plenty of flubs. Trust me. There have been many cakes that have ended up straight in the trash."

Lance took another bite. "Never. I refuse to believe it."

I appreciated his praise. "What are you going to negotiate?"

"The better question is what am I not going to negotiate?" Lance's eye danced with wicked delight. "My salary, a new car, who knows."

"What?" I wondered again about his finances.

"For starters, I'm taking you up on your advice."

"Really?" What advice? I had given Lance a number of suggestions over the last few weeks.

"I've booked myself for a three-week vacation. I leave tomorrow."

"What?"

He grinned so wide it made my cheeks hurt. "You

told me a little time away might give me a new perspective, and I've decided you're right. I asked the board to grant me a temporary sabbatical."

"But what about the new season? What is OSF going to do without you?"

"Won't it be fun watching them deal with that?" Lance winked and folded his arms across his chest.

"What kind of vacation?"

He linked his long fingers together. "Let's just say it's an adventure."

I couldn't believe Lance was really going through with it. Something had shifted. Usually, Lance was all talk, but he was taking off and heading to another continent. I was proud of my friend, even if his motive might have been based on some subtle revenge. I could tell that he hoped that OSF would fall apart in his absence.

"What kind of adventure?"

"One I've been dreaming about for many years. You know what they say, 'no time like the present.'" He finished his cake. "Don't you agree?"

"Absolutely."

Lance looked at his watch. "Darling, I must run. So much to do. Bags to pack. You know the drill."

I gathered our dishes, placed them in the sink, and covered the cake. "I'll follow you out. I'm beat."

He waited for me to close up the bakeshop and linked his arm through mine. "You'll keep me abreast of everything going on while I'm away?"

"Of course." I stopped in mid-stride. "You'll come back? You aren't thinking of leaving for good, are you? What about the wedding?"

Lance patted my hand. "What's that they say about

absence making the heart grow fonder? I think it will do the board some good to miss me, but I assure you I will be back with time to spare for Helen's nuptials. I wouldn't miss it."

"Promise."

He dropped his affected voice and met my eyes. "Promise."

"I'm going miss you." I realized it was true as I said the words.

"Now you know how I felt when you darted off to the Caribbean with that delicious hunk of a husband."

"For a week."

"Darling, I'll be home before you know it. When is the wedding?"

We stopped at Elevation and I filled him in on the fact that both the Professor and Mom wanted to surprise each other on Midsummer Night's Eve.

"Brilliant! But I have an even better idea. Let's twist it up a bit. What if the entire town is in on the surprise? We'll let both of them think that we're collaborating in secret when in reality everyone will know except for the two of them. What do you think?"

I laughed. "I love it! That's pretty perfect and would be so much fun. But there's one looming, giant problem—the venue. We don't have one."

"What do you mean?"

I had forgotten that Lance hadn't heard any of the news about the wedding festivities. We had been so focused on the case and trying to clear his name that I hadn't told him about our dilemma of not being able to find a venue. When I finished explaining how the wineries were already booked and how it was looking more and more likely that Mom and the Professor would have to host the wedding in Lithia Park, he drummed his fingers on his chin and stared at me.

"Why don't you host it at *your* winery, darling?"

"That would be great, except for one minor detail. I don't own a winery, Lance."

He threw his hand over his mouth and gasped. Then he stood back and stared at me. "You don't know, do you?"

"Know what?"

He gave me a look of bewilderment, then he put the back of his hand on his forehead and sighed. "For such a talented chef and sleuth, you can be quite dense sometimes."

"Thanks."

"I mean no offense, but I am surprised you haven't put it together."

"Put what together?"

"The winery. The winery that Carlos bought for you."

"What?" I stepped backward. I felt like he had slugged me in the gut.

"Uva? You know your family friend Jose's winery?"

"Yeah." I nodded, trying to connect the dots.

"Carlos invested in the winery. He knew how much you loved it and Jose needed to sell."

I thought about the key he had given me. It wasn't a metaphor. It was to the winery? "Wait," I said, remembering something terrible. "I thought Richard Lord invested in Uva?"

Lance gave me a pained smile. "He did. You and Mr. Lord are now business partners."

Now I did feel like I had been punched. Hard.

"Don't fret. There's a third partner, and let's just say that he'll have your back." Lance kissed both of my cheeks. "Ta-ta, darling! I'm off."

He continued down the sidewalk leaving me standing with my mouth wide open once again. Carlos had invested in Uva. I was a one-third partner in a winery with Richard Lord. Things were about to get interesting.

Read on for an excerpt of the next installment in the
Bakeshop Mysteries

Till Death Do Us Tart

Now available
from St. Martin's Paperbacks

They say that love makes the world go round. Given the contagious feeling of love in the air in my warm-hearted town of Ashland, Oregon, I suspected that the saying might be true. Ashland's amorous tendencies were heightened with preparations for what locals were calling "the wedding of the century." My mom and her longtime beau, the Professor, had finally decided to tie the knot and everyone was humming with eager excitement. Torte, our family bakeshop, was no exception. For the past few weeks, we had been hand-pressing dainty lemon tarts with mounds of fluffy whipping cream, testing new recipes for strawberry sponge cake, and finalizing the menu for the wedding feast. Mom and the Professor had agreed on an inclusive guest list. That meant that anyone in our little hamlet who wanted to come to the wedding was invited. That also meant that my team and I were going to be baking around the clock to ensure that we had enough food to feed the masses.

To complicate matters, Mom and the Professor had a trick up their sleeve. They were each planning to surprise one another with a Midsummer Night's Dream wedding on the summer solstice. But the trick was on them. The entire town was in on the secret—we were surprising them. Keeping the festivities a secret from Ashland's lead detective and my very astute mom was going to be no small feat. After tossing around several white lies, we decided our best cover story was to say we were hosting a party. I'd recently learned that I was a third owner in Uva, a gorgeous hillside vineyard on the outskirts of town. We had sent invitations for a re-opening bash, asking guests to come in Elizabethan attire for a celebratory feast under the stars. At last count, we had over two hundred and fifty RSVPs.

Time to get baking, Jules, I thought as I unwrapped sheets of filo dough. The sun had yet to rise. There was something calming and almost magical about baking in the quiet predawn hours. I loved the idea that while I was kneading bread dough my friends and neighbors were fast asleep. It was as if mornings were exclusively mine. Not many people ever witnessed the sun's slow ascent, the way the sky shifted from deep purple to pink and how light drifted across the tree tops. Every sunrise was slightly different. Some days the bricks on the plaza across the street glowed a burning orange, like the sun was begging villagers out of their beds. Other days it lagged behind wispy clouds, encouraging a lazy lie-in. Sunrises were like pastry. No two scones or turnovers ever came out exactly the same. Sure, the average connoisseur might not notice a nuisance of slightly thinner crust or browning of crystalized sugar, but each sweet and savory treat that I pulled from our ovens had its own unique signature.

I glanced outside Torte's steamy windows. Antique street lamps cast soft halos on the sidewalk. A banner with Shakespeare's bust flapped in a hint of wind. The new season of the Oregon Shakespeare Festival had kicked off last month, bringing tourists and theater lovers to our small Southern Oregon town. From now through the end of summer the bakeshop would see a steady stream of customers. This was our busy season, so adding in a wedding, launching a new winery, and finishing our basement expansion was going to be challenging, to say the very least.

Dusting my hands with flour, I set to work placing thin layers of the filo dough on the kitchen island. Then I brushed them with melted butter. I planned to create a stacked strawberry pastry with honey, a touch of salt, and almonds. If it went according to my vision we would serve it for the morning rush, and potentially add it to the ever-growing list of desserts for the wedding. Once I had brushed the sheets of dough with butter, I layered fresh sliced strawberries, drizzled them with honey, and sprinkled them with toasted almonds and coarse sea salt. I repeated the layers until I had a four-inch stack. I finished it with a final coating of butter and slid it into the oven.

With my test pastry in the oven, I turned my attention to our daily bread and specialty cake orders. Soon the kitchen was alive with the scent of sweet bread. I was so lost in the process of twisting braids of challah dough that I didn't even realize that the sky had lightened until I heard Stephanie and Andy come inside.

"Morning, boss," Andy called in his usual chipper

tone. He wore a Southern Oregon University T-shirt, cargo shorts, and flip flops. "It's already warm out there. I think it's going to be a cold brew kind of day."

"That works for me," I replied with a wave.

Stephanie trudged in after him. Even though they both attended SOU, their styles couldn't have been more different. Her violet hair had been dyed black at the tips. She wore a pair of skinny jeans and a black tank top that matched her surly attempt at a smile. "Hey," she gave me a nod and headed to grab an apron.

Andy stared at the racks of bread. "Dude, how long have you been here, boss?"

"I don't know, a couple of hours." I glanced at the clock on the wall behind me and gave him a sheepish look. "I couldn't sleep. Too much to do." That was true, but there was more to my lack of sleep than just our bakery production. As excited as I was about Mom's wedding, I had a lot on my mind. My estranged husband, Carlos, was arriving with his son Mateo in two days. I had never met Mateo, and while I was confident that we would get along, I couldn't silence a small, nagging fear that he might not like me. They were coming for the wedding, but I had to find some time to talk to Carlos alone. He hadn't told me about how he'd purchased a share in Uva. I wasn't sure what that meant for his long-term plans, and quite honestly what that meant for me.

After a quick return to the Amour of the Seas, the cruise ship where we first met, and eventually married, I had come home resolved that it was time for me to leave that life behind. Did buying into Uva mean that

Carlos had different plans? Was he thinking of leaving the vagabond lifestyle of the sea too?

Then there was the issue of Richard Lord. Richard was a third partner in the winery and had made it crystal clear that he would do whatever he could to buy us out. For some reason Richard had been extremely accommodating with Mom's wedding plans. That should have given me peace of mind, but instead it had me on edge. I didn't trust Richard's motivation. Maybe there was a small chance that he had changed his ways, but I suspected his sickening sweetness was part of a bigger plan. The question was what?

The sound of Andy firing up the espresso machine shook me from my thoughts.

He adjusted his well-worn baseball cap. "Okay, if you've been here for hours you need a cold brew—stat."

"You know that I'll never turn down your coffee," I said, brushing my hands on my cheery Torte apron. Our current space included the kitchen which opened to the espresso bar and pastry counter. The front of the bakeshop housed a variety of bistro tables and window booths. My parents had painted the dining area in teal and red—royal colors—in honor of my dad's love of the bard and all things Shakespeare. Short of freshening up the paint and modernizing our equipment, Torte hadn't changed much since the day my parents first opened the front doors. I liked it that way and intended to keep the same welcoming vibe in the newly renovated basement.

Progress had sped up over the past couple of days. The electrician was due later in the afternoon for the final inspection. After that it would be a matter of paint, trim, and then the fun stuff—like arranging furniture and artwork. Our goal was to move wholesale baking operations downstairs within the week. Once we had the new kitchen up and running we could tear through the current kitchen to create stairs between the spaces. The dining room, espresso bar, and pastry counter would all expand and customers would have additional seating options downstairs with a view of the brick pizza oven and bakers at work. Our architect, Robert, had found a way to add in a woodstove in the seating area so that customers could cozy up with a latte and pastry on cold winter afternoons. I felt like a kid at Christmas every time I went downstairs to check on progress. We were so close I could hardly wait.

"What do you want me to start on? It looks like you're almost done with all the wholesale orders." Stephanie stared at the whiteboard that had the day's tasks outlined and then back to the racks of bread. "Weren't you just lecturing me about not getting enough sleep?"

"True," I replied with a chuckle. "But I'm the boss, so the rules don't apply, right?"

Stephanie scowled. "Ha!"

"Promise me that if I start acting loopy, you guys will keep me in check?"

"Oh, we'll keep you in check," Andy replied before Stephanie had a chance. He handed us glasses of iced coffee with a lovely layer of something creamy on the top. "You don't have to worry though. This is my toasted coconut cold brew. One glass of this will have you revved up and ready to bake."

Stephanie dunked a spoon into her coffee and swirled the thick coconut milk together with the dark brew. "I don't know about the coffee, but we've got your back, Jules."

I fought a tightness in my throat. Stephanie's outward appearance and aloof attitude sometimes gave the impression that she didn't care, but nothing could be further from the truth. I don't know how Mom and I had lucked out with such a stellar young staff, or what we would do without them.

"Thanks," I said, taking a sip of the coffee. The rich espresso and bright coconut flavor were a perfect pairing.

Andy returned to his post while Stephanie and I reviewed what I had already completed and what needed to be tackled next. We fell into a familiar rhythm. One of the many things that I appreciated about our team was everyone's ability to take initiative. I didn't have to remind Andy to wipe down the espresso machine at the start of his shift, or ask Stephanie to whip buttercream for our specialty cakes. It wasn't long until Sterling and Bethany, the two other members of our small but mighty staff, arrived. Sterling had been taking on a bigger role as kitchen supervisor. He didn't have formal chef training, but was a quick study and had an innate ability to know what flavors worked well together. Finding Bethany had been serendipitous. We met at Ashland's annual chocolate festival where she debuted her drool-worthy brownies. Mom and I had asked her to help out at Torte while we were away on the cruise. She was such a natural fit that we ended up inviting her to stay on permanently. To my surprise and equal delight, she and Stephanie hit it off instantly. They had teamed up to expand Torte's social media with daily contests and gorgeously styled pictures of our culinary creations.

I knew that we were going to have to hire more staff with the expansion. The thought of interviewing potential candidates made my head swim. That could wait, at least a little while longer.

"What's on the lunch menu today?" Sterling asked, folding his apron in half and tying it around his waist. Even with the warming summer temperatures he wore his standard black hoodie and skinny jeans.

"How does an Italian sub sound?" I pointed to the walk-in fridge. "I ordered extra salami. You could use the baguettes that are coming out of the oven next."

"Sure." He reached for a spiral notebook. "What do you want on them?"

"Maybe start with an Italian dressing with fresh parsley and basil. Salami, black olives, roasted red peppers, spinach, and mozzarella cheese."

"I'll take two of those," Andy shouted above the sound of foaming milk.

"Do you want them grilled or cold?" Sterling jotted down my list of ingredients.

I thought about it for a minute. Grilled baguettes brushed with olive oil and served slightly charred sounded delicious, but it was supposed to warm up as the day progressed. "Cold," I said. "In fact if you make a few dozen now you can chill them so that they'll be nice and cool by the lunch rush."

"On it." Sterling headed for the fridge.

Bethany offered to tackle muffins and croissants. That left me to deliver our wholesale orders. I enjoyed getting a chance to pop into neighboring businesses along the plaza, especially as the theater season ramped up. It would become harder and harder to find a spare minute once the summer crowds descended. I packaged buttery loaves of sweet bread and crusty sourdough into a box and headed outside. Flowers spilled from window boxes along the plaza. Empty galvanized tubs were secured with a bike lock on the side of A Rose By Any Other Name, the flower shop, owned by my friend Thomas's parents. Soon they would be bursting with colorful, fragrant blooms. The tree-lined sidewalk looked sleepy, but I knew that wouldn't last long. By noon the outdoor bistro tables would be packed with diners and the shops would be bustling with tourists.

I passed Puck's Pub where a bartender was sweeping up the remains of last night's revelry. He tipped his cap. I waved and continued on to the Green Goblin at the far end of the plaza. The pub and restaurant sat across the street from Lithia Park. I was tempted to take a quick spin through the lush grounds before returning to the bakeshop to quiet my mind. Instead, I dropped off the Green Goblin's order and crossed Main Street to finish the delivery route. By the time I made it back to Torte Andy was chatting with a line of customers waiting for lattes and Bethany was packaging up boxes of croissants and sticky buns.

"Are you Juliet?" A woman waiting for her drink order stopped me.

"Yes." I didn't recognize her.

She extended a manicured hand with diamond so huge it took over half her ring finger. "Clarissa." She didn't exactly smile.

"Nice to meet you. Did you need something?" I nodded to the pastry counter.

"No. This young gentleman is making me a non-fat

latte. I wanted to introduce myself because I believe you're working with my husband?"

"Really?"

Her penciled lips turned downward. "Yes, Robert. Your architect."

"Oh, Robert. Of course. We love Robert. He's done an incredible job."

"He's the best." She twisted the brilliant diamond. "You're lucky that he agreed to take on a project . . ." she paused and glanced around the bakeshop. "Of this size. Typically, he prefers to focus his efforts on larger, more profitable endeavors."

The way she spoke made me feel like we were a charity case. "He never mentioned that."

Andy put Clarissa's drink on the bar. "Non-fat latte is up." He glanced at me and rolled his eyes.

"I'm meeting Robert shortly. Have you had a chance to see what he's done with the basement?" I tried to keep my tone upbeat.

Clarissa shook her head. "No."

"You should come say hello and take a look. He added a woodstove that is going to be the centerpiece of the seating area downstairs. I can't wait to arrange cozy couches and pillows around it."

"I'm sure it will be charming. It's such a quaint space you have here." She turned her attention to the front door and motioned to a woman in her mid-forties with bleached blond hair and a black leather biker jacket. "I must go. I'm meeting someone." Clarissa dismissed me.

She and the woman in the leather jacket made their way to one of the booths in the front. They were an odd pair. I got the sense that Clarissa wasn't impressed that her husband was designing a bakeshop. She obviously wanted him working on more prestigious projects than our quaint bakery. Robert had never seemed disinterested in his design work. If anything he'd been enthusiastic and was constantly bringing Mom and me new ideas and suggestions. Oh well, I sighed, and returned to the kitchen. Clarissa could turn her nose down on Torte. I knew how lucky I was to get to spend my days in the comfortable and welcoming space.

Grandma J's Coconut Cream Pie

Ingredients:
- 1 cup sugar
- 1 cup half and half
- 1 cup coconut milk
- Three eggs
- 2 tablespoons cornstarch
- 1 teaspoon vanilla
- 1 teaspoon coconut extract
- Pinch of salt
- 1 cup of coconut
- Whipping cream
- 1 pre-made pie crust

Directions:
Heat oven to 200 degrees and spread coconut on cookie sheet. Toast until golden brown. Usually 4 to 5 minutes. Remove and set aside to cool. Then turn oven temp up to 475 degrees. Press pie crust into a pie plate. Poke holes in the bottom with a fork and then fill with pie weights or dried beans. Bake for 8–10 minutes, or until edges are light

brown. Remove from oven and allow to cool for 30 to 40 minutes before filling.

While the crust and toasted coconut are cooling, beat eggs and sugar together. In a saucepan add coconut milk, half and half, coconut extract, vanilla, salt and cornstarch. Stir in eggs and sugar and whisk together. Bring to a gentle rolling boil. Stir continually until thickened (approximately 5 minutes). Remove from heat and allow to cool. Fill baked pie crust with coconut pudding. Spread mounds of whipping cream on the top, and then sprinkle on the toasted coconut.

Chicken Tortilla Soup

Ingredients:
  2 large chicken breasts (cut into small pieces)
  1 14.5 oz. can of fire roasted tomatoes
  1 14.5 oz. can of chili beans
  1 2.25 oz. can of diced green chilis
  1 large onion
  3 cloves garlic
  A bunch of fresh cilantro
  2 cups frozen corn
  2 cups chicken stock
  2 teaspoons chili powder
  1 teaspoon cumin
  1 teaspoon salt
  1 teaspoon pepper
  Olive oil

Directions:
Add a large glug of olive oil to a stock pot, and turn burner onto medium-low. Wash cilantro. Cut and dice the stalks.

Reserve the cilantro leaves for later. Chop onion and garlic and sauté with the cilantro stalks until the onions become translucent. Add chicken and brown on both sides. Add tomatoes, beans, chicken stock, and spices. Bring to a boil and then turn the heat down and simmer on low heat (covered) for 30 minutes. Remove lid and add corn. Simmer for another 5 to 10 minutes.

Garnish with fresh sprigs of cilantro, tortilla strips, and a dollop of sour cream.

Avocado Wraps

Ingredients:
  8 flour tortillas
  4–5 avocados
  1 red onion
  1 tomato
  1 lime
  A bunch of cilantro
  Salt and pepper
  1 14.5 oz. can black beans
  2 cups of grated Monterey jack and sharp cheddar
    cheese

Directions:
Dice tomatoes, onion, and garlic. Wash and chop a handful of cilantro. Mix together in a bowl. Slice avocados and use a fork to cut together with onion, tomato, garlic, and cilantro. Squeeze in juice of one lime and season with salt and pepper.

Grill tortillas. Spread with guacamole and then add a layer of beans and cheese. Roll and serve immediately.

Carrot Cake with Cream Cheese Frosting and Candied Ginger

Ingredients for cake.
  1 ¼ cups canola oil
  ¼ cup buttermilk
  2 cups sugar
  1 teaspoon vanilla
  1 teaspoon vanilla butter extract
  2 cups flour
  2 teaspoons baking soda
  2 teaspoons baking powder
  1 teaspoon salt
  2 teaspoons cinnamon
  1 teaspoon cardamom
  1 teaspoon nutmeg
  3 cups grated carrots
  Juice of one lemon (reserve zest for frosting)
  Juice of one orange (reserve zest for frosting)
  Small piece of ginger root (grated)
  1 cup pecans
  1 cup walnuts

Directions:
Preheat oven to 350 degrees. In a large bowl add eggs, oil, buttermilk, sugar, vanilla, orange juice, and lemon juice. Beat together, then mix in flour, baking soda, baking powder, and spices. Fold in shredded carrots, grated ginger, and nuts. Spread into two greased nine-inch pans. Bake for 25 to 30 minutes. Allow cakes to cool before frosting.

Ingredients for candied ginger:
  Fresh ginger root
  Sugar

Directions:
Use a mandolin to slice thin pieces of ginger (with the bark removed). Place in a saucepan and simmer in ¼ cup of water for 30 minutes or until ginger is tender. Remove from heat and drain water. Return ginger to pan, add ¼ cup water and ¼ cup of sugar and bring to a boil, stirring frequently. Reduce heat to low and continue to stir until the syrup begins to look dry (almost as if it has evaporated). Remove from heat and allow ginger pieces to cool on a wire baking rack.

Ingredients for frosting:
    ½ cup butter (at room temperature)
    1 8 oz. package of cream cheese (at room temperature)
    1 teaspoon vanilla
    1 teaspoon orange juice
    1 teaspoon lemon juice
    Zest of lemon and orange juice
    3 ½–4 cups of powdered sugar

Directions:
Beat butter on high speed in an electric mixer for 5 minutes. Add cream cheese and whip for another 2 to 3 minutes. Add vanilla, lemon and orange juice, plus zest and sift in powdered sugar one cup at a time until blended and creamy. Spread immediately on cooled cake. Top with candied ginger pieces.

Doughnut Latte

Andy's up to new tricks at the espresso bar. Pair his morning latte with your favorite jelly doughnut and sink into sugar heaven.

Ingredients:
    Good quality dark espresso
    2 % milk
    1 teaspoon white chocolate syrup
    1 teaspoon vanilla syrup
    1 teaspoon raspberry syrup
    ½ teaspoon cinnamon

Directions:
Prepare espresso and steam milk. Mix syrups and spices together in the bottom of a cup. Once milk is steamed, pour into the cup and stir together. Pour over espresso. Top with a dusting of cinnamon.